To Lesley
Much love
Emily Royal
x

HAWTHORNE'S WIFE

London Libertines, Book Two

by Emily Royal

Published by Dragonblade Publishing, an imprint of Kathryn Le Veque Novels, Inc

Additional Dragonblade books by Author Emily Royal

London Libertines
Henry's Bride, Book 1
Hawthorne's Wife, Book 2
Roderick's Widow, Book 3

★★★ Please visit Dragonblade's website for a full list of books and authors. Sign up for Dragonblade's blog for sneak peeks, interviews, and more: ★★★
www.dragonbladepublishing.com

Dedication

To Francesca who, thanks to having inherited her mother's penchant for procrastination, is unlikely to read the love scenes in this book until she's old enough not to be embarrassed by them.

Acknowledgements

A book is never the effort of just one person. I have so many people to thank who helped make it possible.

First, my fabulous Beta Buddies: Amanda, Frances, Jennifer, Julie, Kate B, Kate S, Liz, Lorraine, Pauline and Sara. Thank you for your feedback and support, as always. To the wonderfully positive and encouraging Sarah Painter: thank you for your continued encouragement and company when I seek solace in tea, wine and nibbles. And to Neil, Jasmine and Frankie, thank you for everything.

I'm also grateful to Lys & Nicola, who inspired my love of life drawing and thanks, as usual, to all at Dragonblade for keeping the faith in a new author, to Violetta for the crisp edits and Dar for the stunning cover art.

A nod to Abby & Hawthorne, for unknowingly naming my hero while this book was only a spark of an idea. And lastly to Fred, for naming my heroine.

CHAPTER ONE

Hampshire, England
1809

F REDERICA STANFORD STEPPED out from the darkness of Radley woods into the sunshine, disappointed not to have caught a glimpse of *him*.

Hawthorne Stiles, the most beautiful person in the world.

But he was Viscount Radley, the only son of Earl Stiles, the land-owner of the Radley estate. He existed too far above Frederica in station to notice her.

But she noticed him. She could always recognize the sound of his horse's hooves—the rhythm of a practiced horseman. The air would shift as if to herald the arrival of a perfect specimen, tightening her skin with a thrill almost like she experienced when diving from the trees overhanging Radley Lake into the clear waters. That brief moment of weightlessness was the nearest she would come to flying, except in dreams.

And her dreams always began and ended with him.

She used to play with Hawthorne's friends at the lake, poking at the water, looking for frogspawn. Jeffrey, Edward and Roger, all sons of earls and viscounts, they had at first tolerated her, a commoner, the merchant's daughter who tagged behind them. But their first term at Eton had opened their eyes to the class divide. Now, they teased her from their elevated positions atop their mounts, while Hawthorne sat astride his own horse, casually looking across the landscape as if she were of too little consequence to merit his attention.

In her whole life, he'd spoken to her once, but just four words. If those four, precious words were all he'd give her, she would make a treasure of them.

Are you all right?

It had been last winter, when the farm twins had taunted her over a hedgehog. The creature had needed a friend, but to the twins, it had been an object of amusement. Tom, the better mannered of the two, had merely taunted her, but John had attempted to kick the creature across the field, the animal's protective spines no match for his thick boots. A fit of rage had overpowered her, and she'd launched herself at him, ready to fight for a life no one else would defend. John, with his thick-set frame, had thrown her to the ground, but before he could land a blow, the roar of authority and the crack of the whip had stayed him.

Like an avenging angel, Hawthorne had stood before her, whip in hand, eyes black with fury. John fled, wailing like a baby from the lash mark across his cheek, while she'd plucked the hedgehog out of the grass.

Hawthorne's eyes had focused on her for the first time, taking in her disheveled hair and mud-spattered gown. She ran away, unable to overcome her shame.

Since then, he'd not noticed her at all.

But why should he, a man whose company was in such high demand from ladies of his own station? Countless debutantes, with their adoring mamas, rode past Frederica in their carriages on their way to take tea at Radley Hall. Other women visited him outside. Only last week she'd been exploring the woods and heard an unmistakable male voice reading love poetry, followed by a lighter voice whispering his name over and over until those whispers escalated into passionate cries. All the time he recited beautifully constructed verses, telling his companion of her divine beauty.

What would it be like to be loved by one such as he?

"FREDERICK, YOU INDULGE that girl."

"I know, Benedict, but she's my only child."

Frederica crossed the hall. Grandpapa's voice came from the parlor, warring with Papa's lighter, love-fueled tones. But her father always deferred because Grandpapa was a baronet whose title dated back to Queen Anne who, according to Papa's history books, had spent her life giving birth to children only to lose them.

She stopped by the parlor door. Conversations were always more interesting when the participants were unaware of being heard, particularly when the observer was the subject of their discussion.

"She won't be a child forever," Grandpapa continued. "Even I can see she's almost a woman. Ladies don't go grubbing among the hedgerows."

"She's happy," Papa argued. "She's free."

"Nevertheless, she must prepare herself for an entrée into the world."

"It's not a kind world."

"It's the world in which we live. Her dowry will increase her chances of a good match. But a woman does not secure a home through fortune alone. By acting appropriately, she's more likely to secure the attention of a man of quality than a cad."

"Are there not cads among your class, Benedict?" her papa asked.

"Of course, Frederick, but she's less likely to fall prey to a cad by acting like a lady. Has she been practicing her accomplishments?"

"Of course."

"Bring the child to me."

She darted back, but not quickly enough. The door opened.

"Frederica." Papa rarely addressed her by her full name.

"What have I told you about eavesdropping? Nothing good comes of it. When unobserved, we reveal more than we wish. And no man alive can handle the absolute truth."

His stance softened. "Come, Rica. Grandpapa wishes to see you."

Grandpapa rose as she entered the room. His expression bore the usual inconsistency—disapproval coupled with fondness, as if he disliked what he saw but loved her regardless.

"Sit by me, child."

His voice resonated through her body, constraining it as the corsets she wore. But a kindly smile stretched across his face, and she complied.

"Tell me about your studies."

Papa inclined his head, but Frederica had no need for the unspoken signal.

"I've been learning music and drawing, Grandpapa."

"And your progress?"

"Papa says I have no talent for music."

"The drawing, then?"

"She has a good eye." Papa pointed to a picture on the wall. "She painted that landscape last week. Would you like to see her sketchbook?"

"Papa…"

"Hush, child," Grandpapa said, "bring it over."

Papa held the sketchbook out, and Grandpapa opened it. The first pages contained basic sketches, pencil drawings of an inkpot, a signet ring, and one of Papa's coat buttons, etched with a distinctive crisscross pattern. Later sketches depicted the human form. She had always been drawn to the hands, where the skin crinkled around each knuckle. She could imagine the structure beneath the skin, the bones interlocking. Hands were an expression of the soul. Her tutor always said the eyes represented the soul. But hands revealed almost as much, their beauty being that they could be studied with little notice. Who cared if their hands were under scrutiny?

Callouses, like Papa's, were a reflection of honest toil. But callouses on the knuckles indicated a less than savory existence, a lifetime of fighting in the drinking establishments frequented by the likes of the farm twins. Hands of the aristocracy, men like Grandpapa, were smooth and characterless, though the skin on his was paper-thin and translucent.

Except *his* hands. The skin might be smooth, but the fingers were long and lean, the sinews showing strength as they had curled around the handle of the whip the day he'd thrashed John. The knuckles had whitened with tension before panic had overcome her and she'd fled. But what if she'd stayed? Would he have touched her?

"Child, these are exquisite." Pride sounded in Grandpapa's voice as he returned her to the present.

"She sketches likenesses, also," Papa said.

Page after page revealed a new sketch, until Grandpapa turned to a portrait.

"Eleanor," he choked.

It was Mama. The sketch was a copy of the portrait which hung over the drawing room fireplace. Moisture glistened in Grandpapa's eyes, their amber hue darkening with grief. He shifted away from her. Did he still blame her for Mama's death which Frederica caused by coming into the world?

Papa had never once made Frederica feel responsible for Mama's death. Perhaps what he'd once told her was true. A man might expect to lose his wife, but no parent should have to bury their child.

"Grandpapa, would you like the picture? To remind you of Mama?"

The old man closed his eyes, his chest rising and falling, then reopened them and smiled.

"No, child. You keep it. I have you to remind me of her. You look just like her."

She hadn't the heart to tell him he was wrong. Mama's portrait showed a woman with dark blonde hair, amber eyes, and a rosy complexion. Frederica's skin was paler, her eyes a vivid, sea green, her hair a warm hue of red.

"What's this?" Grandpapa asked.

He'd reached the final portrait in the sketchbook. Boldly sculpted features swept across the paper. Deep-set eyes stared out from the page. Thick, dark hair framed the face. The nostrils were slightly flared, just as they had been the day he'd spoken to her. A strong, capable mouth completed the likeness, curled into a slight smile.

It wasn't the Hawthorne Stiles who rode past her without even a backward glance, or the man she'd spied declaring love to another in the woods. It was the Hawthorne who reigned over her dreams.

Grandpapa closed the book and sighed. "Frederick, it's time she was introduced into society. A greater acquaintance will cure her of any girlish fantasies beyond her station."

⫸⫷

"ONE MORE INDISCRETION, son, and I'll pack you off to the army before you've changed your breeches."

Father's words rang in Hawthorne's ears as he steered his mount onto the lane. What did he know about being a parent? Having no mother, either, he might as well have been a bloody orphan.

Perhaps Father still blamed Hawthorne for Adam's death—wished the Almighty had taken Hawthorne instead. By virtue of having arrived in the world twenty minutes ahead of him, Hawthorne's twin brother had been the heir. But Adam had survived only three hours. Father still visited Adam's memorial, as if the power of prayer could resurrect his firstborn. In Father's eyes, had his heir survived, he'd have been blessed with the perfect son.

In all likelihood, Father wished God had taken Hawthorne instead. But as it was, Father's hopes were pinned on Hawthorne. Mama had left the world before delivering another spare, so there was no younger sibling to snap at his heels for the title of Earl Stiles. The inheritance mattered little to Hawthorne, but his freedom did.

Having been suspended from Eton for what his housemaster had described as "indiscretions with a maid," Hawthorne's prospects for Cambridge had sustained a small bullet hole. He'd have to listen to Father if that hole were to heal rather than fester. Hawthorne's passion for justice—a quality which the world lacked—fueled his desire to become a magistrate. And the study of law—not a life spent shooting the French—was the most straightforward path to that goal.

Why couldn't Father be more indulging? But the restrictions of aristocracy were the price to pay for the privileges. Entry into White's could never compensate for the lack of parental affection.

Unlike Frederick Stanford. He had the advantages of money, having made his fortune trading in wine, much of which lined the cellars at Radley Hall. But his status as a tradesman spared him the suffocating niceties of the aristocracy.

And Stanford himself could not be described as anything but an indulgent parent.

A movement caught Hawthorne's eyes—a small, brown creature scuttling across the lane.

He dismounted and scooped the hedgehog into his hands. The animal folded itself up until it resembled a large, brown conker, steely spines projecting outward to ward off predators, though they failed to penetrate his riding gloves.

Unlike *her*. The steel spines she wore managed to prickle underneath his skin.

Perhaps this creature was the same one she'd defended so passionately against those two ruffians. Her voice had been full of fire and vengeance as she'd flown at a bully twice her size. But it had softened when she cradled the little thing in her arms, seemingly oblivious of the mud smears on her gown. Perhaps she saw the creature as a kindred spirit, soft and tender on the inside, eyes radiating wary intelligence while they calculated whether the object in their path was friend or foe.

Though it appeared impenetrable, some creatures could breach its defenses. For hedgehogs it was the badger—sharp-teethed animals whose claws were impervious to the spines and could tear through soft flesh.

Might *she* be torn apart by such a predator? Her father might dote on her, but he lacked her ferocity. Stanford's mild brown hair and sensitive features were so unlike his daughter, who was all red fire and passion. Perhaps she was a changeling left by the faeries to live in the world of men. In such a world, she had none to protect her as fiercely as she protected the hedgehog.

Little grub, his friends called her—idle young men who judged her by what they saw—a dirt-ridden creature whose parent let her run wild. They missed the spark of intelligence within those eyes, the flame of passion in her hair which glowed red in the sunlight.

Were it not for her bright aura, he'd never have known how often she followed him. Like a skittish fawn, she darted away when she thought she was being observed. But Father had taught him that to catch his quarry, a hunter needed to lull it into thinking he hadn't noticed it, to look in the opposite direction until she came within reach.

But she never did. At one time, he'd noticed her watching while he pleasured Lady Swainson in the woods. The brief moment of male completion hadn't been worth the sense of shame when the familiar shock of red hair had flitted across his vision. Father insisted that a man's affairs were maintained behind closed doors. Had he known Hawthorne rutted married women against the ancient oaks which had graced the Radley estate for over five hundred years, he'd have a fit of apoplexy.

But nobody knew except the ladies themselves, who had good reason for discretion.

And his silent, fleeting shadow.

The creature in his hands relaxed, and a shiny black nose appeared among the spines. Hawthorne held his breath, and the nose was followed by a face. Two, sloe-black eyes regarded him thoughtfully. Was he friend or foe?

"Friend, little chap, definitely a friend."

"What are you doing?" The voice came from behind. His body tensed, and the creature tightened into a ball. A spine penetrated his glove, and he dropped the animal. It disappeared among the grass.

He turned and faced her. In all the years he'd been aware of her, he had never looked directly into her eyes. But now, his gaze fixed on her, it was if the final link in the invisible chain between them locked into place. Predator and prey were face to face at last. But which was which?

Hoofbeats rattled in the distance and cracked the silence.

"Hey! Little grub!"

Jeffrey appeared at the end of the lane, flanked on either side by Edward and Roger. They might be the least disagreeable male companions Hawthorne could spend his time with, particularly when compared to the odious Roderick Markham and his friends, but that didn't mean he had to relish their company.

She stepped back, her gaze darting about, until she spotted a gap in the hedge.

"Don't go, I..."

Before he could finish, she slipped through the hedge and disappeared.

CHAPTER TWO

T HE RAIN HAD begun to spatter as Frederica slipped inside the barn, sniffing at the scent of ripening straw. The last thing she wanted was to be caught in a downpour too close to Radley Hall, where she'd be in danger of discovery. Ever since he'd looked at her— *really* looked at her, it was as if her body had come alive with a need she couldn't fathom.

"Little grub!"

The voice came from behind.

Jeffrey stood by the door, blocking her way out. Though barely a year older than her, his shadow towered over her. The upper levels of the barn, accessible via a ladder, had a number of windows through which she could crawl.

"If you run, we'll catch you," he said. "I know where you'll come out. We used to climb that wall together."

He held out his hand. "Come on, little grub. I'm inviting you to join us. Roger, Ed, and I, just like old times. Hawthorne has pointed out the error of our ways."

Her breath caught at the mention of his name. She swallowed to disguise her reaction, but Jeffrey had seen it. His smile broadened.

"You like him, don't you? Do you want him to like you, too?"

She shook her head. "I thought you didn't want me hanging around you anymore."

He lifted his shoulders. "Sometimes we don't, sometimes we do."

Another shape appeared. *Edward.*

"Is she coming with us?"

Frederica had learned from Grandpapa that Edward had once been thrashed so hard at school for cheeking his housemaster, he'd been unable to sit without crying for the rest of the term.

With a grin, he held up his hand. Sunlight glinted on the bottle he was holding.

"Something to tempt you, little grub."

"That's port wine," she said, taking a closer look at the bottle. A tawny port Papa sold, most likely stolen from Earl Stiles's cellar.

"Ever tried it?" Edward asked.

She shook her head. The port was expensive, and not even a taste was worth the back of Papa's hand. Earl Stiles was one of the few men among Papa's clientele who could afford it; him, and his neighbor, the Duke of Markham.

"Well, I have," Edward said.

That much was clear. His breath bore the sour undertones of wine and his words the slur of inebriation. The light shining through the glass betrayed the extent of his thievery, the liquid level in the bottle was almost at the bottom.

"You'll get a thrashing, Edward," she said.

"It's Lord Mulberry, to you…"

"Be quiet, Ed!" Jeffrey interrupted. He turned to Frederica. "Are you going to rat on us?"

"Why shouldn't I?"

"We'll share it with you," Edward said. "You can have some now."

He held out the bottle, and she took it. Edward's hands had acquired the habit of appropriating things which did not belong to him.

She sniffed at the bottle. Sticky liquid covered the neck, and she licked her fingers. Like wine, only sweeter—rich, deep notes of ripe fruit. Papa always said the flavor came through years of aging, hence the cost.

But the inebriated young man in front of her had not been savoring the taste.

"If you wanted to get drunk, you should have stolen Stiles's whisky."

Edward wrinkled his nose. "Whisky's disgusting. I prefer this." He nodded toward the bottle. "Go on, finish it. It's almost gone."

"If you drink it, you can play with us," Jeffrey said. "Like old times. We'll even tell you what Hawthorne thinks of you."

Her fingers tightened around the bottle.

"Oh, yes!" Edward said. "He speaks of you an awful lot. If you come with us, you'll get to see him. He's in that abandoned cottage we used to play in."

She lifted the bottle to her lips and tipped it up. The liquid burst into a flame of taste, and she sputtered and swallowed.

"Good girl!" Edward exclaimed. "Now you're one of us."

He took her hand and led her out of the barn. The rain had almost stopped, light smatterings of water stinging her skin which had come alive, though she didn't know if it was the effects of the port or the prospect of being at close quarter with Hawthorne Stiles.

Hawthorne...

His features swam into view in her mind—the imposing, dominant stare which immobilized her. If she were to face him, she'd need to strengthen her courage and dull her fear. As they approached the cottage, she finished drinking what was left of the port. The man she worshipped waited for her inside.

"WHERE IS HE?"

The building was empty apart from Roger who sat cross-legged atop a crate, a bottle in his hand.

"Our damsel has arrived!" The pitch of his voice and the absent cork told her all she needed to know. He held the bottle out to her, but she shrank back, the predatory look in his eyes making her shiver.

"What are you doing?" she asked.

"Playing a game," he replied. "You're our damsel in distress. And Hawthorne's going to rescue you. Like in the stories."

"What stories?"

"The princess and the dragon..."

"Andromeda and Perseus!" Edward exclaimed.

"Oh, shut up, Ed," Jeffrey said. "You're a poor Greek scholar. You're only interested in that story because the princess is stripped naked. Dirty bugger."

A shiver of apprehension rippled through Frederica, and she pulled her hand free.

"See what you've done?" Jeffrey said. "You've frightened our damsel." He gave her a kindly smile. "Our little grub's to be treated like a lady. No stripping. But we must tie you up so Hawthorne can rescue you properly."

He put his arm around her. "Have some more port. It'll help your nerves. We'll tell you all about Andromeda, how Perseus rescued her, and they lived happily ever after."

A few mouthfuls later, the apprehension scratching at Frederica's mind had diminished, dulled by the sweet intoxication of the port, and finally driven away by the image in her mind, of her rescuer—of dark, chocolate eyes filled with determination and love as he unbound her and lifted her into his arms to take her to paradise.

A warm hand engulfed hers. "Come on, little grub. Let's get started."

They took her to the back of the cottage where a broken staircase led to the upper floor. The world shifted out of focus and rocked sideways as if she were in one of the small rowing boats on Radley Lake.

"Here, let us help you, fair damsel." Roger said.

At the top of the stairs, they led her into a small room, empty save for a single chair beside a fireplace. Throaty echoes rattled through the fireplace, the cawing of crows roosting in the chimneypots. Black and white spatters adorned the floor, and the occasional downy feather nestled among the ash in the hearth. Her nostrils wrinkled at the acidic stench.

"Sit her down." Jeffrey ordered. "The monster awaits our sacrifice."

Fingers of dread ran along her spine. "I don't want to do this anymore."

"Silly little grub," Jeffrey teased. "We're just playacting. Take some more port, it'll make you feel better."

A new sensation rumbled in her stomach, like the time she'd eaten oysters for the first time and had promptly expelled her supper over the dining room floor, much to Papa's distress. She took a deep breath and the sensation subsided.

Two pairs of hands steered her toward the chair.

"Got the rope?"

"Rope..." Her tongue thickened in her mouth, the paralyzing effect of the port hampering her speech.

"Don't worry, little grub. We won't tie proper knots."

Blurred shapes moved in front of her. The stench of bird dung rolled over her like a wave, and she swallowed.

"I feel sick..."

"You'll be fine," Roger said. "Your hero will soon be here."

"Hawthorne..."

"Yes, that's right. When Hawthorne gets here, everything will be fine."

Hands took her wrists and ankles, securing them to the chair.

"Good work, boys!" Jeffrey's voice was muffled, almost inaudible. "Come on, the monster awaits!"

Male laughter swirled around her, a door closed, and footsteps receded. She closed her eyes and another noise penetrated her mind, scratching and scuffling, accompanied by a cackle, as if the witches in Shakespeare's tales had come to slay her. Was it Jeffrey and his friends playing at being the monster of the sea?

She opened her eyes, and dark shapes flitted about the room. The flap of wings grew more intense, followed by screeching and cawing. A shape flew at her, claws outstretched. With a cry, she tried to move, but the ropes binding her wrists only pulled tighter. More shapes filled the room, dark demons pouring out of the fireplace. Dust and ash exploded in the air, cutting out the sunlight as the demons danced around her.

She let out a scream as she fought for freedom, but the ropes had morphed into serpents, thick, black serpents covered in spines that tore at her wrists.

With a screech of laughter, the demons flew at her once more. She jerked sideways, and pain exploded in her head, then the darkness claimed her.

⪻⪼

HAWTHORNE STEERED HIS horse toward the stables, dismounted, and handed the reins to the groom.

"Give him a good rub down, Bartlett. I'm afraid I rode rather too hard today."

"Of course, my lord."

As he crossed the stable yard, a familiar voice called out. "Ah, there you are!"

Jeffrey stood flanked by his two friends, a satisfied smile on his face. Edward and Roger seemed a little worse for wear. Roger, the fool, still clutched the cause, an empty port bottle in his hand. When term time came around again and these three were packed off back to Eton, it couldn't come too soon. At least the age gap meant he'd never have to suffer their company at Cambridge.

"We've a surprise for you, Hawthorne," Jeffrey said.

Hawthorne sighed. "Shouldn't you be at home?"

Jeffrey lifted his shoulders. "I think you'll like it. We've caught a wild animal."

Roger waved the bottle at him. "Don't you want to know what it is?"

"Don't you mean *where she* is?" Edward laughed.

"I doubt she's still there," Roger said. "That little grub's more slippery than the trout in your father's stream."

Little grub...

A pulse of fear rippled through him. His little changeling...

"What have you done?"

"Nothing she didn't want," Roger laughed.

"She only agreed because she thought you were coming," Edward added. "You're as much to blame as us."

"Where is she?" Hawthorne drew out his riding crop.

Jeffrey, the soberest of the three, at least had the wit to recognize danger.

"The empty cottage near the barn. She'll have freed herself by now..."

Ignoring them, he broke into a sprint.

⟫⟫✳⟪⟪

THE COTTAGE WAS silent save for the cawing of crows circling the chimney pot. Soon the sun would disappear behind the horizon and they'd descend to roost.

Hawthorne pushed open the door.

"Frederica?"

The only response was cawing and scuffling from upstairs.

"Frederica!"

His words echoed off the stone walls, mocking him. Where was she?

Fresh footprints formed a path to the staircase. He took the stairs two at a time until he reached the upper floor. The cackling and flapping came from behind a door.

He pushed the door open. A rush of wings beat in the air and black shapes flew past him. He entered the room and recoiled at the sight before him.

A young woman lay on the floor. She had been tied to a chair, her skin red and raw where she must have fought against her bonds.

He dropped to his knees beside her. Her lips parted, and his body weakened with relief as a warm rush of air escaped them, tainted by the sour odor of liquor.

She was alive but unconscious. Close to, her skin seemed like porcelain, as if one of Mama's delicate figurines lay before him, the bloodless hue almost rendering her translucent. He ran a knuckle along her skin, its soft innocence so unlike the worldly aura of the women he'd experienced.

A changeling child indeed, a faerie creature too good for the world.

He ran his hands over her head. Sticky wetness adorned the side of her head where it had hit the ground. The chair must have fallen sideways and taken her with it. He withdrew his hand. His fingertips were smeared with blood.

He picked at the bonds on her wrists. The ropes, stained with her blood, too, worked free, and he pulled her to him.

"Frederica…" he breathed.

A small groan escaped her lips and she stirred, shifting her body closer to him; the instinctive act of a creature which recognizes a source of warmth. Or did she recognize her savior?

Savior indeed! What had he done to prevent this? Nothing. He'd watched while those three fools had taunted her, but not once had he prevented them. Had he paid attention, he'd have known what they were planning.

This was his fault. If Father discovered what had happened to her, he'd pack Hawthorne off into the army.

Damn! His future disintegrated in front of him as he watched the young woman in his arms stir to life. His best hope was to return her to her father's house and leave her there to be discovered. He could deny all knowledge and secure his friends' silence by threatening to tell Father about the stolen port.

A course of action, albeit that of a coward. But what else could he do? One day, when he was independent of Father, he'd atone for his cowardice.

With these thoughts in his mind, he picked up her body and carried her out into the open.

Frederick Stanford's home was a modest house, nestled between the Radley and Markham estates. Hawthorne had visited it only once, the night Frederica was born. Out of curiosity, he'd slipped out and hidden in the shadows, wanting to understand what happened when a child entered the world. He'd heard servants' gossip about the dangers of childbirth and that Stanford was in danger of losing both his wife and child.

As Hawthorne moved along the edge of the driveway, cradling that very child in his arms, some fourteen years later, the memories resurfaced, his four-year-old self hiding in the bushes, peering through the window, the echoes of screams from the house. But the anticipated cry of a child had not come. Instead, the deep wail of loss had thickened the air.

Two men had stood in the parlor, Frederick Stanford and his father-in-law, comforting each other. The next day, Father had told Hawthorne over breakfast that Eleanor Stanford had been delivered of a daughter but died bringing her into the world.

A coward he'd been then, skulking in the bushes to witness a man's grief. And a coward he was now, delivering that man's daughter under cover of darkness.

He brushed his lips against her forehead and placed her on the ground beside the main doors. Raising his hands, he pummeled on the doors, then sprinted back into the shadows.

A vertical shaft of light appeared and stretched across the ground, picking out her form. A female voice screamed.

"Fetch the master, quickly! It's the little mistress!"

A second silhouette appeared.

"Frederica!" Stanford's wail of anguish cleaved Hawthorne's heart in two, the voice of a man who'd lost his beloved wife and now feared for his daughter.

What made Hawthorne any better than Jeffrey and his friends, or even that reprobate, Roderick Markham, who lounged about the ducal estate and had inherited his father's cruelty and sport for seeking gratification between the thighs of unwilling women?

Stanford lifted his daughter in his arms and took her inside, calling for his horse to be saddled. Moments later, a figure rode past Hawthorne. Stanford, riding as if the devil were on his heels in his desperation to fetch the doctor.

Hawthorne might exist above her in station, but when it came to honor and purity of the soul, he could never be her equal. Even now, his concern for her was tempered by his fear of discovery. A dark, little voice in the corner of his mind told him that as long as news of the incident did not reach Father's ears, he could go up to Cambridge and secure his future.

"Forgive me, little changeling."

CHAPTER THREE

"**B**EGGING YOUR PARDON, my lord, your father has asked for you."

Hawthorne looked up from inspecting his new gown, complete with mortar-board and hood emblazoned with the colors of Caius College Cambridge. Tomorrow, he'd be leaving to enjoy three years' freedom studying law, subject neither to the whims of Father nor the rules of the regiment.

"What does he want?"

"I don't know." The footman bowed. "But Mr. Stanford is with him."

Stanford…

Hawthorne dropped the gown on the floor. He should have known that justice caught up with all men eventually.

"AH, THERE YOU are, boy."

Three men waited in the morning room, Father in his chair by the fireplace, and two guests. Hawthorne's stomach clenched in anticipation of punishment as two pairs of eyes turned their attention on him.

Frederick Stanford and his father-in-law, Sir Benedict Langton.

"Sit down," Father said.

Hawthorne took the chair beside Father. For once, the safest position in the room was the closest to his parent.

"Mr. Stanford has something to ask you."

Stanford's brow wrinkled with concern. "My daughter was involved in an *accident* five days ago," he said. "I wondered if you saw anything last Saturday."

An accident...

Hawthorne shook his head.

"I told you, Stanford," Father interjected, "my son knows nothing about it."

Sir Benedict touched his son-in-law's shoulder, and Hawthorne's heart tightened at the gesture of affection.

"Was she harmed?" To his ear, Hawthorne's voice sounded high-pitched, but his companions failed to notice.

Sir Benedict leaned forward. "My granddaughter appeared on her doorstep unconscious, drunk, with lacerations on her wrists and ankles, and scratches on her face."

"Has she recovered?"

"Physically, yes," Sir Benedict said. "But she's been unable to speak until this morning. She jumps at the slightest noise and has gained a fear of confined spaces." He turned to Stanford and patted his hand. "We're optimistic she'll recover, and we must be thankful she was not violated."

"I want those ruffians found," Stanford interrupted. "I cannot let such treatment go unpunished. She's my only child."

Shame and guilt warmed Hawthorne's cheeks, guilt which surely Sir Benedict would recognize even if Stanford, in his distressed state, could not.

"As you see," Father said, "my son knows nothing. I'm sorry for your daughter, Stanford, and I wish her a complete recovery. I will, of course, do everything I can to ensure it doesn't happen again. I'll have my man scour the estate."

"Thank you," Stanford said, "but..."

"Leave it be, Frederick," Sir Benedict interrupted. "It's as the child said this morning. She drunk herself into a stupor and was taken advantage of by gypsies. I always warned you she'd acquire a taste for your wine."

Hawthorne's shame intensified. For some reason, she hadn't ratted out his friends. Or him.

"You won't punish her?" Hawthorne asked.

"No," Stanford said. "She's suffered enough." He stood, scraping the chair against the floorboards. "I've left her alone too long. It's time I returned."

"She'll be fine, Frederick," Sir Benedict said. "You left her painting in the garden, she's calmer when outside."

"Nevertheless." Stanford said. "Are you coming, Benedict?"

"I'll join you later, Frederick. I wish to discuss something with Stiles."

Hawthorne leapt to his feet. "I can show Mr. Stanford out."

He followed Stanford into the hallway.

"Will she recover, sir?"

Stanford's features softened with gratitude. "You're kind to ask, Viscount Radley. I believe she will. The fresh air is already doing wonders for her constitution, and her occupation with her paint box will cure her mental state."

He smiled. "But now's not the time for melancholy. I hear you're off to Cambridge. You must be looking forward to it. You're at Caius College?"

"Yes."

"Your father was at St Johns, as was every Earl Stiles since the sixteenth century."

"And Sir Benedict, of course," Hawthorne replied. "Father often talks of how he helped him during his freshman year. Rumor has it that St Johns college is so rich that you could walk from St Johns, Cambridge, to its namesake in Oxford without stepping off their land."

"But you had no wish to follow your ancestors and attend St Johns?"

"Traditions should not be maintained merely for the sake of it," Hawthorne said. "Life's riches can only be savored when new tastes are introduced. Otherwise, one's palate would grow lazy."

"Your father wouldn't agree," Stanford said.

"Then he's wrong, and history is against him. One is not remembered for following in the footsteps of others, but in striving for betterment. In celebrating, not hiding one's differences. Only then can we distinguish ourselves."

"You have the means to distinguish yourself, Viscount Radley," Stanford sighed. "Make the most of your time at Cambridge."

I will.

Stanford bowed and disappeared down the drive, his body tightening with determination as he left to tend to his daughter.

I'll do it for you, little changeling. Your silence has bought my freedom.

Crossing the hallway, Hawthorne froze at Father's voice coming from the morning room. He moved closer to the door and held his breath.

"I tell you, Benedict, my son thinks nothing of the girl. She's just a child. Though I cannot deny he's developing a taste for women."

"Like father, like son?"

"My rakehell days are over," Father said. "My constitution couldn't stand it."

"Your heart still troubles you?"

"A little."

Hawthorne heard the chink of glass and the soft musical notes of liquid being poured.

"Here, drink this. Whisky's supposed to be good for the heart."

"Not the amount you drink, Benedict."

After a pause, Hawthorne heard Father sigh. "Should we tell Stanford the truth?"

"No, George. It would destroy him. And her. Some secrets should

23

stay buried."

"But they have a way of unearthing themselves. Weeds have the knack of sprouting where one least expects it."

Hawthorne's chest tightened. What secret were they harboring? How did it involve Stanford and his daughter?

"Weeds? You see Frederica as a weed?"

"If you're worried about her dowry, Benedict, then don't. I'll honor my promise. Her mother died in my care, after all. But I often ask myself why you're so fond of her."

"Blood isn't everything, George. Despite her origins, I see her as my granddaughter. She's a bright little thing, kind, spirited, and ideal prey for the young men who prowl society like feral cats."

Father spluttered, and Hawthorne could almost imagine the whisky dribbling from his lips. "I trust you're not referring to my son." Indignation dripped from his words. "He'd never touch someone of her station."

How ironic that Father, in the first defense of Hawthorne that he could remember, did so by insulting his little changeling.

Sir Benedict sighed. "Nevertheless, it would be prudent to tell Hawthorne about her. After all, he stands to be trustee."

"He's not mature enough, Benedict. And despite my weak heart, I have no intention of joining my late wife just yet. Perhaps when he's returned from Cambridge."

"Caius, eh?"

Father sighed. "My son was never one to follow in his father's footsteps. I decided to let him have his little rebellion. He'll be constrained enough when he inherits the earldom."

A chair scraped back, signaling the end of the conversation, and Hawthorne darted toward the stairs.

A mystery surrounded Frederica Stanford. His little changeling was not what she seemed.

>>>>><<<<<

ON THE DAY Hawthorne left for Cambridge, the morning dawned bright. A myriad of color shone in the sunlight as if to bid him farewell on his way to freedom. The carriage drove past the beech hedge lining the driveway from Radley Hall. Muted tones of green formed the palette, interspersed with accents of red and yellow.

Colors to lift the spirits. Colors which only an artist's eye could fully appreciate.

One like hers.

As if his thoughts conjured up the image of a sprite, a figure came into view. Clutching a sketchbook under one arm, she drifted along the hedgerow.

She had lost weight, but he'd have recognized her anywhere. Tones of red and ochre reflected off her hair which hung loosely round her shoulders.

The driver slowed the pace, and at the very moment the carriage passed, she looked up and their eyes met.

The pull of recognition forced the air from his lungs. Her eyes reflected the potency of their connection, and the colors faded until only one remained. A rich, sea-green, longing and understanding shimmering in their depths.

He opened his mouth to speak, but words would be insufficient to convey his feelings. Before he drew breath, the carriage had passed. He looked out of the window. She had resumed walking, almost as if he were not there, but before she reached the end of the lane, she turned her head and watched as he rode out of her life.

Father was right. They came from vastly different backgrounds. Hawthorne was destined to become Earl Stiles with all the traditions and constraints of that role. He would return with his degree, settle into society, establish a mistress, and find a wife to secure an heir to continue the cycle. His little changeling was a wild rose who would ramble across the countryside, destined to pursue whatever fate she chose.

In all likelihood, they would never meet again.

CHAPTER FOUR

Dorset, England
1814

T HE BUZZ OF voices spiraled around the ballroom, morphing into caws and screeches. Frederica closed her eyes against the assault of gaudy silks, colors which occurred only in hothouses, the women wearing them trying to emulate nature's beauty but failing. None of them would possess the ability to see properly, to understand the subtle hues which adorned the landscape.

The images assaulted her mind, black shapes circling around her, feathers and arrows of black and red, beaks wide open, sharp edges ready to tear her to pieces while she lay powerless to prevent it, her wrists burning…

"Frederica!"

The voice returned her to the ballroom with a jolt. Pale blue eyes surrounded by a bland, colorless face, regarded her with curiosity and want of understanding.

"Are you all right? Shall I fetch Lady Axminster?"

She took a breath, the air partly dissipating the demons. "No, thank you Alice. I'm well now." As Grandpapa's cousin, Lady Axminster made the ideal chaperone, but her deafness rendered conversation impossible. Her attentions, though well-meant, only added to the thickness of the air which Frederica suffered every time she was indoors.

"I imagine the prospect of spending an evening among society must be overwhelming," Alice said.

Frederica smiled at her companion, bestowing a bland upturn of the lips, the uniform of a lady, to conceal the turmoil underneath.

Alice de Grecy was harmless enough and meant no disrespect, but as the daughter of a viscount, she was far above Frederica in station. The *ton* would always look down on men like Papa who earned their fortune, rather than inherited it. In the eyes of society, idle frivolities were valued more greatly than hard work or compassion.

The music stopped and the dancers dissipated, ladies simpering on the arms of gentlemen, pleading with their bodies for attention, while the men who were lucky enough to effect escape from grasping females, sought sanctuary at the card tables.

"Viscount Radley!" The announcement was followed by a murmur of anticipation.

Hawthorne...

The atmosphere shifted, and heat pricked Frederica's skin. A familiar sharp itch lingered at her wrists, and she adjusted her gloves, fighting the urge to relieve it with her fingernails.

"I can't think why you insist on wearing those thick gloves," Alice said. "They must make you so hot in this weather."

"I–it's a fancy I have," Frederica replied.

"Not very *a la mode*," Alice said. "Don't you know the best way to secure a man's attention is to be fashionable?"

"What, by following the crowd? Doesn't that render one invisible?"

"Invisibility is a virtue, Frederica. Once we marry, we're expected to blend into our husbands' backgrounds."

"As if we no longer exist? What about definition of character?"

"A woman is never valued for her character. When we marry, we become the property of our husbands. But while we vie for a man's attention, we must possess the talent of achieving the delicate balance between prominence and inconspicuousness."

Alice rose to her feet with all the elegance of a well-schooled lady. "Come on, we'll not fill our dance cards sitting by the terrace doors. I can't understand why you insist on being so far from the center of the room."

"I like fresh air."

Alice huffed. "Fresh air! I suppose you must be forgiven for your country upbringing."

"There's nothing wrong with wanting to be close to nature."

"If I want a relationship with nature, all I have to do is look at one of your paintings. In that aspect, at least, I envy you. How you manage to portray such good likenesses is beyond me. I imagine every member of society is clamoring to see one of your works on their parlor walls."

Frederica smiled at Alice's praise. "I trust you're not alone in that sentiment. I hope to earn a living from my work."

"Good lord!" Alice exclaimed. "You'd paint for *trade*? A lady only paints for accomplishment. Though I suppose you're not really a lady. Does your papa object to your fancies?"

"He encourages it." Frederica smiled at the memory, of how, with Papa's gentle persuasion, she had sought color, air, and light and found a pathway out of the darkness. As soon as he'd seen the restorative effect of drawing and painting, Papa had procured the best quality artist materials for her.

"Perhaps I could prevail upon you to paint some of Father's birds?" Alice said. "He has some exquisite specimens in his aviary."

"No!" Frederica cried.

Alice recoiled, and Frederica placed a hand on her companion's.

"Forgive me, Alice. I'm not fond of birds."

"A portrait, then?" Alice asked. "I've always wanted my likeness taken, though my stepmother tells me I'm too vain."

"Isn't vanity a quality prized in society?"

Alice smiled. At least the vanity bred into her hadn't completely obliterated her good nature. "In which case, my dear friend, let us fuel each other's vanity. My pride in my appearance and yours in your accomplishment. And it would enable us to further our friendship, for I intend to ask Father if you may come to our house party next month."

A house party… Rooms full of people, chattering masses, the insipidity of witless words thickening the air, choking her…

Alice gave her a nudge. "Sit up! Now's the time for a woman's prominence to come to the fore."

A tall, silent form stood in the center of the ballroom, his stance emanating a casual disregard of his surroundings. Had she not seen the dance floor empty five minutes before, Frederica might have thought the ballroom boasted a marble sculpture. He dominated the room, a treacherous rock in the sea which the waves were drawn to, dashing into pieces against him, before reforming only to approach him again, a never-ending cycle of relentless worship.

Slowly, he turned, and their eyes met. The warm admiration which she'd once felt for him had matured, along with her body, into a burning need and a wicked pulse of warmth radiated through her.

Roaring and cackling rushed through Frederica's head. Her corset grew tight, and she fought for breath.

She had to escape, away from the rush of heat and beating of wings, from the demons which waited in every room. She leapt to her feet and slipped outside onto the terrace. The fog of terror dissipated, and the colors returned. The bright, fresh green of the finely manicured lawn surrounded by the richer, deeper shades of the plants lining the borders of the garden, interspersed with accents of color from early summer flowers.

Colors to defend her against the black.

Alice appeared at her side, laughing.

"Viscount Radley may be a catch, but I'll swear he's never made a woman swoon so badly that she has to run from the room!"

Foolish, frivolous Alice thought she had fainted at the sight of a man! But Frederica could use that folly to her advantage. A fanciful lady was always acceptable in London society. A madwoman, however, would be reviled.

"He's a fine catch for any woman," Alice continued, "though I fear with your social position, you could never aspire to him. Which is a pity. I hear he's looking for a wife. One would put up with a good deal of invisibility to be owned by him."

Heat rose in Frederica's cheeks, shame at her flight from the ball-room, and at her body's wanton reaction.

"I believe you're blushing!" Alice laughed good-naturedly. "Your secret is safe with me, but only if you accompany me back inside. I'm eager to fill my dance card. Mr. Trelawney has secured me for the first dance, but I've not seen him yet."

Frederica took Alice's arm. Returning to the ballroom was the lesser evil when the alternative was to have Alice de Grecy gossip about her.

⯮⯮⯮⯬⯬⯬

As HAWTHORNE SURVEYED the ballroom, he caught a flash of red. Not the gaudy silks which hammered at a man's senses, but a richer, warmer hue, one which a man could never replicate.

He'd recognize that color anywhere, even though he'd not seen it for five years.

But when he blinked, she had disappeared.

She must have been a product of his imagination, brought forth as a result of Father's revelation last week. Despite Hawthorne's recent ascendance into the magistracy, Father had shown little pride in his achievement. Hawthorne had berated him over his lack of affection, comparing him unfavorably to Stanford, pointing out that he, at least, acted the parent, showing unconditional love for his daughter.

And what had father said?

She's not Stanford's daughter.

He'd then refused to elaborate, dismissing Hawthorne with a cursory wave.

"Ah, Hawthorne, old chap. I wondered whether you'd be here tonight."

Hawthorne's friend, Ross Trelawney, approached, holding two glasses of champagne. Ross had entered Cambridge the same time as Hawthorne, and they'd studied law together. More intelligent than most men of Hawthorne's acquaintance, Ross had expanded his father's businesses and earned a fortune.

"I almost didn't make it here," Hawthorne said. "Samson nearly threw me yesterday."

Ross sipped from one of the glasses and offered the other to Hawthorne. "Your new Arabian?"

Hawthorne took the proffered glass. "I should have called him Satan." He drained it in a single gulp. "Next time he throws me, I'll shoot him. Not even Bartlett can control that horse when he's spooked. Bloody thoroughbreds. They're all insane."

Ross let out a laugh. "If you think a creature should be shot for being inbred to the point of insanity, you'd have to take your pistol to most of the company here tonight!"

Hawthorne cast his gaze over the crowd; row upon row of debutantes accompanied by adoring mamas.

"Good God, Ross. Look at all those desperate women. I'd rather be trampled by Samson than endure their company."

"If you wish to secure a wife, my friend, you must inspect the prospective purchases. What better marketplace than Viscount Hartford's ballroom?"

"I'd prefer a private viewing."

Ross chuckled. "I can well believe it. Gentlemen are supposed to vie for the services of a mistress. You, by all accounts, have the pick of the crop when it comes to courtesans."

"I had an early start."

"Even so, experience is no match for talent. You, sir, have a natural ability for delivering pleasures most creatures can only dream of."

"You flatter me."

"I speak the truth," Ross said. "Perhaps you'd care to be generous and share the secret of your success in persuading women with no more than a single look, to part their thighs."

"I give them what they need."

"Riches and fine gowns? I shower my Kitty regularly with trinkets, yet her eyes wander in your direction. I'll wager she's waiting for you to dispose of Cherise so she can defect into your bed."

Hawthorne sighed. Ross, though intelligent, lacked the ability to see deep inside a person to understand their innermost desires. "I didn't say I give women what they want, Ross. I give them what they *need*."

"Which is?"

"A firm hand."

Ross choked on his champagne. Hawthorne patted him on the back, then resumed his attention on the crowd.

She was nowhere to be seen.

He'd not seen her for five years, but his memory had imprinted the vision of her in his mind. At night he would wake wanting to touch her, but every time he opened his eyes, he found himself reaching into thin air. On the occasions he was not alone, the women in his bed satisfied physical needs but left his soul unfulfilled.

A young woman drew near. Pale blue eyes cast a hungry glance over him before turning their attention on Ross. She was pretty enough—porcelain skin and fine cheekbones—delicate features surrounded by a cascade of blonde ringlets. Her gown fitted her form perfectly, showing just the right amount of flesh, modesty with a small promise of temptation as her lace tuck caressed the swell of her breasts. Her jewelry was the right level of ostentation, enough to broadcast the prospect of a dowry but not so much as to stray into vulgarity.

In short, she looked like every other young lady in the room, bearing the uniform of the huntress eager to tempt a suitor with her looks, her adherence to etiquette, and her dowry.

Which boiled down to nothing more than trinkets, manners, and cash.

"Miss de Grecy, what a pleasure!" Ross's demeanor changed from predatory seducer to gallant suitor. He lifted her hand to his lips and kissed it.

"I believe we're engaged for the first dance, sir."

"I've thought of nothing else all day," Ross said.

She issued a coy smile before retreating.

"Good Lord, Ross," Hawthorne said. "Has the prospect of matrimony turned you into a simpering fool?"

Ross laughed. "Of course not, but do you think these fine creatures would appreciate our more *sophisticated* talents? A man purchases a wife solely to secure an heir."

"You're going to offer for that bland de Grecy girl?"

"Why not? Her dowry would make a fitting investment into my business if Viscount de Grecy is willing to part with it."

"Then you might argue it's the viscount who makes the purchase, and you're the commodity."

"And a willing commodity I'd be, Hawthorne. I only need find a similarly bland partner for you."

"I'm not looking for a wife."

"A man must marry," Ross said. "I'd introduce you to Miss de Grecy's friend, but she's too eccentric, even for your tastes." He nodded toward the French windows. "There she is now. An intriguing creature, but there's something about her I find rather unsettling."

Hawthorne lifted his head, and the breath caught in his throat.

Frederica…

"She looks well enough," Hawthorne said, the pitch of his voice higher than usual, though Ross didn't seem to notice.

"Miss Stanford is her name," Ross continued. "Half the time, she looks right inside you, and the other half, she stares into the distance as if she's no longer there. I can't make her out. I've seen her at two parties, and have yet to see her dance. She spends the whole evening sitting at the edge of the room. But you must know her? She lives near your father's estate."

"I know of her," Hawthorne replied, clenching his hand to dispel the stirring in his groin. "We never mixed in the same circles."

The years had turned the intriguing child, his little changeling, into a beautiful woman. She sat in the corner of the room, an other-worldly creature unlike the ladies of Hawthorne's acquaintance. Most women of his acquaintance fell into two classes: the ladies who hungered for his attention in ballrooms and drawing rooms, and the harlots who offered their attentions for a coin, in bedrooms and boudoirs. But Frederica was neither. In Hawthorne's eyes, she would never fit into any form of society. Her uniqueness set her apart.

Ross nudged him. "See her gloves? Even in hot weather she wears them. I've never once seen her remove them. I fancy lodging a wager at White's. What do you say? Ten guineas to the first man who persuades her to take them off?"

"Leave her alone," Hawthorne growled.

Ross laughed good-naturedly. "So speaks the magistrate."

"Perhaps she's just cold, Ross."

"Then why is she sitting by the door? You can see her headdress moving in the draught."

She looked uncomfortable in her surroundings. Her gaze darted in every direction, most often directed toward the door. Without thinking, he crossed the floor, as if she drew him to her.

Unattached ladies milled about the perimeter, and eager eyes lifted as Hawthorne passed them, but his focus was directed at the lone figure by the French windows.

Though she sat still, he noticed the change in her stance. She kept her focus on the center of the room, and any casual observer would have seen a young woman watching the dance. But the atmosphere thickened with the spark of tension which preceded a storm, the charge lifting the hairs on Hawthorne's neck.

She dipped her chin, and long lashes fluttered as she closed her eyes. Perhaps she thought he'd not see her if she couldn't see him. He moved toward her slowly and held his breath. One more step and he'd be close enough to touch her.

She opened her eyes as her head snapped up. His senses were assaulted by the intense, sea-green eyes which had tormented his dreams.

He paused, transfixed by her stare. Shame warmed his blood, shame at the last time he'd seen her, the day he'd abandoned her on her father's doorstep.

He'd won his place at Cambridge, secured his degree, and his position as a magistrate. But the price was too great. The young woman sitting before him had paid with her peace of mind.

Hawthorne's future was set. He had wealth, the prospect of an earldom, the pick of heiresses for a wife, and a position in society where he could affect, in a small way, some justice in the world.

But what about justice for her?

She smoothed her expression, and her eyes took on a vacant look as if she'd retreated so far into herself, she was no longer in the room.

But Hawthorne recognized it for what it was. Some animals, when under threat, disguised themselves to blend in with their surroundings, to convince predators they were no longer there.

She had every cause to believe him a predator.

He gestured toward the chair beside her. "May I join you?"

She flinched, but he drew encouragement from her lack of refusal and sat beside her.

"Are you engaged for the next dance?" he asked.

She shook her head and resumed her attention on the dance, as if a stranger had sat next to her. But the quickened pace of her breathing told him she knew who he was.

"Do you not remember me, little changeling?"

"Little grub," she corrected.

"Excuse me?"

"You called me little grub."

"That was my friends." His shame increased at the memory, of how they'd teased her while he'd pretended not to notice.

"They're not here," he blurted. "You are quite safe. Ed's up at Oxford, how his father managed to buy his place is beyond me. Roger was packed off to the army. Whereas, Jeffrey…"

"I feel ill." She tried to stand, but her legs buckled. He leapt to his feet and caught her. Her warm body trembled in his arms, and the rush of desire to protect her dispelled the lust which had afflicted him the moment he'd spotted her in the ballroom.

He circled an arm round her waist and led her deeper into the room where a footman stood to attention, a tray of wine glasses in his hand.

"No!"

"Hush," he admonished. "Once you've had something to drink, you'll feel better."

"Out!" she cried. "I must get out!" Her body jerked.

He'd only seen such terror once before, mirrored in the eyes of a fox surrounded by a pack of dogs. As a child, he'd joined one of Father's hunts and witnessed the kill. The outnumbered animal had screamed in terror at the fate awaiting it.

A proud Father had bloodied Hawthorne in honor of his first hunt, dipping his fingers into the mangled flesh which had once been a fox before running them along Hawthorne's cheeks.

Those marks were no different to the stripes of honor he now wore, his degree and magistracy, which had originated from the suffering of the woman in his arms.

Taking her hand, he strode toward the French windows and pushed them open. She threw back her head and drew breath, the color returning to her cheeks.

He lifted a hand to her face, and her skin almost burned him.

"Good God, feel how hot you are!" he cried. "No wonder you're distressed. Let me remove your gloves."

"No!" She snatched her hand away.

"I mean you no harm," he said. "It's one of the quickest ways to cool the body."

She fended him off. "Please go."

Had her childhood ordeal completely broken her?

"Daughter!" A man appeared at the doorway. Frederica released herself from Hawthorne's grip and ran toward her father, who took her in his arms.

Frederick Stanford had changed little in five years, save a slight thinning of the hair at the temples. But the love in his voice was exactly the same as it had been the night he'd found her unconscious form on his doorstep.

"Papa..."

"Where is Lady Axminster?" Stanford asked. "What good is a chaperone if she leaves her charge to the mercy of the crowd?"

"Papa, don't distress yourself. I'm quite well. I just needed to be outside."

Stanford's focus shifted, and he met Hawthorne's gaze. His eyes radiated anger until recognition glowed in their depths.

"Viscount Radley, what a pleasure to see you. I must thank you for taking care of my Frederica. I trust she was not too distressed?"

"Not at all," Hawthorne said. "She became overheated. It's easily done. Perhaps she would appreciate a turn about the gardens."

Stanford's shoulders relaxed, and he nodded in unspoken gratitude.

"You're very kind," he said.

Frederica relaxed in her father's arms, her eyes glowing with trust. If only she might trust Hawthorne as much. But it was not something he should expect. It was a privilege he must earn. And Frederica's trust was a prize few men would be able to win.

Father's words echoed in his mind.

She's not his daughter...

But Stanford loved her nonetheless.

"I've heard much of your exploits at Cambridge," Stanford said. "And now you're to be a magistrate."

"Yes, sir."

"Your father must be proud. You must tell me how you intend to dispense justice."

Stanford continued to question Hawthorne on his studies and the magistracy. He did not ask the bland, polite questions a mere acquaintance might ask for the purpose of exchanging remarks, but the genuine questions of a man who showed a keen interest in another.

With their attention diverted away from her, Frederica blossomed like a flower in the sun's warmth.

Stanford was a clever man, capable of showing interest in others, yet maintaining his main focus, the restoration of his daughter's peace of mind.

At length, Stanford drew her into the conversation, letting her steer her own way, nurturing her confidence until he gave her the chance to exercise it.

"Frederica has been active in pursuing her accomplishments."

She met Hawthorne's gaze, and he smiled at her.

"Do you still draw and paint, Miss Stanford?"

Her lips lifted into a smile of surprise. "You remember?"

"How could I not? I hear you're quite the proficient."

"You flatter me."

"Your papa has every reason to be proud of you."

Stanford squeezed her hand. "My daughter is the most precious thing I have in the world."

"Papa…"

"I mean it, Rica," Stanford said before addressing Hawthorne again. "She needs people she can trust. I would count it a great favor if you were to watch over her if ever I am not around. I fear society would treat her ill. She has her grandfather, of course, but Sir Benedict isn't getting any younger. I would hope for the sake of the friendship between your father and Sir Benedict, that you would treat her as your ward if anything were to happen to me."

"It would be my honor, sir," Hawthorne said.

"Promise to keep her out of harm's way, away from rakehells and men who prey on a young woman's virtue for sport."

Frederica laughed, a delicate musical note of merriment. Hawthorne's blood warmed at the sound. Would that he could hear her laugh every day!

"Papa, Viscount Radley would find it impossible to keep rakehells at a distance from me, because it would mean he would also need to keep away."

She lifted her gaze, and a firebolt of desire jolted through his body. "How many mistresses do you have?"

"Frederica!" Stanford admonished, but Hawthorne held his hand up. "She has every right to ask. My reputation precedes me."

He met her gaze as bravely as he could, bearing his soul to her scrutiny. "Miss Stanford, a man may have a reputation, but one must always search deeper within to fully understand the calling of his heart."

She colored under his attention and blinked, breaking the spell between them.

"Perhaps I should take you home, Rica," Stanford said.

"Yes, Papa. I'm a little tired."

"I hope we'll meet again, Viscount Radley." Stanford held out his hand. "Are you attending de Grecy's house party?"

"I believe so." Stanford bowed and ushered his daughter inside.

Yes, Stanford was right, danger lurked in every corner of society, and Frederica was exposed to it. Unscrupulous men would take advantage of her.

But Hawthorne was also in danger, very great danger of falling in love with Frederica Stanford.

CHAPTER FIVE

D AWN HAD LONG since broken, but the sun had yet to penetrate through the clouds. Frederica skipped through the dew-soaked grass and headed toward the oak tree at the opposite side of the field. She'd spotted it from the carriage on the journey to de Grecy's estate. Its distinctive silhouette had attracted her eye. She clutched the posy of wild flowers in her hand. Infinitely preferable to the orchids from de Grecy's hothouse, the untamed blooms would brighten up her bedchamber.

The rainfall, which spattered against her skin when she left the house, had grown heavier. By the time she returned, she'd be soaked, the walk back would take at least half an hour. Papa would admonish her for venturing out alone, and Lady Axminster would spend the rest of the day lecturing her on proper decorum. But, after only one day at the house party, Frederica was in need of fresh air to cure her suffocation from the company of idle creatures whose self-worth was defined by their membership at Almack's.

She froze at a deep moan coming from the direction of the tree.

"Dammit!" someone cursed, followed by a splashing sound.

As she drew close to the source of the noise, she spotted a huge horse, saddled and without a rider, standing beside the tree.

"Curse you, animal!" he said, then muttered further obscenities.

A deep ditch ran behind the tree, and Frederica moved toward the edge and looked over.

A man sat at the bottom.

"Hello there!" she said.

He lifted his head, and her stomach flipped. Deep chocolate eyes looked back at her, the intensity of their gaze darkened with pain.

Hawthorne Stiles.

"What's happened?" she asked.

"I'd have thought that was obvious," he growled. "Bloody animal threw me."

She crouched and held out her hand. "Let me help you out. Can you stand?"

He struggled to his feet and reached up, but his leg gave way beneath him, and he fell back with a groan.

"Are you hurt?"

"My ankle. I think I've broken it," he said. "I can't climb up on my own. You'll have to fetch someone to help."

"That'll take too long," she replied. "I can't leave you alone in this rain."

"Then what do you propose? I can't stay here forever."

His gruff tone might have concealed the pain in his voice from most people, but not her. She swung her legs over the edge of the ditch and slipped down to land beside him.

"What the devil are you doing?" he asked.

"Helping you out."

"Don't be a fool."

"It's no different to mounting a horse," Frederica said. She cupped her hands, interlocking the fingers to form a makeshift step. "Here. Place your foot here, and I'll give you a push."

"I can't do that…"

"Yes, you can," she interrupted. "I won't leave until you're out, and *I* don't intend to stay here forever, either."

She bent over, lowering her hands until they were a foot from the ground. "On the count of three."

"It wouldn't be proper," he said.

"Propriety be damned."

"A lady shouldn't curse."

"And neither should a gentleman," she said crisply. "Not even when he's lying in pain in a ditch."

His mouth twitched into a smile, then he placed his hand on her shoulder, and lifted his foot into her hands.

"On the count of three," he said.

"One…two…three…"

She pushed her hands up as he launched himself into the air, then he scrambled over the top and disappeared. Moments later, his head appeared, followed by an outstretched hand.

"My turn to help you."

Ignoring his proffered hand, she climbed up after him, digging her toes into the wall of the ditch to gain a purchase.

"I see you needed no help from me," he said.

"A childhood spent climbing trees better equips one for the world than one frittered away in the schoolroom."

He sat beside the edge of the ditch, pulled off his boot, and inspected his ankle.

"Let me," she said. Ignoring his protests, she knelt beside him, and touched his foot, feeling the bones beneath the skin. He drew in a sharp breath as she pressed her fingers around the ankle bone.

She lifted her skirt and tugged at the hem of her petticoat.

"What the devil are you doing now?" he asked.

"I need something to bind your foot with."

"Here…" he reached for his necktie, "…take this." He unwound it and handed it to her.

As their fingers touched, a shiver rippled through her. Their eyes met, and his fingers curled round her hand. An unfathomable need pulsed within her, and she broke free. She lifted his foot and wound the cloth round his ankle.

"I don't think it's broken."

"Are you a doctor?"

"Of course not," she said, ignoring the rough edge to his voice, "but I've sprained my ankle more times than I can remember. I believe I can tell the difference. It's a little swollen, but the bones seem sound."

A smile danced in his eyes. "I suppose a lifetime spent falling out of trees has equipped you to make such a diagnosis."

"Are you making fun of me, sir?"

"Of course not," he said. "But I rather wonder at your education, Miss Stanford."

"Not all of us are fortunate enough to be admitted into Cambridge."

"No, but a lady needs to be educated if she is to succeed in life."

"The definition of an education is an activity one engages in to learn the skills necessary to survive adulthood," she said. "Given that I am, by no means, a lady, my educational needs differ from those of Alice de Grecy, for example."

"I'll wager your chaperone would disagree with you."

"Lady Axminster is concerned with nothing more than my footing in society. She seeks to enhance it, with a view to securing a suitable match for me."

"Isn't that what every chaperone wants for her charge?"

"And are the wishes of her charge to be discounted?"

"Don't all women wish to secure themselves a husband?"

She blushed at his words and bit her lip to conquer the image in her mind—Hawthorne taking her hand, offering his heart, as she'd once heard him professing love to another, years ago.

"Some of us just wish to be happy," she said.

"Is that not one and the same thing?"

"For a man, perhaps. In a wife, he wants a helpmate to run his home and produce an heir. If she fails to satisfy his other needs, he's at liberty to seek them elsewhere, and society will applaud him for it."

"Such as?"

"Company and conversation. Those he can find at his club, together with brandy and cigars. Affirmation of his power can be provided by his gun, to fell pheasant with, and his ability to dictate to his servants. As for love, he can find that in a mistress."

"There's no guarantee a mistress will love her protector, Miss Stanford."

"No," she said, "but with the freedom to choose as many mistresses as London can afford him, a man's chances of finding love will always surpass those of his wife."

"You have a rather bleak view of matrimony, Miss Stanford."

"Quite the contrary, I assure you," she said. "I'm merely championing the case for marrying for love. I'm optimistic enough to believe that the perfect partner exists in the world for each of us. But I question the chances of finding them, when most marriages are solely based on title and fortune. In my view, unrequited love is the worst pain a living soul can endure."

"Then where do you suggest I find my perfect partner, Miss Stanford?"

He took her hand and squeezed it, and she closed her eyes against the rush of longing which coursed through her. She had already found her perfect partner. She now had to protect her heart.

She secured the makeshift bandage with a knot and stood. "We must return to the house and send for a doctor."

He sighed and reached for his boot, wincing as he pulled it on.

The horse had remained by the tree during their exchange. Frederica smoothed down the front of her gown, grimacing at the mud smears, and approached the animal, her hand outstretched.

The animal's ears flattened as it watched her approach.

"I wouldn't go near him if I were you," Hawthorne said. "I'd rather walk."

"You can't," she replied, keeping her voice soft so as not to frighten the horse. "Not with a sprained ankle."

"I'd rather let the animal go," he said sharply. "I told him I'd have him shot if he threw me again."

"And you think threats are an appropriate method of getting someone to listen?"

"Samson's a horse, not a person," he said, exasperation in his voice.

"And he deserves a chance," she said. "Don't you, boy?"

She moved closer to the horse, holding her hand out, palm upward.

"You're a beautiful boy, aren't you?" she asked. "I'm sorry I have nothing for you, but I'm sure I could find you something back at the house, if you came with me."

The horse snorted and tossed its head.

"Did something frighten you, Samson?" she asked.

"A flock of birds," Hawthorne said, "and not for the first time."

Her stomach clenched, and she gritted her teeth to dispel the image, and took another step forward. "I don't like birds, either, Samson," she said. "Most of the time I know they won't harm me, but when they get too close, it's as if my body freezes and I can't move."

Samson stilled and lifted his head, as if to sniff her hand. One step closer and she'd be able to touch him.

"You understand, don't you?" she said softly. "It's like a wall of water building up inside, until a word, an image, or a flap of wings causes it to burst, and you have to run. Or fight."

She reached out and stroked the animal's nose, smooth and velvety against her fingers.

"Perhaps we can help each other," she said. "Would you let me help you?"

She reached out and took the reins, while continuing to stroke Samson's forehead with her free hand, coaxing him to come to her.

Hawthorne remained silent as the horse took a step forward.

"Brave boy!" she said. "There's no shame in fear, Samson. True bravery lies in conquering that which makes us afraid. Those who profess to be brave, most likely have never had to face their fears. And they will be poorly equipped when the time comes."

She took a step back, resisting the urge to pull on the reins. Samson needed to follow her of his own free will.

She cast a glance over her shoulder. Hawthorne watched her, his eyes dark. Then she resumed her focus on the horse.

"This man won't hurt you," she said. "He didn't mean what he said. Perhaps he's a little frightened of you? But we can help him, can't we?"

The horse took a step toward her, then another. She moved back, and he followed her to where Hawthorne stood, waiting.

"What form of education taught you to do *that*?" he asked.

"None," she replied. "I'm his advocate, so I merely needed to consider his view of the world. As a magistrate, you must have witnessed lawyers doing the same with the accused."

"You see him as the accused?"

"His life is at stake."

"Not anymore," he said. "It seems as if I've benefitted from an education this morning, for you have taught me the error of my ways. Now, if I may prevail upon you to help me mount, I'll take you back to the house, before we dissolve in this rain."

THE CHIMNEYS OF de Grecy's manor came into view, and the woman in Hawthorne's arms grew silent. Her courage, which had come to the fore in the face of his predicament, seemed to diminish with each step closer to the house.

Or was it the closer they came to society? As a child, she'd seemed so carefree, skipping across the fields, thriving in the outdoors. But when confined in a room full of people, such as a ballroom in London, she became skittish, not unlike his horse.

Her body shook with tension. How had she described it? A wall threatening to break, after which she'd bolt.

He reined Samson to a halt.

"Do you wish to dismount, Miss Stanford?"

"I–I don't know," she said. "If anyone sees me…"

"I understand," he replied. "I have no wish to ruin your reputation. I'll take you to one of the back doors where you can slip inside, unseen. Nobody will challenge a young lady wandering inside the house on her own. Send for your maid as soon as you return to your chamber, and she can see to your gown."

She shook her head, distress in her expression. "I don't have a maid," she said. "One of the chambermaids here has been tending to me."

"You cannot be assured of her discretion." He sighed. "My valet can deal with it and will swear anyone he encounters into silence."

He steered Samson toward the back of the house, then helped her to dismount.

"You should put ice on your ankle," she said.

"De Grecy's icehouse will be empty this time of year."

"Not quite," she replied. "Alice told me we're having sorbet to-night. She was rather proud of the fact, given that Lord Darlington's ice ran out last month, and Viscount Hartford's the month before."

"Then I must see if Rawlings can procure me some, and relieve our Miss de Grecy of some of her pride."

Miss Stanford frowned, but a hint of mirth showed in her eyes. "I must admonish you, sir. Alice is my friend."

"Then I shall honor her, Miss Stanford, for her taste in friends."

A voice called out in the distance, barking an order. Another re-plied.

"You must get inside before you're seen," Hawthorne said. "Go straight to your room. I'll send Rawlings directly. Don't open your door to anyone but him."

"Thank you," she said. "I am in your debt."

"And I, yours."

She looked up at him, and his senses were assaulted by her eyes, against which the drab, gray landscape faded into nothing. His body had hardened with need the moment he'd lifted her onto his lap in the saddle and felt her warm body against him. Now, as he yearned to drown in those eyes, his manhood surged against his breeches, and he shifted his position to ease the ache.

If only she weren't so far beneath him! Once more, he cursed the ill fortune of his birth. He had no need to find his perfect match. She stood before him, glowing with compassion and a love of all things living. But she had spoken the truth about matrimony. Society expected the heir to an earldom to marry well. Perhaps if Adam had lived, Hawthorne, as the second son, would have been free to marry for love.

CHAPTER SIX

A N INHUMAN SCREAM split the night air.

Hawthorne froze, and his companion clutched his arm.

"What's that?"

"I suspect it's an owl, Clara."

Clara, Lady Swainson, relaxed her grip.

"You go on ahead," he said, "in case the noise roused anyone. I'll backtrack."

"What if someone sees you?"

"I'll tell them I'm an avid ornithologist."

"Always the model of discretion, Hawthorne, darling."

She blew him a kiss and scurried into the darkness. De Grecy's house party gave him the ideal opportunity to service the needs of his body, and he was practiced enough in the art of seduction to predict the precise moment of her climax, silencing her shrieks of pleasure with his mouth as her body rippled around him. Widowhood certainly agreed with her. Twenty years after the demise of Lord Swainson, she'd never remarried, despite numerous offers.

Hawthorne's own release tonight had not come. He'd shown an ungentlemanly penchant for fantasizing that he was buried inside an altogether different female body. When he'd opened his eyes, his body had winced in disappointment that the eyes looking back at him were brown, not green, that the hair he clutched in his fist was silver-blonde, not red.

He straightened his breeches as the thought of *her* made him harder than he'd been all night.

Why in God's name had Stanford foisted that old goat on his daughter as chaperone? Deaf as a barn door and twice as wide, Lady Axminster was a poor companion for such an enigmatic young woman. With her connections to Lady Jersey, the woman might present Frederica's best chances for acceptance in London society, but it would not make her happy. Miss Stanford needed freedom and love, neither of which would be found at Almack's.

Alice de Grecy might be an unremarkable creature compared to Frederica, but at least their friendship drew Frederica away from the rest of the party. Only that afternoon, he'd stumbled across them in the drawing room, every conceivable square inch of floor covered in sketches of Miss De Grecy, ranging from simple outlines to more detailed studies of a single feature, an eye, her upturned nose, or that petulant little mouth.

Both artist and sitter had been too occupied to notice him. Frederica's focus was on the sitter herself, tutting in frustration as her pencil swept across the page until a smile of satisfaction crossed her lips. Then she'd tossed the completed sketch aside and begun a new one.

Alice De Grecy had noticed him first.

"Viscount Radley! What do you think of these likenesses? Do they portray me in a good light?"

In the artless manner of a woman fishing for compliments, she turned her eyes on him, widening them in that maddening manner of unattached ladies schooled to appear alluring to the opposite sex.

"You're a beautiful woman, Miss De Grecy," he'd said, "and these likenesses say a great deal about the subject."

Miss De Grecy had failed to grasp his true meaning, but a smile had twitched on Frederica's lips while she'd concentrated on her easel.

"Of course," he'd continued, "it is what the likeness tells us about the artist which is of more interest to those with a true appreciation for art."

Her hand had stilled, and she'd reached for her sketchbook, holding it to her chest in a protective gesture.

"Alice, I've finished the preliminary sketches. Perhaps I might begin the painting tomorrow?"

Before he could stop her, she'd slipped out of the room.

A second scream ripped through the memory and returned him to the present.

It wasn't an owl.

He broke into a run, toward the source of the scream.

Doors opened as guest after guest was roused by the noise.

"Did you hear that?"

"What is it?"

"Return to your beds," Hawthorne raised his voice and addressed the crowd. "I'm sure it's just one of the maids taken ill."

"Shouldn't we fetch Lord de Grecy?"

"His lordship sleeps in the west wing. By the time he gets here, I'll have dealt with the matter."

Reassured by his authoritative tone, the guests slipped back into their rooms, like a wave receding.

The screams had died down to a whimper accompanied by a male voice, soothing, coaxing.

At the end of the corridor, a shaft of light stretched across the floor where someone had left a door ajar. In the flickering light of a candle, he could make out two shapes in the bedchamber. One knelt on the floor, rocking back and forth. A second crouched beside it.

"Hush, daughter."

"I–I must get out."

"Rica, it's over, now. I'm here."

She let out another wail. "Birds, they're in here!"

Frederica...

Her nightgown had been torn down the front, exposing her body.

But her father didn't seem to notice her state of undress, which tightened Hawthorne's body with want.

Dear God, had someone compromised her?

"Can't breathe…" she gasped. "…Make them go away…"

Stanford drew her into his arms.

"Hush, sweet one. Papa's here."

"The room, the door. They're closing in on me!"

Stanford stroked her hair. "Come back to your Papa, dearest."

A maidservant appeared next to Hawthorne, rubbing her hands against the cold.

"What's happening, sir? I heard a scream. Is someone ill?"

Another cry rang out, and the maidservant shrank back. "That's no illness. I know madness when I hear it."

Hawthorne grasped her arm. "It's not madness."

The voice wailed again. "The door, the birds!"

"Is she lacking in wits?" the maid asked. "It's Miss Stanford, isn't it? I've heard tell…"

"Keep your tales to yourself," he snarled, "and I'll thank you not to divulge anything of what you've seen."

The maid's expression grew sly. "What's my silence worth?"

Fueled by a need to protect his little changeling, he reached out and took the maid's throat. The greed left her eyes, replaced by terror.

"Breathe a word about this and I'll have you dismissed.

"My family…" she choked, "I can't, they'll starve…"

"Then promise me you'll be silent," he said. "Or I'll break your neck."

Her body trembled, and she nodded. "I promise."

"Good. Now go."

He released her, and she scuttled into the darkness, sniffing.

Hawthorne looked at his hands, hands meant to dispense justice, not terror. What had come over him?

An overwhelming need to protect *her*.

Her father rocked her to and fro as one might soothe a fevered infant.

"There, sweet one. All over!"

"Papa," she said, her voice deepening as the terror of her nightmare loosened her throat. "Oh, Papa, I'm sorry! I had the dream again. Does anyone know? Did they hear?"

"No, my love."

"What about Lady Axminster?"

"Lady Axminster is deafer than a brick and half as intelligent. Why do you think I chose her as your chaperone?"

Stanford picked her up in his arms and carried her to bed. A ripple of emotion threaded through Hawthorne's body. The need to ease her pain burned through him, for he was responsible for her nightmares.

"Forgive me, Papa," she said, her voice muffled against her father's chest as he lowered her to the mattress.

"It's not your fault."

Stanford looked up, and his gaze focused on Hawthorne in the doorway. A warning in the older man's eyes told Hawthorne to keep his distance.

Her body stilled, and she closed her eyes.

"Sleep now," Stanford whispered.

He placed a kiss on her head and blinked, and a tear slid down his cheek.

Hawthorne pushed the door open more fully and slipped inside the chamber. Stanford shook his head.

"Hush. You mustn't wake her."

"Can't I help?" Hawthorne asked.

"I'll be fine. She should sleep for the rest of the night, but I'll stay with her for a while until she's settled."

"Let me," Hawthorne said. "You look exhausted."

"I've done this before," Stanford replied. "I cannot risk her waking and seeing you. It would destroy her if she knew an outsider witnessed this."

She shifted her arms, revealing a wrist. Hawthorne's breath caught at the scars. Absent-mindedly, Stanford caressed her skin as if to soothe them away.

"Her wrists…"

"Aye," Stanford said. "She was injured during her ordeal—you remember? Just before you left for Cambridge. My brave child fought against the ropes those gypsies bound her with and broke free."

"Gypsies?"

"She's stronger than she looks," Stanford continued. "She made it all the way home before collapsing. Her physical scars will never completely heal. But I would hope that, in time, her invisible scars will fade and her peace of mind will be restored." He set his mouth into a grim line. "I'll do everything in my power to keep her safe. Society would have her committed to Bedlam if they knew."

Frederica murmured in her sleep, and Hawthorne moved closer, compelled by the need to comfort her.

"Don't come any closer," Stanford said, his eyes pleading.

He retreated to the door, but before he left the room, he turned and bowed. "Sir, what you asked me at the ball, to take care of her. It would be my honor."

"Thank you."

Hawthorne didn't deserve Stanford's gratitude, but if he could protect his little changeling from herself as well as society, he could atone for the part he'd played in her destruction.

"OF COURSE, IT'S nothing compared to the Duke of Markham's aviary in London, but Papa's very proud of it."

Alice linked her arm through Frederica's and led her further into the aviary toward a display of brightly colored flowers.

The best cure for a weakness of the mind was to face one's fears. Hadn't she told Samson that, yesterday? In the aviary, in the company of the other guests, Frederica could test her resolve. The occasional flap of wings clenched at her stomach, but the chatter of the guests obliterated the sounds of the birds of paradise which resided there.

"What do you think?" Alice said. "Wasn't I right about the colors? You wouldn't find flowers such as this in the woodlands."

"But they're brought about by mother nature."

"Mother nature needs a little help," Alice said. "Or at the very least, she must be trained to show herself in the best light, how society wants her to be."

"Should everything adapt itself to conform with society?"

"Good gracious, Frederica!" Alice laughed. "But I suppose you can be forgiven considering your background."

"But you must admit, Miss de Grecy, that your friend is right."

A clear baritone resonated within Frederica's bones. Together with the flutter of wings, it resurrected a long-hidden memory of dark eyes full of fear and concern, and of strong arms carrying her home across the fields, before abandoning her on the ground.

"Viscount Radley!" Alice's voice lifted a tone, her body subtly changing into the stance of female availability and desperation.

"Society may give mankind a structure within which they must operate," Hawthorne said, "but society must also accept that which is different."

He moved closer to Frederica. "Are you well, Miss Stanford?" he asked.

She nodded.

"Miss de Grecy!" a voice called out from across the aviary.

"Tend to your guests, Miss de Grecy," Hawthorne said. "Your friend is in safe hands with me."

As Alice retreated, Hawthorne held out his arm. Frederica took it, and he placed his hand over hers and squeezed her fingers.

"Miss Stanford," he said brightly, "perhaps you'd be so kind as to show me the flowers you were discussing so animatedly with Miss de Grecy."

His grip tightened, and a thrill of possession coursed through her blood, as if his strong, muscular frame would safeguard her from her nightmares, if only she'd surrender to him.

He stopped beside an orchid. "Such an extraordinary looking object," he said. "By all accounts, difficult to cultivate in England. What purpose does it serve here, do you think?"

"Other than feeding the vanities of the idle rich who are too foolish to appreciate the natural world?"

"Aren't flowers the symbol of love?" he asked. "They're the means by which the plant attracts the instruments of procreation. The bee gathers the nectar and moves from plant to plant, spreading pollen so the plant can reproduce."

Her cheeks warmed at his words. "Should you be speaking of such intimate topics with a woman?"

He squeezed her hand again. "My little changeling is no ordinary woman. And we were speaking of such matters during our excursion outdoors, yesterday."

"I don't appreciate the imprisonment of living things which have been removed from their natural habitat. No creature should be incarcerated or confined."

"Are you speaking of yourself?" he asked.

"Perhaps."

A bird flew in front of her, and she stiffened at the memory of her nightmare. A warm hand squeezed her fingers, and he steered her toward a different plant, a single stem sprouting from a number of spike-shaped leaves, covered in a cluster of flowers.

"According to the label, it's called a hyacinth," he said. "What do you think of the color, Miss Stanford? Would it be easy to replicate in paint?"

"Such a gaudy shade of purple is easy to reproduce," she said. "A simple mixture of red and blue would suffice, though at the edges of the petals, the blue becomes more prominent." She sighed. "Alice wants me to paint some of them for her, but where's the challenge in something so easy? What are hothouse flowers compared to grasses? The subtle hues of green and brown which adorn the countryside are ignored by society. They would only appreciate the green if it were gone."

A shadow passed overhead, followed by another, and she froze, swallowing to battle the wall of fear which swelled inside her.

"Are you well, Miss Stanford?"

"I can't breathe…" A ball of fear knotted in her stomach, and she closed her eyes.

A number of voices drew near, exclaiming with enthusiasm.

"Oh, what pretty colors!"

"Did you see it fly past?"

"I say! What's wrong with *her*?"

Hawthorne's arm tightened around her waist, and he pulled her outside, crossing the pathway in swift, confident footsteps. "That's better," he whispered.

His eyes shimmered with concern and understanding. Her cheeks warmed with shame. The man she worshipped had witnessed her spell of madness.

"You became overheated, as did I," he said brightly. "I find glasshouses unbearably stuffy. Personally, I loathe a confined space. I cannot understand anyone who'd rather be indoors on a day such as this."

She drew a deep breath, the fresh air dissipating her panic.

"I see we are of one mind, Miss Stanford."

Footsteps approached as the other guests joined them.

"Good Lord, Miss Stanford!" Lady Axminster's sharp tones cut through the air.

"Rica?" Papa's concerned face came into view.

"What's going on?" Alice appeared beside her. "Are you all right, Frederica?"

"Of course she is!" Hawthorne's voice dominated the others. "It's unpleasantly hot in there, and I was most anxious for Miss Stanford's opinion on the flowers outside and how their colors compare to your orchids."

He squeezed her hand. "Isn't that right, Miss Stanford?"

"I–I suppose so," she stammered.

He steered her toward Papa, who took her arm.

"Thank you, Viscount Radley," Papa said. "I'm indebted to you."

"You're welcome, sir." Hawthorne leaned forward, and his breath caressed the skin of Frederica's neck. He lowered his voice to a whisper. "My little changeling will always be safe with me."

She lifted her head to answer, but he'd already moved away.

"Viscount Radley!" a voice cried out from the direction of the house, and a groomsman came into view, waving a piece of paper.

Hawthorne strode toward him, grasped the note, and tore it open. His body stiffened, his mouth set into a hard line. His eyes turned almost black, and he cast a quick glance at Frederica. Anger and regret glittered in their depths, then he closed his eyes, blinking to clear the emotion. Opening them again, his face showed the same impassive expression he bestowed on society.

He returned the note to the groom whose eyes widened as he glanced at it. He delivered a bow.

"I–I'm sorry for your loss, Viscount Radley. Forgive me, I mean, Earl Stiles. You'll want your carriage, I assume?"

"Yes," Hawthorne said, his voice strained, the words forced through gritted teeth. "I'll need to leave immediately."

He turned to their hostess. "Lady de Grecy, forgive me, I must return home." He bowed, then crossed the lawn in quick, purposeful strides.

So, Hawthorne's father was dead. The only link between Frederica and Hawthorne was broken, the friendship between Grandpapa and the old earl. Doubtless, he'd now want nothing more to do with her.

>>>><<<<

AS SHE REACHED the landing at the top of the stairs on her way to supper, Frederica collided with a solid wall of muscle. She drew back as long fingers curled round her wrist. She looked up into his eyes. A small glimmer of pain lay beneath the veneer of the cold aristocrat.

"My...my lord," she said. "I mean, Earl Stiles."

His jaw tightened at her formality with him.

"I thought you had returned to Radley Hall."

"I'm leaving now."

"I'm sorry."

"Don't be."

He appeared carved from marble, cold, passionless, and impenetrable.

"Please accept my condolences on the loss of your father," she said.

He remained unmoving.

"Your father was a good man..."

"Spare me the witless speech of a lady, madam. Tomorrow I'll suffer condolences and empty words, but I thought *you* better than that." He loosened his grip and sighed. "A man doesn't feel the sorrow a woman harbors."

"I understand," she said quietly. "I never knew my mother. You and I—we have—had our fathers to guide us. Papa is everything to me. If I lost him, it would rip my heart out."

Understanding the grief he needed to hide for the sake of proprietary, she took his hand.

"I know you must be strong," she said. "But a beloved parent de-

61

serves to be remembered and grieved."

His mouth tightened.

"I shall grieve," she said. "On your behalf."

"Oh, little changeling," he whispered. "You understand." He coaxed her closer until their lips met. "Only you…" he whispered.

Longing coursed through her body as his lips brushed against her mouth. She let out a soft cry, overwhelmed by feelings.

"Frederica …"

His tongue traced the seam of her lips and gently probed.

She granted his wish, opening up to him. Her Hawthorne, her perfect partner…

He wanted her.

What was she thinking? He was too far above her in station to ever view her as anything more than an object of lust. She could never subject herself to that. Not from him.

"Forgive me." She stepped back. "I should not have kissed you."

"Frederica, I…"

She would not willingly give in to her desires. Better to love him from a distance, to wonder what might be, than to give herself to him only to be cast aside when he grew weary of her. Ignoring his pleading tone and beautiful eyes, she fled.

CHAPTER SEVEN

HAWTHORNE SET HIS glass on the desk and shook his head.
"It cannot be true."

Sir Benedict stubbed out his cigar. "Surely you must have had your suspicions. Frederica looks nothing like Stanford."

"Father said she wasn't his daughter, but I hadn't known Eleanor wasn't her mother. That means not even you are related to her."

Hawthorne had almost finished going through Father's papers. There was just one last bundle to review, the bundle Sir Benedict had brought in this morning.

He picked up a document covered in elegant handwriting containing both Father's name and Frederica's.

"What's this?"

"It's what it says," Sir Benedict said. "A promissory note."

"But it notes Father's intention to give her five thousand on the occasion of her marriage."

A cold hand clutched at his insides. There was only one reason Father would pledge such a large sum of money on a young girl.

"Don't even think it, young man," Sir Benedict admonished. "Your father merely felt a sense of obligation toward Frederica's *natural* mother."

"Why?"

"The girl died in his care. She was a cousin of Mrs. White's."

"Father's old housekeeper?"

Sir Benedict nodded. "Read on, my boy. You'll find a letter from Mrs. White. But I cannot bear to speak of it aloud."

Hawthorne pulled out the letter, written in the poorly-fashioned script of a servant. The heartfelt words spoke of a young woman who had been driven to insanity by her ruination.

The last line chilled his blood as he read the name of the man who had caused such destruction, Frederica's natural father.

"Ye Gods..."

He curled his fingers into a fist, the paper crackling in his grip, and dropped the letter as if it burned his skin.

"Does Stanford know?"

"No," the old man said. "He believes she's his daughter. Your father and I agreed to maintain the deception."

"Why?" Hawthorne exclaimed. "You deceived a respectable man into believing her to be his, and have been lying to him for nineteen years! Not only that, you've deceived yourself. She's not your granddaughter. What you've done is unlawful."

"There speaks the magistrate," Sir Benedict scoffed. "But what of the compassionate man I've grown to admire, the man who would champion the cause of justice, irrespective of the law of the land?"

"Stanford loved his wife to distraction," Hawthorne said. "You've betrayed that love."

The door opened to reveal a footman.

"Begging your pardon, my lord, your solicitor has arrived."

Hawthorne pinched the bridge of his nose to dispel the ache in his head. "Thank you, Watson."

"Is everything all right, sir?" Concern etched the servant's face, and he cast a glance at Sir Benedict. "I heard raised voices."

"Of course," Hawthorne barked. "Now, get out."

After the door closed, Sir Benedict raised his head, his amber eyes meeting Hawthorne's gaze.

"I loved my daughter more than life itself," he said, pain hoarsening his voice. "I never believed a man would love her more until Stanford came asking for her hand."

He waved toward the decanter. "Why do you think I consented to the match between her and a wine merchant? She had her pick of the young men, but I saw how deeply Stanford loved her. The night she was taken from us, it broke him. As it broke me."

A sigh rattled from his chest, and he grimaced in pain, rubbing his left arm.

"Frederick had lost his wife, and I was damned if I was going to see him lose his child."

"What happened to the child? Eleanor's real child?"

"She died. Stanford was too grief-stricken to understand he'd lost his daughter as well. Doctor Baines had sedated him."

"Then surely the doctor knows…"

"Doctor Baines died of consumption some years ago. I paid him handsomely and swore him to silence. The very night the Almighty saw fit to take my daughter and grandchild, he delivered salvation in the form of that baby. Stanford believes her to be his, and I will not have him broken again."

"And her?"

"I love her as if she were my flesh and blood." Sir Benedict leaned forward, his expression grave. "And I expect you to honor your father's memory by not revealing her true identity to anyone. Not least, her natural father. It would do more harm than good."

Sir Benedict was right. Sometimes the truth was best kept buried.

But the truth had a way of revealing itself. Like water contained behind a wall, it eventually seeped through to conquer the barriers with which man sought to control nature.

His breath caught at the memory of those words—Frederica's words—uttered in the De Grecy aviary.

His little changeling. Only now did it become clear what sort of changeling she was. Not a child from the otherworld delivered by the faeries, but one brought into the world by an act of violence. By the devil himself. The devil whose name taunted him, written in stark, black letters.

He smoothed out the letter, wetted his thumb, and rubbed at the name until it faded into obscurity.

He placed his elbows on the desk and steepled his fingers. Sir Benedict's eyes met his, a plea in their expression. It was the expression a defendant bestowed on him in court, one accused of a deed committed out of desperation. One must always look beyond the deed to understand what had driven the perpetrator. Hawthorne could use his discretion for the good of society, a small gesture, but to one person it meant the world.

And Frederica meant the world to Stanford and to Sir Benedict.

"I'll do anything you ask," he said. "These papers shall remain under lock and key."

The old man's body relaxed, the breath leaving his body in a sigh.

"I have one more favor to ask, my boy."

"Go ahead."

"Your father's pledge. A dowry of five thousand is too much. Reduce it to one thousand." Sir Benedict raised his hand to stem the protest on Hawthorne's lips. "I'm not asking it because of her illegitimacy."

"Father made the pledge. And Stanford is aware of it."

"But it was not notarized," Sir Benedict said. "It's not legally binding."

"How can you profess to love her if you wish to reduce her fortune?"

"Believe me, my boy, I do love her. While she was growing up, I petitioned the trustees of my estate to bestow a much larger fortune on her, and they refused to break the terms of entailment. But recently, I have understood how a fortune would bring her no good."

"But a fortune is her best chance at a prosperous and happy life."

"Surely you don't think money the only key to happiness? Just look at Markham! *He* married a woman for her dowry and drove her into an early grave. That profligate son of his has been brought up to enjoy all the comforts and vices money can buy. Roderick's even worse than his father. He'll indulge in debauchery for years to come and will never suffer the benefit to one's character brought about by a lack of funds. You cannot wish for Frederica to be tainted by such a lifestyle?"

"All women must marry."

"Can you see her making a successful marriage?" Sir Benedict asked. "Name one man in the world who would both understand and love her. She sees the world through different eyes. Five thousand from you along with the thousand her father will bestow on her, would attract the attention of fortune hunters. I want her to have enough to enjoy independence, but not so much as to attract a man unable to appreciate her qualities. Qualities which you must admit are unique."

Unique indeed. The thought of Frederica being wasted on the fops which prowled the edges of society, her inquisitive mind stunted by the life of a woman destined to serve her husband in the home, confined by the chains of matrimony…

Sir Benedict spoke the truth. Not a single man in the world valued her for what she was.

Except you.

"Very well," he said. "But *I* must bear responsibility for the decision. I'll reduce it on one condition, you tell Stanford it was my decision."

"Why would you do that?"

"She may never forgive the man responsible for reducing her fortune. An act of love should not be rewarded with hatred."

Sir Benedict smiled. "Your father would have been proud of you. I suppose it's little matter to you whether she blames you, for you're so far above her that she'd never enter your thoughts." He reached for his cane and struggled to his feet. "I can rest in peace now I know someone other than her father will watch over her."

With a groan, the old man shuffled to the door.

"Are you all right, sir?"

"Just age, my boy. I never believed I'd outlive your father. We often talked about it. He surpassed me in so much when we were together at Cambridge that I'd laughed about death being the only force he couldn't conquer."

After the door closed, Hawthorne slumped in his chair. In one aspect, Sir Benedict couldn't be more wrong.

She would always reside in his thoughts.

But his little changeling would soon hate him. He had just brought about Sir Benedict's peace of mind, but at the cost of his own.

A clatter echoed from outside, followed by a low cry.

Hawthorne leapt to his feet and burst into the hallway. A prone figure lay on the floor, body twisted, mouth open as if straining for air, his right hand curled around his left arm. Lifeless eyes stared up at the chandelier which hung above him, the sunlight winking on the facets of the crystals.

Sir Benedict had outlived his best friend by only a few days.

"GRANDPAPA..."

Frederica averted her gaze from the coffin being lowered into the ground and closed her eyes, reliving the memory of the man: the smell of old cigars and port, the deep hum of his voice, and the sparkle of love in his eyes, even when he'd turned a disapproving look on her.

That was how he should be remembered, not as a cold mass of flesh and bone concealed inside a wooden box.

"Come, dearest." Papa said. "It's time to return home. Your grandpapa's lawyers are waiting."

The body was still warm, yet the officials already circled around him, vultures wanting to pick over the remains, to secure profit and further their businesses.

Papa held out his hand. He might appear stoic as the earth swallowed his father-in-law's body, but his fingers trembled as they curled around hers. Grandpapa was the last remnant of the mother Frederica had never known, the woman Papa had loved so deeply that he'd refused to marry again.

Perhaps one day Frederica might find someone to love, and to love her as deeply as Papa loved Mama. Someone prepared to defend her against society and accept her affliction.

Someone like *him*.

"Come on, Papa, we'll face them together."

He helped her into the carriage. "My darling child, I'm so proud of you."

"CURSE HIM! HOW could he do this?"

Papa's body shook with indignation.

The lawyer shifted uncomfortably. "Forgive me, Mr. Stanford, but Earl Stiles is entitled to do what he wishes with his money. There was no legal obligation to bestow anything on your daughter. Be thankful he's agreed to one thousand."

"It would have been better to bestow nothing at all, Mr. Stockton," Papa scoffed. "To reduce a sum his father had promised, what clearer indication can he give of his contempt? He has ample funds, five thousand is nothing to him."

The teacups rattled as Papa slapped the desk. "Not only has he insulted my daughter, he's insulted his father's memory. To send you round to tell us the day I've buried her grandfather. I cannot articulate into words how this makes me feel. I'll never forgive him, never!"

The lawyer set his teacup aside. "The earl travels to London to-morrow. He's asked you to wait on him before he leaves."

"For what purpose? To insult me further?"

"Mr. Stanford, may I remind you the earl is under no obligation. The deed has yet to be signed. I would respectfully ask you to set aside your pride for your daughter's sake and Sir Benedict's memory. By all accounts, it was Sir Benedict who argued in her favor."

Papa sighed, his stance softening. He could never withstand confrontations. His wish for peace and harmony surpassed the materialism which festered among the upper classes.

"Very well," he sighed. "I'll see him." He nodded to Frederica. "Stay here, Rica. I will not suffer you to attend the earl."

The amount itself mattered little to Frederica. It was enough to ensure a comfortable life. But sorrow shuddered through her at the motivation behind Hawthorne's action. The late earl must have valued her for a reason, perhaps due to his friendship with Grandpapa. But Hawthorne, in going directly against his father's wishes, had demonstrated that, to him, she was worth considerably less.

CHAPTER EIGHT

FREDERICA PACKED HER paints up and rinsed her brushes, stretching her arms to relieve the tension in her muscles. When focused on her artwork, she entered a different world. Her physical body lost its awareness of her environment and in her mind, she drifted into the painting, where rich reds pulsed against green. The contrasting colors gave the picture depth even though it had been painted on a flat surface. It was a trick her tutor had taught her, difficult to master, but after years of practice, she had achieved it.

Even though winter had set in, there was always something interesting to paint, the leafless trees and strong trunks splitting into slimmer branches, reaching outward. When snow fell, the contrast of white against the dark branches lent a new richness—small diamonds sparkling as the sunlight caught the snow.

And Samson... Hawthorne may have affirmed that Frederica was too far beneath him to be worthy of his notice, but he couldn't prevent her from befriending his horse. Most people would view Samson as uninteresting to look at. But his coat, though unremarkable at first glance, bore dappled marks in subtle shades of gray and blue, growing darker closer to the tail. Had Mr. Stubbs, the famous painter, still been alive, he would have replicated Samson's spirit in oil, and his portrait might have graced Hawthorne's drawing room at Radley Hall. But the horse would have to settle for being immortalized in watercolor, hung in Frederica's considerably less impressive parlor.

Painting was not simply the means to replicate what she saw before her, but to represent her love for the subject or, in this instance, her love for Papa. It would always say more about Frederica herself than the subject she painted.

It is what the likeness tells us about the artist which is of more interest to those with a true appreciation for art.

Those words—*his* words—resurfaced in her memory, and she closed the lid of her paint box with a snap.

Hawthorne always resided in her mind.

Would she never be free of him?

Her current painting, a Christmas gift for Papa, was almost finished. But before the two of them could celebrate together, their first holiday without dear Grandpapa, she faced the ordeal of the house party at Radley Hall.

His residence.

The day of Grandpapa's funeral, Papa had returned from being summoned to Radley Hall, his attitude toward Hawthorne having mellowed. He'd argued, as the lawyer had, that she had no need for a large fortune.

And he was right. All she needed was freedom and the opportunity to live an unrestricted life where she could openly express her joy at the natural world and not suffer the fear that her instances of madness would be viewed by those who wouldn't understand. She had enough bestowed on her to achieve just that. While she had Papa, there would be someone to protect her, but with no other living relatives, her father had explained that Earl Stiles had repeated his promise to oversee her wellbeing.

What distressed her most, was the fact that Hawthorne knew of her situation—perhaps even of her madness.

She heard a rap at the door.

"Frederica?"

"Come in, Papa." She turned the painting to face the wall.

"Is it finished?"

"Almost, but it's supposed to be a surprise. No looking until Christmas."

"Very well." He smiled. "Come, now. It's time to go. You mustn't keep the earl waiting."

"I don't see why we have to go."

"Because he's invited us. The company will be good for you. A house party is always to be preferred over the crush of a ball."

"Can't you come with me?"

"I'm sorry, Rica, love," Papa said. "It's my busiest time of year. I'm overseeing a large order for the Duke of Markham. I'll join you once it's concluded."

"But why would the earl invite us, invite me?"

Papa took her hand. "Perhaps he wishes to help you widen your acquaintance before we go to London in the spring."

"Why would he do that?"

"Because he's a kind man, Frederica, and because London is never so daunting if one already has friends there. And since Lady Axminster's gout has driven her to Bath, we must replenish your list of acquaintances from his list of guests."

His guests...

Would that list include his mistress, the sophisticated Lady Swainson who Frederica had seen, more than once, riding along the drive to Radley Hall in her barouche?

Her stomach tightened with apprehension. The image of him courting another sent a spike of agony through her heart. She had always prided herself in being fearless. Though the demons tormented her at night, she wasn't afraid of a man or woman alive.

Except him. That fear lurked within her, fear of the power he had over her body and the need which burned within her whenever she looked into his eyes. In order to conquer her fears, she must face them.

"Very well, Papa," she said. "I'm ready to go."

"THIS IS YOUR room, miss. Dinner is at seven. Will you be requiring help with your evening gown?"

"I can dress myself, thank you."

The maid dropped a curtsey, then scuttled away as if she couldn't escape quickly enough.

Frederica's chamber was in a different part of the house to the other guests. The room was furnished elegantly enough, with a lit fire, but lacked the opulence of the rest of Radley Hall. Her trunk sat forlornly in a corner as if it, too, recognized the insult. The bare-paneled walls of the corridor outside were dotted with candle sconces. Functional, rather than decorative—as befitted the servants' quarters.

Was she so repugnant that he wanted her isolated? Perhaps he'd have her meals brought up so she might not offend the rest of the party with her presence.

She wouldn't give him the satisfaction. If he wanted to remind her of her inferiority, she'd be happy to disappoint him. Closing the door to her chamber, she moved across to her trunk, pulled out a dress of pale blue silk, and draped it over the back of a chair beside the fireplace. She glanced at the clock on the mantle shelf. Dinner was being served late, so she had time to visit the stables and see Samson. With luck, by the time she returned to dress for dinner, the warmth from the fire would have removed the creases in her evening gown.

HAWTHORNE WAVED HIS valet out of the dressing room and finished buttoning his jacket. Rawlings was a good enough man, but the valet's attention to detail rendered the ritual of dressing overly tedious. He could, however, be commended for his powers of observation as he was able to tell Hawthorne that Miss Stanford had arrived one hour ago and, shortly afterward, had been seen walking in the direction of the stables.

After leaving his dressing room, he set off in her wake. Whether or not she wished to speak to him, given the events following her grandfather's death, Hawthorne still owed it to Sir Benedict's memory to ensure her wellbeing.

And he owed it to her father. Stanford deserved to know the truth about Sir Benedict's request to reduce her dowry, and Hawthorne had found himself unable to harbor yet another secret about Frederica. The day Stanford had buried his father-in-law, Hawthorne had offered to enter into partnership with his business, to ensure its continuation, with Frederica as the sole beneficiary. A regular income, secured under trust, would grant her more financial independence than a dowry ever could. Untouchable by a future husband, it would render her safe from fortune hunters. Having initially resisted, arguing that Hawthorne knew nothing about the business of wine other than how to drink it in vast quantities, Stanford had acquiesced, on the condition that Hawthorne left the business decisions to him.

The snowflakes, which had scattered in the winter air, grew in density. Rather than melting, a light dusting covered the ground. The clouds hung overhead, their purple hue the promise of more snow to come.

Ahead, a slender figure emerged from the stables, a book tucked under her arm. Even in the dwindling light of the winter afternoon, her hair glowed as if on fire. She waved and blew a kiss toward the stable.

"Until next time, beautiful man!" she cried.

A deep voice answered, and she waved again. Laughing, she set off in the direction of the kitchen gardens and disappeared.

What game did she think she was playing?

He crossed the stable yard and called out.

"Who's in there?"

The head groom appeared at the door.

"Bartlett! What the devil are you doing with Miss Stanford?"

Bartlett glanced behind him. "I'm not supposed to say."

"Good God, man," Hawthorne said. "In whose employ are you? Mine or hers?"

The groom sighed and gestured toward the stall. "She came to see Samson."

"For what purpose?"

"She helps groom him."

"And she asked you to keep it a secret?" Hawthorne asked. "You must know I wouldn't be angry with her for visiting."

"She didn't ask me for her sake, sir, but for Samson's," the groom said. "You've said yourself you'll get rid of him if he didn't improve. She wanted to make sure that doesn't happen, and I was to tell her if you spoke of it again, so she might petition her father to purchase him."

Beyond Bartlett, the large Arabian stood placidly in his stall. Since the animal had thrown Hawthorne on de Grecy's estate, he had grown calmer. He still suffered from high spirits, but Hawthorne had found himself increasingly able to control him. Until now, he'd attributed it to his own skills as a horseman.

"She grooms him, you say?" he said.

"And talks to him, sir," the groom replied. "She's brought Samson tidbits every time she's visited, as well as ointment for my hands. It was her grandfather's, but Sir Benedict has no need of it now, God rest his soul." He held up his hands, sadness in his expression. "Such a kind young woman, if I may say so, sir. I don't care what they say about her. You said the same about Samson here, and he's turned out all right. They both just need a little understanding, that's all. Kindred spirits, you might say."

The groom approached the horse and patted his flank. "Lately, our Samson's been still enough around her that she's been able to draw him. Ever so good she is, too. She gave me this."

Bartlett pulled out a piece of paper from his pocket and handed it to Hawthorne.

It was a drawing of an eye. Hawthorne had always thought eyes were perfect circles, but the shape on the page resembled a plump almond. The white of the eye contrasted against the skin of the lids. The pupil, though dark, glowed from within with flecks of light where the white paper peeked through the pencil strokes. Thick lashes curled over the upper eyelid. Had anyone asked him, he'd have sworn Samson's eyelashes were black, but they stood out, a soft grey against the dark pupil.

How could a simple drawing of an eye convey so much?

It was as if the very essence of Samson stared back at him.

With a few pencil strokes, she had expressed her love and admiration for the animal.

Bartlett was right. All Frederica needed was a little understanding, which she would not get from the sharks who circled the waters of society. In one aspect, at least, Sir Benedict had spoken the truth. No man alive would ever be worthy of her.

»»»«««

FORTIFIED BY A glass of sherry, Frederica soldiered into the dining room and headed to her place next to where a young man stood, his hands resting casually on the back of a chair.

"Ah, my dinner companion." His face broke into a smile.

Pale, blue eyes glittered with merriment and an overindulgence of liquor. He held out his hand. She took it, and he brushed his lips against her fingers. Breeding bled though his voice and finely crafted features.

He had the countenance of an angel, save for the mischief in his eyes, a marked contrast to the silent, darkly brooding figure at the head of the table.

Their host gave the signal to sit. Frederica's companion pulled out her seat for her with an air of dandified gallantry. "Fair lady," he said. "I fear I'm the only eligible gentleman among the company. Unless, of course, you count our host, Earl Stiles." He leaned forward and winked. "Which I don't…"

The man at the head of the table glowered in her direction, eyes so dark they looked black.

"Neither do I," she said bitterly.

"Ah!" he whispered, "I have an ally. What sins have *you* committed to merit Stiles's disapproval? I find it hard to believe such a virtuous-looking creature as yourself could have committed any transgression worthy of note."

"My lineage."

"My greatest sin is my behavior," he said.

"You're fortunate, sir," Frederica replied, sipping her wine. "You can modify your behavior, whereas the circumstances of my birth are permanent."

"Which are?"

"My father is a merchant."

"Is he here tonight?"

"He's overseeing the delivery of a consignment of port."

"Ah! Then he must be Mr. Stanford."

"You know him?"

"I'm practically *related* to him! He has the knack of sourcing the most delectable ports known to man. The pater is the reason for his absence." He held out his hand. "Permit me to introduce myself properly. Roderick, Marquis of Dewberry. My father is the Duke of Markham."

"Are you not ashamed to be seen with the daughter of the trader who serves His Grace?"

"Of course not! Women have qualities other than birth which I place great value on."

For a moment, his eyes took on a predatory look, then he blinked, and the expression was gone.

"I look forward to getting better acquainted with you, Miss Stanford. Rest assured, you needn't fear the disapprobation of Hawthorne Stiles when I'm here to mount your defense."

Perhaps she might enjoy the house party after all.

"COME, LADIES, LET us leave the men to their brandy." Clara Swainson, with all the authority of a hostess, ushered the women out of the dining room.

Frederica rose and followed at a distance.

Roderick Markham gave her a conspiratorial wink. Over dinner, he'd been gallant, charming, animated in his conversation, and well-versed in wine. He appreciated a good claret more than anyone in the room, and told her she was to be envied having a father with such an extensive knowledge of wines. His gentle praise of Papa who, by all accounts, was revered by the duke for his tastes, was balm to her soul compared to the disapproving looks Hawthorne cast in her direction.

Why had he invited her if only to make his dislike of her so obvious?

She took a teacup from Lady Swainson and moved toward the French windows. Freedom and fresh air were only a few feet away, even if separated by glass.

Whispers shuffled about the room, broken by the occasional chink of china as the ladies sipped their tea. Frederica remained set apart. After a few awkward remarks about the weather, the women exhausted their repertoire for conversing with the lower classes and left her alone.

Only Lady Swainson made any genuine attempt at conversation, but Frederica resisted her efforts at friendship. She'd seen how the woman had looked at Hawthorne. And he had done the same toward her. Frederica could only compare herself to Lady Swainson and find herself wanting. Clara was the woman he desired. Frederica was merely a plaything to amuse himself with when he was a child, something to discard once he'd left the schoolroom.

In which room had he placed Lady Swainson? Or did she reside in his bed?

Perhaps as the evening progressed, Hawthorne would disappear, and Lady Swainson would find an excuse to absent herself from the party, then return later, a well-calculated minute or two after him.

Jealousy was an ugly emotion; it ensnared the souls of the inadequate and inferior and destroyed their ability to find peace.

"Is the company of the ladies too dull for your tastes?"

The male voice came from behind. Holding a teacup in one hand and a plate of shortbread in the other, her new friend smiled, showing even, white teeth.

"Lord Markham!"

"Roderick, if you please." He rolled his eyes in mock indignation. "I thought we were friends."

"We've just met."

"Then let my offering seal our friendship forever." He held out the plate. "There isn't much about Stiles to praise, but his cook makes a tolerable shortbread. I brought it for you."

A familiar smell lingered on his breath.

"I rather think you need it more than I, Lord Markham. How much brandy have you had?"

"You impugn my honor," he said. "But one must take advantage when our skinflint host deigns to free it from the incarceration of his drinks cabinet."

"Should you speak of him so?"

"You should hear what he says about ladies. He may be gallant in polite society, but beneath that exterior lies the heart of a rake. The pater always said he was a slippery devil."

Frederica took the shortbread and nibbled at a corner. Too sweet for her, but at least it removed the sour taste of Hawthorne's disapproval.

"What does he say about ladies?"

"You wouldn't expect me to divulge what gentlemen say away from ladies' delicate ears, would you Miss Stanford?"

"I'm no lady," she said. "Neither are my ears that delicate."

"Ha!" Markham laughed. "Stiles was right."

"What has he said?"

"He views you as some sort of wild animal."

Not only did Hawthorne think her unfit for his company, but he shared his views over port and brandy.

"I rather wonder at him inviting me here," she said, sipping her tea to hide her distress, "if he finds me so repugnant."

Markham moved and touched her hand. "I, for one, am very glad he did. Why Stiles prefers the company of one such as Lady Swainson when there are more delectable objects in the room, defeats me."

The rest of the men entered the room and milled about. The air shimmered around Hawthorne as he gravitated toward Lady Swainson.

Frederica's skin prickled, and she lifted her gaze to see Hawthorne staring directly at her. His focus shifted to Lord Markham, and his body stiffened.

Lady Swainson held out her hand, and Hawthorne took it. He smiled at her, but his eyes remained hard and cold.

"Perhaps Lady Swainson can give him what he wants," Frederica said, wincing at the bitterness in her voice.

"Of that I'm sure," Markham replied. "Most likely a good, hard fuck against the drawing room wall."

Frederica's body convulsed, and the tea caught in her throat.

Choking, she lifted her hand to her mouth, dropping the cup. Markham caught it as if he'd anticipated the move.

"You there!" Markham gestured to a footman at the door. "Fetch a glass of water."

She barely registered the voices in the room. Apart from one.

"Stand back!" Hawthorne's voice resounded, rumbling with the undertones of a storm.

Two men stood before her. One dark like a thundercloud, eyebrows knitted together in a frown. The second, with all the countenance of a sunny afternoon, gave her a gallant smile and patted her on the back.

"There!" he soothed. "All better now. Didn't I say I'd take care of you?"

"Markham, a word if you please," Hawthorne urged.

Markham's eyes widened. "Would you relieve the lady of her protector?"

"Hardly that," Hawthorne scoffed, curling his lip in distaste.

"Come, Miss Stanford," Markham said, "permit me to take care of you."

Ignoring the low growl rumbling in Hawthorne's throat, Frederica let Markham escort her to a seat. Though it took her into the center of the room, further away from her means of escape, she drew satisfaction from witnessing Hawthorne's irritation.

CHAPTER NINE

THE EVENING OVER, Frederica was only too relieved to retire. The onset of fatigue, which always plagued her when in the company of strangers, had overwhelmed her. Markham's witticisms about Hawthorne had at first amused her, but when he became imbibed with too much brandy, they'd taken a sour note.

Pleasant company, but rather too fond of liquor. He'd clearly inherited the habit from his father, the duke, who, by all accounts, bore responsibility for the majority of Papa's income given the quantity he ordered regularly.

The maid bobbed a curtsey as Frederica arrived at her chamber door. At night, the passageway looked even bleaker. A shaft of light stretched across the floor from the room opposite her chamber.

"Is another guest in this part of the house?"

"No, miss," the maid said. "That's where I'm sleeping while you're here."

Her words confirmed Hawthorne's view of her. But what did she care? This maid would likely prove to be better company than the other guests, except perhaps Roderick Markham, who had, at least, behaved as if he enjoyed her company.

"What's your name?"

"Jenny."

She fussed about the room, lighting candles and turning back the bedsheets.

"Would you like me to help you undress, miss?"

"No thank you, Jenny," Frederica replied. "You must be tired." The maid looked barely out of childhood.

"Very good, miss." Jenny crossed the room and drew the curtains. "Mrs. Briggs, the housekeeper, told me to look after you special. She was very particular about the windows, said to make sure you had fresh air."

She lifted the sash, and a breeze floated into the room, dissipating the thickening blanket of dread which always threatened to engulf Frederica when she had been inside too long.

"Mrs. Briggs said I must leave the door open for you as well, miss. I hope I'll be able to give satisfaction."

"Thank you, Jenny." Frederica gave her a smile of reassurance. "I feel well-looked after already."

The maid bobbed another curtsey. "If you need anything during the night, you're to call out. Goodnight, miss."

⫸⫷

BLOODY MARKHAM! WHAT the devil was he playing at?

Hawthorne waved his valet away and adjusted his jacket. Voices drifted through the house as his guests stirred into consciousness, accompanied by the footfall of servants.

Despite the pleasures Clara's body had afforded him last night, she possessed one fatal flaw which rendered her efforts futile.

She was not Frederica.

And now Markham was sniffing around his little changeling.

Roderick Markham had always been a sly bastard, displaying the bully's cowardice in trying to reign over those he considered weak and therefore easy prey. The archetypical child who tortured small creatures, just like his father.

At Eton, he'd fancied himself Hawthorne's rival ever since Hawthorne had pulled him off that poor maid. Hawthorne had given her sanctuary in his room, which had resulted in his suspension. Though he'd never known for certain, he'd always suspected that Roderick had ratted him out to his housemaster.

What on earth had possessed Mrs. Briggs to seat Frederica next to Roderick at dinner? Ross Trelawney would have made a better dinner companion, but as he was courting that bland de Grecy heiress, the housekeeper must have thought it improper to seat him next to Frederica. As a result, that self-centered debaucher had secured Frederica's attentions. Worse, she'd come to life, giving Hawthorne a glimpse of the animated creature she might have been among the company of others, had she not suffered the incident of her childhood.

Perhaps that was his punishment, to sit by and watch while the very worst of men courted her.

Why couldn't she see the folly of her actions? Markham didn't possess an honorable drop of blood in his veins. Too many maids left the duke's employ within months of arriving. Hawthorne only had to read the letter concerning Frederica's birth to understand why.

In a lapse of judgement last night, he'd warned Markham to stay away from her. So now, of course, Markham's attention toward her had increased, first due to the pleasure from needling Hawthorne and second, out of curiosity.

He should never have invited her.

Where was she now? He'd had no reports during the night from Mrs. Briggs or the young chambermaid she'd assigned to her.

Securing his buttons, he smoothed down the material of his jacket unnecessarily, for Rawlings had pressed it that morning. He headed to the breakfast room.

The clatter of porcelain told him he'd arrived too late. Which of his guests was up this early?

A solitary figure stood by the serving table, the morning sun illuminating her face, speaking in a low voice to the footman in attendance. Hawthorne found himself envying the man for being close enough to look into those lovely eyes. What color would they be in the sunlight?

Her body stiffened as Hawthorne walked in, the hem of her gown trembling as if a breeze ran through the room. She turned her clear gaze his way. The warmth in his blood burst into flame.

Curse his body!

"I didn't think to see a guest about this early," he said coolly in an effort to fight his feelings.

"We commoners cannot spend our time idling in bed in anticipation of being waited on," she countered.

The force of her hostility fanned the flames inside him. He sat at the head of the table and waved the footman over. "I trust you slept well, Miss Stanford."

"Perfectly, thank you."

She resumed her attention on her breakfast, but rather than eat, she pushed the food around her plate. Her body vibrated with suppressed emotion, and he waited for the outburst. The clatter of metal against porcelain signaled the release as she dropped her knife on the plate.

"Why did you reduce my dowry?"

The question was unexpected.

"I fail to see that's your concern, Miss Stanford."

She waved a dismissive hand at him. "I don't care for the money, but I'm curious to comprehend the message you intended to convey by reneging on the promise your father had made to Grandpapa? Did you intend to insult me, his memory, or both?"

"I deemed it prudent at the time."

"Prudent? Is that all you can say?" she cried. "Does it matter so much to you, to draw the line between me and the rest of the world?"

"Of course not."

She bit her lip and lifted her teacup. Hawthorne saw the action for what it was, an attempt to calm herself.

"Did Grandpapa not argue on my behalf? Did he also view me as worthless?"

She may be a survivor, but vulnerability and pain radiated from her voice.

"No, of course not. Your grandfather loved you very much, little changeling." She flinched at his pet name for her.

"Then why?"

"It was my decision."

"Did you bully him as you do everyone else? Did you think so little of him?"

"No." He sighed. "It was a matter of honor."

"Honor? In what way do you honor him? I..." She broke off and sat back in her chair.

"Frederica..."

"I say!" a new voice cried. "Breakfast sounds rather lively this morning!"

Of all the guests to interrupt them, it had to be Roderick bloody Markham.

"Miss Stanford, permit me to replenish your plate. You must maintain your strength for today's excursion. Or perhaps you'd let me teach you how to play at cards instead? We can put that intelligence of yours to good use."

She smiled. "Lord Markham, I'm capable of serving my own breakfast."

"I'm sure you are, Miss Stanford, but your humble servant would be honored to assist you. You've just as much right to be treated as a lady as the other guests here. I'm sure Stiles would agree." Throwing Hawthorne a smile of triumph, Markham sat beside her.

"Of course, I agree," Hawthorne said. "Miss Stanford is my guest as much as the rest of you." He lifted his teacup to his mouth and took a sip. The liquid caught in his throat, and he coughed.

Markham winked at Frederica. "I believe our honored friend struggles to convince himself of the credibility of his last statement."

She stifled a giggle and accepted the plate he pushed in front of her and began eating with relish. Though it was good to see her eating, the fact it was due to Markham's attention, stuck in Hawthorne's chest.

How could she not see what he was doing? Markham's gallantry came from a desire to irritate Hawthorne.

And other desires…

Dear God, did she not understand the danger?

One by one, the other guests joined them until the table was full. Clara sat beside him, as usual, but other than casting an acidic glance their way, Frederica paid him no more attention. His little changeling who he'd once been so assured of being bound to him, was severing the link and forging a new bond with the man who flattered and amused her.

Not even Clara's conversation, nor her captivating body, could stem the tide of dread. Hawthorne's instinct told him tragedy loomed on the horizon.

CHAPTER TEN

To HAWTHORNE'S DISMAY, Frederica did not take part in the excursion in the grounds. Instead, she stayed inside, keeping company with Markham along with Markham's two friends and their wives. Markham's friends, James Spencer and Charles Elliott, were cut from the same moral cloth as Markham himself. They were both married, but a rake was a rake. James had a mistress in London, and Charles was such a frequent patron to one of the seedier bawdy houses, that the proprietress had assigned him his own room and was known to make house calls even when his wife was at home.

While under Hawthorne's roof, they wouldn't dare break the rules of decency. With luck, Stanford would arrive soon after concluding his business, and Hawthorne could be assured that at least one person on his estate, other than himself, cared for Frederica's well-being.

Overnight, a further layer of snow had covered the landscape. Her creative nature would appreciate the contrast in colors outside. But she was not there to share his joy.

After ushering the guests into the hall where mulled wine awaited them, Hawthorne went in search of her. Laughter echoed from the drawing room. Inside, James Spencer and Charles Elliott sat beside each other, smoking. Their wives and Markham were nowhere to be seen. Frederica sat near the window holding a glass, full almost to the brim with a dark red liquid.

James took a long pull from his cigar, then pursed his lips. A puff of smoke burst from his mouth in a perfect ring.

Frederica laughed. "An unbroken circle, I win!"

"Then I must take another finger." Charles lifted his glass. "You're too good at this, Miss Stanford. You'll drink me under the table."

She giggled and took a gulp from her glass.

Anger boiled inside Hawthorne, and he strode into the room. "Stop!"

The men flinched and straightened their backs as James stubbed out his cigar.

Frederica seemed unperturbed by Hawthorne's entrance, and the reason was obvious. She lolled forward.

Charles shifted uncomfortably in his seat. "I say, Hawthorne, old chap…"

"Go find your wife," Hawthorne hissed.

"Come on, Charlie," James grumbled. He helped his friend up, and they moved toward the door.

Frederica struggled to her feet, but Hawthorne blocked her path.

"You're not going anywhere in your state."

"Let me pass."

"Not until I've said my piece."

"Not content enough with controlling my fortune, you seek to control my person, too?"

"Don't be a fool," he said, ignoring the surge in his groin at the feel of her body in his grasp.

"What are you doing?" she slurred.

"Trying to instill some sense into you. What on earth are you doing drinking with those men? You shouldn't be with them at all!"

"Why, because they're above me in station?"

"For one thing, yes."

Her eyes darkened at his words, her inebriation doing nothing to temper the anger in their expression.

"Haven't you done enough to me?" she asked.

"Not nearly enough," he said. "Your behavior is reprehensible, Frederica. If I were your father, I'd give you a bloody good thrashing!"

"Then why don't you!" she cried. "Why don't you beat me like an errant servant who seeks to fraternize with her betters?"

She drew back her hand to strike him, but he caught her wrist and pulled her to him. Her body collided with his, but instead of breaking free, she reached up and took his arms.

"Why?" she whimpered. Her knuckles whitened as she dug her fingernails into the material of his jacket.

"Since Grandpapa died, it's as if I'm nothing to you," she choked. "Why do you hate me so much?"

"Oh, Frederica." He stroked her hair, closing his eyes as his fingers curled through the silken strands. He dipped his head, and breathed the scent of her hair—the aroma of nature, freshly cut grass, and lavender.

His little changeling. His, and nobody else's.

"I could never hate you," he whispered.

She tilted her head and looked up at him. His senses were assaulted by a clear, vivid green.

"Hawthorne…"

Her pupils dilated, and she parted her lips.

"Little changeling," he whispered, "my own little changeling…"

He lowered his mouth to hers, tasting the port on her lips, and another taste. Despair—from her belief she had no worth.

But Hawthorne valued her more than the rest of the world. With his tongue, he teased her lips in a gentle plea. She granted him entrance, and her fingers tightened around his arms.

She belonged to him. Not to Stanford, the man who'd brought her up, who believed he was her father, nor to the creature who'd spawned her. Hawthorne wanted her like no other woman before. Clara might have pleasured his body, but the woman in his arms, here and now, was the only one who could satisfy the needs of his soul.

A bolt of fire coursed through him as base desire overcame rational thought as their kiss deepened.

He slipped his hand inside her gown. A cry escaped him at her body's reaction. Her nipple hardened, pressing insistently against his palm.

Dear God! What was he doing taking advantage of her, just like he'd accused that bastard, Markham?

She was worth more than a quick moment of gratification on the drawing room floor. Fighting his instinct to claim her, he broke the kiss, and pushed her away.

"God forgive me, Frederica, I mean, Miss Stanford. I shouldn't have done that."

Hurt and rejection glistened in her eyes. She covered her mouth with her hand and drew a sharp breath.

"You should go to your chamber and rest," he said. "Sleep off the drink."

He reached for her, but she sidestepped him and moved to the door.

"Frederica, let me explain."

"Don't touch me!" She ran out of the room, slamming the door behind her.

There was no point in following her, so he rang the bell for the footman. After issuing orders to send Mrs. Briggs to tend to Miss Stanford, he sat in the chair she had occupied and took her glass and lifted it up, watching as the sunlight caught the facets in the crystal, reflecting the deep burgundy liquid. A red stain smeared across the rim, and he lifted it to his mouth, closing his eyes when his lips touched the glass in the very same place where her own had been.

The door opened, and the blonde-haired, elegantly-attired figure of Roderick Markham sauntered in, brandishing a bottle of port.

Markham's face fell. "What are you doing in here, Stiles?"

"I rather think I should ask that of you." Hawthorne nodded to the bottle. "Where did you find that?"

"You're turning into a miser," Markham said. "A good port like this is wasted on you."

"But not on you and your friends?"

"Don't tell me you've frightened them away."

"They had no right to be here," Hawthorne said. "Not with her."

Recognition glowed in Markham's eyes. "Aha! The little bird. It defeats me what the attraction is, but an earl must have his little idiosyncrasies, I suppose."

Hawthorne curled his hand into a fist, fighting the urge to smash it into the smug expression of the man opposite.

"What game are you playing with those friends of yours, Markham?"

Markham lifted the bottle of port to his lips and took a swig. "A drinking game, Stiles. Miss Stanford was predicting James's ability to blow a perfect smoke ring. If she guessed correctly, we take a finger of port. If not, *she* did. Hence the need for further supplies."

"Christ, Markham, a lady hasn't the capacity for alcohol. You shouldn't be playing boyhood drinking games with her!"

"Lady, indeed! Her father runs the shop which sells this stuff."

"What about her reputation?"

Markham snorted. "Why should it matter to you?"

"While she's under my roof, I'm responsible for her," Hawthorne said. "She's not like the women you seek to seduce."

"That she's not," Markham sneered. "She's a wild creature, but tempting, nonetheless."

"Leave her alone."

Markham's smile broadened. "Don't tell me Earl Stiles has taken a fancy to a local peasant."

"Of course not." Hawthorne turned his head away to conceal his expression.

"I believe the little tart has found herself a protector."

"Don't call her that," Hawthorne growled.

"Why not?" Markham asked. "Doubtless she's opened her legs for more men than she's opened her lips for wine bottles. Her sort usually begs for it by the time they've left the schoolroom."

"Don't make me throw you out, Markham."

Markham laughed. "Let me guess, you've already had her!"

Hawthorne leapt to his feet. "Why you…"

"I say, Rodders," a voice said, "we've been looking for you."

James's head appeared round the door. "Where's our bird of paradise gone?"

Markham held out the bottle to Hawthorne, smiling, his eyes pale and cold. "Forgive me, Stiles. I believe this is yours."

Hawthorne shook his head and gritted his teeth to maintain control. "You're welcome to it."

"Spoken like the host who's willing to share his *possessions* with his guests. Come on, James, time to enjoy that which Stiles's hospitality has to offer."

Hawthorne could still hear Markham's chuckles even after he left the room.

CHAPTER ELEVEN

A N OWL SCREECHED outside, and Frederica froze. But all the windows were closed, and there was no risk of the bird getting inside.

She held her book to her breast as if to defend it against anyone who might accost her.

She'd needed something to read to ease the tension of the evening, and where better to find relief than Hawthorne's library?

Her skin tightened at the memory of his lips on hers. His hands were as commanding as she'd always dreamed, claiming her body as his tongue conquered her mouth. But he had withdrawn, disgust altering his expression as he pushed her away. She'd fled to her room, seeking solace.

He'd magnified her shame by sending his housekeeper to her chamber with a dish of broth to ensure she took her supper away from the rest of the guests. In the servants' quarters, where she belonged.

A sneeze racked her body. All day, her head had felt thick and muffled, as if she were being held under water, hot one minute, then cold the next.

"Hey! Wait, little bird." James appeared and blocked her path. "Aren't you joining us for dinner?"

"I'm going to my chamber."

He took her hand. "Is that an invitation?"

Laughing, she tried to shake him off. "Of course not!"

"Nevertheless, I'll take it as such, little bird."

He pushed her back until her body collided with the wall. Teeth gleaming, he thrust his face close.

"No!"

"Just one kiss," he slurred, "just for me."

"What about your wife?"

"What would I want with that miserable shrew when such a delectable morsel is in my path? If you're seeking a protector, I'm more than happy to oblige. I'd treat you like a princess."

She struggled, but he held her firmly in place. He drew ever closer, ready to claim her mouth.

"Hey!" a voice roared.

A hand appeared and gripped his shoulder. He jerked back and released her.

"How dare you!" Hawthorne bellowed. A fist crashed into James's face, culminating in an explosion of blood and spittle.

Hawthorne stood before them, body vibrating with anger, his broad frame dominating her vision. His eyes were dark, mouth set in a hard line, nostrils flared. Murder raged in his expression, and she cringed.

James seemed to wither under the power of Hawthorne's gaze.

"Leave," Hawthorne said. "You're no longer welcome in my home."

"I say, old chap, it's just a bit of fun," James's voice barely concealed the tremor in his tone. "What say we call it quits? After all, you've given me a damn good shiner…"

"I said get out!" Hawthorne's jaw bulged with tension. "Take your wife and go, before I run you off the grounds myself."

James opened his mouth to respond but closed it again and retreated.

After his footsteps had faded, Frederica drew in a deep breath. Her head throbbed so loudly, Hawthorne must be able to hear it. She lowered her gaze and backed away.

"Don't move."

She froze at his command.

"I wish to return to my…"

"I *said*, don't move." He inched close to her. "What the devil are you playing at?"

"Nothing, I…"

"Don't interrupt! What on earth possessed you to flaunt yourself like a harlot? I thought you possessed a shred of intelligence."

She'd never seen him so angry. Her body recoiled at the force of his voice, but he did not relent.

"To say I'm disappointed in you would be an understatement. I'm disgusted. If I were your father…"

"But you're not!" she cried. "You've no right to…"

"I've every right!" he roared. "When under my roof, you follow my rules. If your father learned of your behavior, he'd be heartbroken."

"What would *you* know of how he feels?"

"It matters not," he said. "He'll be here later. I was coming to tell you that. Once he arrives, you're no longer my problem."

"Your *problem?*"

He sighed. "I'll tell him to take you home. This isn't the place for you."

"Why? Because I'm beneath you?" she cried. "Is that why you're so angry, because I'm fraternizing with your guests when you'd rather I sat in the corner?"

A wave of nausea ripped through her, and she caught her breath.

"I feel sick."

"Then go to your chamber," Hawthorne said. "I'll send Mrs. Briggs to take care of you, *again*."

She turned her back on him and stumbled away.

＊＊＊⫸⫷＊＊＊

NOT LONG AFTER she collapsed in a chair in her chamber, Jenny burst into the room.

"Oh, miss, are you ill again?" She placed her hand on Frederica's arm, the unashamed act of kindness drawing forth the tears Frederica had been able to hold back under Hawthorne's verbal onslaught.

She gestured to the empty fireplace. "Shall I light the fire for you, miss? It's freezing outside, and Mrs. Briggs said there's a storm brewing."

What was she doing? Lounging about feeling sorry for herself while this thin child whose hands were already chapped from a life in service offered to tend to her.

"No, Jenny, don't trouble yourself. I can make do with a blanket."

Before Frederica could object, the maid plucked a blanket from the bed and placed it over her lap.

"Oh, miss!" Jenny exclaimed. "Begging your pardon for being so forward, but is it your grandfather you're so upset about?"

"My grandfather?"

"Yes, I heard how Sir Benedict died in the master's study after they'd had words."

"Words?"

"Yes, miss. He was ever so upset about something."

Dear Lord! What did she mean? Had Grandpapa argued with Hawthorne just before his death? Had it been about Hawthorne's decision to reduce her fortune? A cold hand clutched at her insides. Had their argument brought about Grandpapa's death?

"I shouldn't have said nothing!" Fear etched the maid's features, fear of the beating she'd get if the housekeeper heard she'd been gossiping with the guests.

Frederica took her hand, seeking comfort in the maid's own need for it. "Can you tell me what happened?"

"I—I don't know…"

"You can trust me, Jenny. I'm not like the other guests."

"I overheard Sir Benedict," Jenny said. "Sore angry he was, asking the master to honor his request, and the master refusing. But Mrs. Briggs caught me and shooed me away before I could hear anything else."

"What *did* you hear?"

"I heard mention of money and a letter. They argued over the letter." Her cheeks grew pink, and she lowered her gaze before continuing in a small voice. "And a name."

"What name?"

"Yours, miss."

Frederica's stomach jolted.

A voice called out in the distance, and Jenny stiffened.

"Coming, Mrs. Briggs!" She smoothed down her apron. "Begging your pardon, miss, I must go, but I'll return once I've tended to Lord Markham's room."

"Lord Markham?"

"The master sent him and his friends away. In an awful temper he was, too, so Mrs. Briggs said. The room is to be cleaned to remove all traces of him. Master's orders." She bobbed a curtsey, then fled.

Frederica drew the blanket around her. The cold of the room was nothing compared to the ice which threaded through her veins.

Hawthorne, the man she had worshipped as a child, had not only banished her friends, but he'd been responsible for Grandpapa's death.

What had they argued about? What was in the letter Jenny had spoken of? Did he still have it in his study?

While he dined with the guests he valued, the guest he despised could at least attempt to find that letter. Perhaps it might explain why he hated her so much.

CHAPTER TWELVE

As Frederica approached Hawthorne's study, the bustle of activity told her the meal had begun. The servants would ferry dishes to and fro, replacing dirty with clean as the guests ate their way through a multitude of courses. No one would take interest in Frederica. Her chance had come.

A door opened and shut in the distance, accompanied by a clatter or porcelain, a servant in a hurry to clear the crockery. She froze before the sound faded, and she reached the study door and curled her fingers round the handle. The door creaked in protest as she pushed it open, perhaps wishing to betray her. But what did she care if he caught her? He'd meddled with her life, and she had a right to know why.

A squat, mahogany desk dominated the room, topped with leather decorated with gold leaf around the edges. Two pedestals supported the thick wooden top, each with four drawers. The desk had been neatly arranged, not a paper out of place. An inkpot and quill rested beside a notebook, and a letter opener sat parallel to the spine of the book, as if a servant had taken pains to place it in an aesthetically pleasing pattern for his master. The smell of ink, tobacco, and whisky bled from the very fabric of the desk.

Grandpapa would have spent many evenings here with the late earl. She could almost believe his aroma was in the room, that blend of cigar smoke and musty spices which had always lingered on his jacket.

Her body tightened with loss. Had he died here, perhaps sitting on the wingback chair in front of the desk, while pleading her case to the stone-hearted man who now reigned over the estate? She set her candle down and began searching.

Half an hour later, her search had proven fruitless, having rifled through every part of the desk, save the upper left drawer which was locked. She'd found nothing of consequence, just ledgers detailing servants' wages, legal documents concerning the late earl's last will and testament, and trustee documents for the Radley estate, none of which related to her.

She picked up the letter opener, and before regret and conscience could assault her, she jammed the blade into the gap above the locked drawer and twisted it. With a creak, the gap opened a fraction. Pushing the blade in, she levered it up, and a sliver of wood broke free, and the drawer flew open.

Inside was another notebook containing copies of the estate accounts and a wad of pound notes. But beneath the notebook was a sheaf of papers tied together with a red ribbon. Her eyes wandered over the document on the top, and she froze on reading the name halfway down, written in a cursive script.

Frederica Eleanor Stanford.

She pulled her gloves off and spread the documents on the desk, her fingers trembling as she leafed through each sheet.

The first document was a note from the late earl promising to bestow a sum of five thousand pounds on her in the event of her marriage. It was dated November 1795, not long after she had been born.

Why had he bestowed such a sum on her? Her skin crawled at the only plausible explanation. Men of wealth and title granted money to children to assuage their guilt, payments to remove unwanted by-blows from their lives and consciences.

Dear Lord, did that mean Hawthorne was her brother? Was that why he'd reduced the sum? To punish her for being his father's bastard?

The next document was a letter penned in an irregular hand. The heartfelt words drew her in.

Sir, forgive me for abandoning you, but I must tender my resignation forthwith. Mary nears her confinement, and I must tend to her. She suffers from melancholy, and I fear for her life and that of the child. I feel responsible, for I secured her position with… Someone had scratched out the next few words. *And it's as if I was the one who violated her. Mary's mind is broken. She says she will kill the child as soon as it's born. She tried to throw herself down the stairs again and must be watched. My mother is old and cannot watch her all the time.*

Please forgive me, sir, but I have no choice. My sweet cousin has been ruined. I cannot bear to see the hate in her. She says that any child of his deserves to be strangled. But even the child of a monster deserves to be loved. Perhaps once I am assured of Mary's health and the child's safety, I can return, but I would understand if the disgrace would prevent it.

The words blurred as tears filled Frederica's eyes. A young girl taken advantage of by her employer, who raped and abandoned her. A child born of hatred…

A child of rape…

The next document was written in a clearer hand, and her heart jolted in recognition. Even if the letterhead of Sir Benedict Langton had been missing, she couldn't mistake the distinctive way Grandpapa curled the tails of each letter "f".

My dear Stiles,

I have secured an appointment with Stockton to draw up a document for the settlement and can only express my gratitude once more for all you have done. Were I able to bequeath a portion of my own estate, I would, but I regret it's entailed away from the female line and the trustees have refused my request.

I would ask you say nothing of this to Stanford. He still grieves for Eleanor, and the comfort the child gives him is but a thin thread binding him to reason. I fear for his mind if he discovers our deception. He would cast the child out if he discovered her true identity. For myself, though nothing can bring my beloved daughter back, I am not yet so cold-hearted as to believe that an unwanted orphan is less deserving of compassion than the man who believes her to be his own.

I admire your generosity, my friend, in taking young Mary in. Though she died in your care, Doctor Baines assures me nothing could have prevented it. Your conscience may pain you, but it is a credit to you, and I find myself continually grateful to have you as a friend. I trust that young Hawthorne will, one day, show a similar degree of compassion to his subordinates as his father does.

I pray Mrs. White can be trusted to be discreet, but she strikes me as a most admirable woman and has offered to deliver this letter to you in secret.

Yours ever,

B.L.

The final document was another letter from Grandpapa, dated almost a week later than the first. She blinked, and a fat tear splashed onto the paper, sitting proud for a moment before dissolving to leave a dark stain.

Stiles

The worst is over, and I should be able to leave Stanford's side in a day or so. He appears to have made a full recovery, and Doctor Baines assures me he can only improve. He dotes on the child. She looks nothing like Eleanor, of course. I only hope she has not inherited her natural father's temperament. Her eyes are, I must presume, the color of her mother's. I pray she will not share that poor young woman's fate, but I believe she will thrive in Stanford's care. I have never seen a man love a child more. It would break his heart if he discovered the truth.

Her fortune will help secure her safety, and for that, I am ever gratefully

yours,
B.L.

Frederica collapsed onto the chair, and the papers fluttered to the floor.

The tears did not come. Neither did the pain. A frost spread through her body, and she closed her eyes, wanting to deprive her senses and forget what she had seen.

FOOTSTEPS TAPPED ON the floor outside the study accompanied by male voices. She picked up the papers and rammed them into the drawer, slamming it shut. With luck, her handiwork wouldn't be discovered until after she'd returned home.

The voices stopped outside the door, the first unmistakable, resonating through her body as if it still yearned for him in spite of everything.

"Fancy a brandy, Ross?"

"Best not, old chap. I think your guests have been enjoying rather too much of your drink this week."

"Christ, yes." She heard a deep sigh. "Bloody bastard. Should have been strangled at birth. The father's no better, one of the most loathsome men to walk this earth. With luck, I'll not suffer the misfortune of seeing either of them again after today."

"Is that likely?"

"We move in different circles, Ross. Come on, I need a brandy, but I also need you to ensure I don't finish the bottle on my own."

The door handle moved again, and Frederica's stomach churned. What would Hawthorne do if he discovered her in the study?

A third voice joined the others, then Hawthorne sighed.

"Oh, bloody hell, that's all I need."

"Weren't you expecting Stanford?" Ross asked.

"Yes, but I was hoping he'd arrive after she'd slept off the liquor. Come on, you occupy him in the morning room, I'll send Mrs. Briggs to see if she can make her presentable."

The footsteps faded into the distance.

After waiting a moment, Frederica tiptoed to the door and pulled it ajar, her body trembling.

Papa was in Radley Hall. But how could she face him knowing who and what she was? What had Grandpapa's letter said? The bastard child of a rapist, the product of hatred, the child even her own mother had wanted to murder at birth. She had been spawned from evil, and Papa had been deceived into taking her in.

No wonder Hawthorne hated her. Papa would hate her, too, if he knew.

Should have been strangled at birth.

Hawthorne's words sliced through her heart. But what pained her more was the fact she deserved it. He was right, she should have died. Frederick Stanford's true child was the one who should have lived.

Seizing her chance, she slipped across the hallway to the main doors, then ran out into the night.

CHAPTER THIRTEEN

"WHERE'S MY DAUGHTER?" Stanford's voice obliterated the distant chatter of Hawthorne's guests.

By now, the gentlemen would have joined the ladies for coffee and an evening of music. Clara excelled at the pianoforte, and he'd promised to sing a duet with her. But his heart no longer wished to accompany her. Each time he saw Clara, her face was replaced by another, one with deep-set eyes and framed with red-gold hair. When Stanford took his daughter home, would Hawthorne ever see her again?

"She's resting, sir," Hawthorne said. "She was indisposed and took her supper in her chamber. Why don't you join my guests for coffee, and I'll bring her to you. I'll have a chamber prepared for you, and you can take her home in the morning."

"But..."

"Ross, please take Mr. Stanford to the drawing room."

Stanford's eyes narrowed as he recognized the authority in Hawthorne's voice, the tone of the magistrate.

"Come with me, sir." Ross, with his gentler demeanor, could always be relied upon.

As soon as they left, Hawthorne leapt to his feet. The housekeeper accosted him in the hallway.

"Why is Miss Stanford not with you, Mrs. Briggs?"

"I can't find her, my lord. She's not in her room."

"Where the devil is she?"

"Begging your pardon, sir." A footman approached, holding a tray of port glasses. "I saw Miss Stanford outside your study earlier this evening."

Hawthorne nodded. "Thank you, Watson. I'll try there first. If you find her, please take her to the drawing room."

His study was empty, but a candlestick stood in the center of the desk. Wax had solidified on the leather cover where the candle had burned out, leaving an irregular splash pattern. His notebook and quill were exactly where he'd left them, but the letter opener lay at an odd angle.

The upper left drawer was splintered at the top where it had been forced open. He looked inside and found his ledgers still there, as was the money he kept for when his steward needed ready cash. But the papers which had previously been neatly stacked lay crumpled, as if someone had stuffed them in quickly.

Who would be angry enough to commit such an offence, but not motivated by greed? A pair of gloves lay on the floor at his feet. Only one of his guests insisted on wearing gloves all the time, the one person who was absent during dinner.

He pulled out the topmost piece of paper, smoothed it on his desk, and looked over the written words she must have read and understood.

"Frederica…"

At all costs, he must find her before she did anything foolish.

THROUGH THE KITCHEN door, Hawthorne saw a group of servants seated round the table, snatching a hasty supper, a brief respite while the guests languished over their coffee.

"The master's here!"

The hum of jovial chatter disappeared and silence fell. Several pairs of eyes watched Hawthorne as he descended the stairs, and the air grew cold with apprehension. Watson rose to his feet.

"Did you find her, sir?"

Hawthorne shook his head. "No. Miss Stanford has disappeared."

A young girl at the end of the table let out a gasp, and the woman seated next to her gave her a nudge.

"Be quiet, Jenny!" she hissed.

"Jenny," Hawthorne turned to the girl. "Have you something to say?"

She shook her head. "No, sir," she said, her voice shaky. "She wasn't in her room when I looked in on her after clearing Lord Markham's room." She wiped her nose. "Forgive me! I should have said something. She seemed ever so upset."

"Has nobody seen anything?" Hawthorne asked. "No matter how trivial. You see and hear what I and my guests are likely to miss."

One of the under-gardeners shifted in his seat. "It's probably nothing, sir…"

"Tell me," Hawthorne said.

"Outside. I thought it was an intruder, but they were moving away from the house, not toward it."

"Where?"

"Near the main entrance. Too slight to be a man. I dismissed it as a fancy, but…"

Before he could finish, Hawthorne turned and rushed up the stairs.

"Watson, tell Bartlett to saddle Samson immediately!"

Within moments, Hawthorne entered the stables, pulling his long coat around him. The temperature had fallen and snow whirled in a devilish dance.

The groom walked his horse out and handed him the reins. Issuing a gruff word of thanks, Hawthorne placed a foot in the stirrup, swung his leg over the horse's back, and set off.

The gardener had not imagined it—a trail of footprints led toward the gardens. The snow was falling more steadily, the wind whipping it into a frenzy, forming drifts which had already obliterated some of the features of the garden. He had not ridden far before the footsteps disappeared.

He could only hope she was still a creature of habit. As a child, he'd often seen a flash of red on his estate where she'd drifted into the rose garden and hidden in the gazebo. He used to watch over her while she sat alone, a silent sentinel never revealing himself lest he frighten her.

He urged Samson into a canter.

He heard her before he saw her. Amid the roar of the blizzard lashing his face, he detected heartfelt cries. He dismounted and tethered the animal to a sapling twenty feet from the gazebo. His little changeling was wounded, even if those wounds were invisible. She needed a careful hand if he was to return her inside where she could be tended to by those who loved her.

But would they love her when they discovered the truth? Or would Stanford abandon her mourn his real child that died nineteen years ago?

She sat huddled against the gazebo wall, thin arms wrapped around herself to battle against the cold. Gloves missing, the scars on her wrists stood out against her pale skin.

"Miss Stanford."

She didn't react, and he moved closer until he almost touched her.

"Little changeling..."

Her body stilled, and she lifted her head. She blinked, her eyes red and swollen from crying.

He ran his hand along her arm until he reached her wrist. Her skin was hot and smooth under his thumb, except for the scars, an ugly reminder of his cowardice.

"What are you doing here?" he asked, his voice gentle.

"Leave me alone."

"I can't do that. The cold will kill you if you stay here."

"It's what I deserve."

"No…"

"I come from evil!" she cried. "Is that why I suffer from madness, why I'm vilified? Do they all know what I am?"

"Nobody knows, Federica, apart from me."

She shook her head. "My mother hated me!"

"No, little one," he said. "She would have loved you had she lived. Eleanor was a wonderful woman."

"I mean the woman who gave birth to me."

He drew his arms round her. "Your papa loves you, Frederica. He's at Radley Hall now. Come back with me, and he'll take care of you."

"Does he know the truth about me?"

"No, and there's no need to tell him."

She shook her head. "He has a right to know."

"I'd advise against it, Frederica, though I know he'd love you just the same."

She must have heard the doubt in his voice. It was too great a loss to risk telling him the truth. Some secrets needed to remain hidden.

"I cannot stay with him," she said. Her body shook as a sneeze overcame her. "He won't love me. I'm nothing." The despair in her tone tore at his heart.

"Don't say that!" he cried. "There are people who love you. Your grandpapa loved you despite knowing the truth. And I…" He broke off, biting his lip. "I want you safe and well. Don't tell your father the truth."

She shook her head, and he grasped her chin.

"Listen to me," he whispered. "Listen to one who cares."

Tears ran down her cheeks. He traced the outline of her mouth, and she parted her lips. His skin tightened at her warm, sweet breath.

"Hawthorne..."

"Oh, Frederica..."

He leaned forward and covered her mouth with his own. Her body softened in his arms, and she reached out to him, curling her cold fingers around his arms.

He claimed her sweet taste with his lips. A small groan escaped her lips, and he swallowed it, a natural response to her kiss.

"Frederica," he breathed. "You need a protector. Let me take care of you."

She pushed him away. Her face was still flushed from arousal, but fear flashed in her eyes.

"A protector," she repeated, her voice hard. "The best offer a bastard can hope for."

"Forgive me, Miss Stanford," he said, forcing the emotion out of his voice. "I don't know what possessed me. It won't happen again." He held out his hand. "Come, your father awaits."

With a sigh, she let him lead her to his horse. Her compliance not out of regard for him, but because her spiritedness had diminished.

By the time they reached the hall, she had grown lethargic. Mrs. Briggs waited by the entrance armed with blankets, and she wrapped Frederica in them tenderly, as if she were her own child.

There was no possibility of her returning home in her current state. Stanford must wait until the morning to see her. With luck, Hawthorne would be able to speak to her in the morning before Stanford saw her, and persuade her to keep the secret of her lineage to herself.

Chapter Fourteen

WARM LIPS CARESSED Hawthorne's mouth as vivid, green eyes drew him in. He reached out, and they disappeared, shattering into the darkness with a splintering crash which sharpened into a steady hammering.

He opened his eyes and sat up. He was in his bedchamber. The other side of the bed was empty. He hadn't invited Clara into his bed and was unlikely to do so again. Last night she'd understood no invitation was forthcoming, and after their duet in the drawing room had finished, she'd drifted away from him, taking a glass of whisky to her own chamber.

The embers in the fireplace had long since died, but the flickering light of his candle told him he could only have been in bed two hours at most. Dawn was several hours away, and even the servants would still be asleep.

What had woken him?

A shadow moved underneath the door. Hawthorne climbed out of bed and padded across the floor, opening the door.

Watson stood in the corridor. His hair stuck out at odd angles, and his jacket was unbuttoned, the mark of haste.

"One of your guests has taken ill, my lord."

"Have you sent for a doctor?"

"I took the liberty of rousing Bartlett. He's already on his way to Doctor McIver."

"Then I don't understand why I needed to be disturbed."

Watson shifted from one foot to the next. "Mrs. Briggs said you were very particular about the guest."

Icy fingers clutched at his heart. Watson could only mean one person.

"I trust I did the right thing, sir," Watson continued. "She's been taken ever so bad."

Dear lord...

Watson was not prone to exaggeration, unlike the rest of the staff, except, perhaps, for the stoic Mrs. Briggs.

If anything happened to her...

"Has her father been informed?"

"I sent Jenny for him as soon as I'd dispatched Bartlett."

"I must go to her." Panic tightened Hawthorne's throat. "The moment Doctor McIver arrives, send him straight to her chamber."

Fear reignited the impending sense of tragedy he'd seen circling round Frederica. Uttering a silent prayer, he set off at a sprint.

When Hawthorne reached her chamber, the door was open. Mrs. Briggs and the young maid she'd given the task of tending to Frederica, were moving about. The maid wrung out a cloth in a bowl of water before handing it to the silent man who sat on the bed.

Stanford.

Hawthorne had eyes only for the woman in the bed. Her breath rattled in her chest. Outside, the wind howled against the window.

"My child," Stanford cried.

It transported Hawthorne to the past, to that long-ago evening when he carried her battered little body home and abandoned her on her father's doorstep. Frederick Stanford was a broken man, his most precious possession, his beloved daughter, in danger.

Stanford lifted his head. He stared at Hawthorne. "What have you done to my child?"

Hawthorne moved closer to the grief-stricken man and took his hand. His fingers were ice-cold. Stanford withdrew his hand and resumed tending his daughter.

No, *not* his daughter. But he loved her. Because he didn't know the truth.

Unwilling to let others witness the man's disintegration, Hawthorne shooed Jenny and Mrs. Briggs out of the room with instructions they were not to be disturbed until the doctor arrived.

"Birds, birds! They're smothering me. Keep them away!"

Hawthorne reached for a cloth, wrung it in the basin, and placed it over her forehead. The heat of her skin burned through the material.

"She has a fever."

"I know," Stanford said, his voice hoarse. "She's been ill before but never this bad. What shall I do if she's taken from me? My child, my life..." A low sob resonated in his throat.

Hawthorne drew up a chair and sat beside the bed. "The doctor is on his way, Mr. Stanford. He'll do everything he can. I'm sure she'll recover."

"Can you guarantee that, Stiles? You cannot understand even the smallest proportion of what I'm feeling. You don't have children. She's my world."

Stanford lifted her hand to his lips and kissed the scar on her wrist.

"I can't untie the rope," she murmured. "They said he'd rescue me. Where is he?"

"Hush, Rica!" Stanford soothed. He turned to Hawthorne. "She's had nightmares ever since those cursed gypsies terrorized her."

Guilt stabbed through Hawthorne's heart.

"I can't lose her," Stanford croaked. "The Almighty is cruel if he wishes her to suffer any more."

Hawthorne leaned over to place the cloth on her forehead again, and she opened her eyes. They were dulled with fever, unseeing.

"He raped her!"

Stanford squeezed her hand. "Who, Rica—who?"

"My mother!" she wailed. "You must tell Papa, I can't lie to him!"

"Don't listen to her, Stanford," Hawthorne said. "Fever drives out reason, like a nightmare."

"Nightmares are based on reality, are they not?" Stanford asked quietly.

Hawthorne placed a hand on the older man's shoulder. "Your late wife was not raped."

"I know," Stanford replied. "But Frederica's mother was."

"I don't know what you..."

"Would you attempt to deny it, Lord Stiles?"

Hawthorne withered under the steel in Stanford's voice, and he shook his head.

Stanford caressed Frederica's hand. "I've always known she wasn't my natural child," he said. "She looks nothing like me or my Eleanor. The night my wife died, the doctor said to prepare for the worst, that both mother and child were at risk. As Rica grew, so did my suspicions. Tonight has only confirmed those suspicions."

He turned to Hawthorne. "How did she discover the truth? Did you tell her?"

"Of course not. She found my papers." He sighed. "I should have realized, she's inquisitive and intelligent, unrestricted by the confines of society. She doesn't deserve the hand fate dealt her. But Sir Benedict acted in your best interests, Stanford, not just hers, when he replaced your dead child with her."

"I know," Stanford said. "There are countless children abandoned and unloved. Sir Benedict united a bereaved man and an unwanted child, knowing we could save each other. And we did."

Hawthorne nodded. "Sir Benedict begged me not to tell you the truth. He wanted you to believe she was yours so you'd always love her. It warms my heart that you love her, regardless. Do you wish to know who her father is?"

Stanford set his jaw into a hard line. "*I'm* her father."

"But…"

"Speak no more, Stiles." Stanford sighed and caressed her forehead. "I suppose this means you'll renege on your promise?"

"Of course not," Hawthorne said. "The deeds are with the copyist. Stockton will have them ready next time he comes. Your business, and your daughter, will be protected in the event of…"

"…my death." Stanford said.

Before Hawthorne could reply, he heard voices outside the door, including the familiar Scottish burr.

"Doctor McIver has arrived."

The door opened to reveal the welcome sight of the doctor.

"Well, don't just stand there," McIver said, the crisp efficiency in his voice exuding a tone of calm.

"Who's he?" He gestured to Stanford.

Stanford issued Hawthorne a look of warning.

"He's her father," Hawthorne said. "Do whatever's necessary for Miss Stanford. Whatever you need, I'm at your disposal."

The doctor moved toward the woman on the bed, touching her face and hands before he lifted the bedsheet. At length, he drew out a phial from his case and tipped the content into her mouth.

"She has an unnaturally high fever, but I've given her something to help ease it," McIver said. "She's taken a chill. Tonight should dictate whether she recovers. If she survives, I'd recommend a healthy diet. Plenty of red meat. She needs to put on weight."

Stanford let out a low cry.

"I'll return in the morning," McIver said. "Have you someone to tend to her should she need it?"

"I can…" Hawthorne said, but Stanford pushed him aside.

"Yes," he said firmly. "I'll always be here to take care of her."

"Very well, Stanford. I'll visit you in the morning. I pray she'll recover."

Stanford nodded, then resumed his attention to his daughter, as if

Hawthorne were no longer in the room.

Shaking the doctor's hand, Hawthorne retreated and closed the door.

≫≫≪≪

BEFORE SUNLIGHT BROKE through Hawthorne's window, he was up and dressed. Still buttoning his jacket, he climbed the stairs to the upper floor toward Frederica's chamber. He'd have to suffer his valet's disapproval, but he couldn't rest until he knew how she'd fared during the night.

A man stood outside her door. A beard darkened his features, and he looked generally unkempt. His eyes were closed, but Hawthorne knew how exhausted Stanford was, how sad he must be...

The breath left Hawthorne's lungs, expelled by grief. His prayers had been ignored.

"Stanford." Hawthorne held out his hand. "I don't know what to say."

Stanford opened his eyes. "There's nothing to say, Lord Stiles. It was probably for the best."

Dear God...

Hawthorne clenched his hands. "What's happened?"

"The truth would have emerged eventually," Stanford said. "We can put this behind us and enjoy a new life.

"We?"

Hawthorne pushed past Stanford and opened the door. She lay on the bed, propped up against the pillows, eyes closed. Her chest rose and fell with a gentle, rhythmic motion.

"She's alive," Hawthorne breathed. He turned to Stanford, moisture blurring his vision.

"Her fever broke in the night," Stanford said. "She's sleeping peacefully now."

"Did she say anything of her origins?"

"Yes," a female voice said. "I did."

Hawthorne blinked and turned back to the bed. Clear eyes focused on him, the intensity of their gaze rendering him speechless with guilt.

"And it matters not," Stanford said firmly, "does it, Rica, my love?"

Stanford approached the bed, and they embraced.

"I want to go home, Papa."

"Of course, my love. But we must continue to impose on Stiles until you're fully recovered."

She visibly stiffened, and her eyes met Hawthorne's. "We must leave today."

"No, you must remain here, Rica. I'll not risk your life again."

"Your papa is right," Hawthorne said. "Doctor McIver should be here shortly. Only when he's declared you fit will I entertain the prospect of your going home."

"Papa, might I have a word with Lord Stiles? In private?"

"I–I don't know. It wouldn't be proper."

"I merely wish to thank him, Papa."

"Very well."

As soon as the door closed, she slumped back against the cushions, the mark of an actress playing a part to convince her father that her mind, as well as her body, had recovered.

Hawthorne sat beside the bed. "You've no need to thank me, Miss Stanford. If there's anything I can do…"

"There's only one thing I want from you," she whispered. "A name."

"A name?"

"Papa says he cares not. But I care. I want to know who my natural father is."

"Nothing can be gained from your knowing."

"That's my decision, not yours."

"Can't you trust me to make the right decision for you?" Hawthorne asked. "I want what's best for you. I've always…"

She lifted her gaze, and his resolve withered under her silent scrutiny. At length, she looked away.

"Send Papa in."

"Miss Stanford…"

"Please."

The pain in her voice tore at his heart.

"I'll tell you, Miss Stanford, but no good will come from you knowing."

He took her hand. Her fingers were cold.

"Your father is the Duke of Markham."

Her breath caught in her throat, and she closed her eyes. Hawthorne waited, but she said nothing.

"Miss Stanford, are you all right?"

"Send Papa in, please."

"You won't tell him, will you?"

"No. He's suffered enough."

Hawthorne opened the door, and Stanford rushed in. They were a true father and daughter, sharing the unconditional love Hawthorne could only dream of ever having in his life.

CHAPTER FIFTEEN

"**M**ISS STANFORD?"

Frederica barely registered the voice as she watched a blackbird cross the thin layer of snow in the garden, leaving behind perfect imprints of his feet, the likeness of which she was able to capture with a few strokes of her pencil.

A month had passed since her ordeal at Radley Hall, and today marked the first signs of spring. Small green spikes had pushed through the layer of snow, stretching upward like drowning men gasping for air as they broke the water's surface. In a week, the delicate flowers which everybody described as white but were really a subtle shade of green, would grow. She was already planning the combination of colors on her palette to replicate the hue. Snowdrops were her favorite flowers. Often overlooked yet resilient, they always marked the end of the cold season.

"Frederica!" Papa stood at the parlor door, the doctor by his side.

She stood and dipped a curtsey.

"Doctor McIver. How good to see you."

The doctor gave her a warm smile.

"And you, my dear." He took her hands and turned them over to inspect them.

"I trust you're keeping warm? Winter may be on the wane, but you're not out of danger. The chill could return."

"She's taking good care of herself." Tenderness shone through

Papa's words. Since the revelation of her lineage, his love for her had intensified, not diminished. How could she have thought he'd disown her?

He gestured to a chair. "Will you take tea, Doctor McIver?"

"I cannot stay long, Mr. Stanford. I'm due home. I spent rather longer than expected at Radley Hall this morning."

"A small brandy, then?"

"I'd appreciate a dram of whisky if you have it."

"Of course."

Papa filled a glass and handed it to the doctor, then settled into the chair beside Frederica.

"I trust all is well with the earl?" her father asked.

"I would imagine so."

"You didn't see him?"

"He's spending the rest of the winter in town. But his steward has settled my account and has instructed me to tend to your daughter until you move to London for the season."

Frederica's stomach jolted. "London?"

"We've discussed this, Rica, my love," Papa said. "A season in London will improve your health and your spirits."

"Aye." Doctor McIver nodded. "I'd recommend it. I will be in London myself for the season and can tend to your daughter there."

He rose, and Papa followed suit. Frederica pushed her chair aside, but Papa held up his hand. "No, Rica, stay there and rest."

"Good day, Miss Stanford." The doctor bowed.

Papa shook his hand. "I cannot thank you enough, Doctor McIver."

"I can't take all the credit, Mr. Stanford. Earl Stiles is very persuasive when intent on having his way."

The door closed behind them, and their voices faded into the distance.

Frederica resumed her attention on her sketchbook and flicked through it. She stopped after the first few pages and ran her fingertip across the outline of a sketch. Over the years, the edge of the paper had frayed, more so than any other page in her book.

Even after five years, the likeness wrenched her heart. The features had matured, the face filling out with a masculinity which came when a boy turned into a man. But the eyes were the same—the dark intensity which broke through her defenses no matter how impenetrable a barrier she'd formed around herself.

Sighing, she snapped the sketchbook shut and set it aside.

The dark features and brooding gaze of the man in the sketch were in direct contrast to the golden features and clear blue eyes of Roderick Markham. Her friend.

No, not her friend, but her brother. And as soon as the weather grew warmer, she would pay him a visit.

THE GRAY STONE building of the ducal residence seemed to swallow the sunlight.

As Frederica approached the main doors, her nerves battled with her resolve. What harm could come from her visit? If Roderick were not there, she would leave her card and return home.

He was her friend. She would reassure him she wanted neither inheritance nor recognition, only friendship. She had no wish to see his father, the duke.

Her father. The man who had taken a woman unwilling.

But what made the duke different to other aristocrats? Even Hawthorne had mistresses, and Frederica had seen him firsthand taking liberties with Lady Swainson in the woods. Liberties Frederica willingly offered herself, before her conscience had intervened.

The door opened to reveal a liveried footman. His stance exuded contempt from the tips of his polished shoes to the top of his powdered wig. Gold brocade adorned his jacket, the product of many hours of hard labor of young girls like Jenny.

His jacket likely cost more than Frederica's best evening gown, which had been packed into her trunk, ready for the journey to London.

"I'm here to see Lord Markham."

"Is he expecting you, miss?"

"No, but we are acquainted."

The footman shook his head as if the notion of his master being acquainted with someone who arrived on foot, rather than in a carriage, was unsupportable.

"Who shall I say is calling?"

"Miss Stanford."

He wrinkled his nose and led her inside.

Overstated elegance bled from every corner of the interior, from the black and white tiles forming an intricate pattern on the floor, to the marble columns flanking each door leading off the main hall.

Only the chandelier brought color to the room, but that was a trick of the sunlight reflecting off the facets of the crystal, sprinkling accents of color onto the floor.

Without taking her cloak, the footman crossed the floor in sharp, impatient strides and ushered her into a parlor.

"Wait here."

He turned his back and left her alone with the door ajar, as if she couldn't be trusted in one of the rooms unobserved.

When he arrived, Roderick would likely share a joke with her at the footman's expense.

She didn't have to wait long. The approaching footsteps had a determined, if irregular, gait, not the strong strides she'd have expected from Roderick. Perhaps she'd called at too early an hour. The children of dukes could afford to languish in bed.

Bastard she may be, but she was also the child of a duke.

The man who opened the door was not Roderick.

He was tall, a little over six feet, but his physique displayed evidence of a life of decadence. His face was fleshier than the norm, full, sensual lips stained red. His jacket was even more ornately decorated than the footman's, with thread upon thread of gold glittering in the sunlight.

His body leaned to the left, his weight supported by a cane. His left foot was bandaged, and he bore the expression of a man in pain; pain brought about by a lifetime of port and rich sauces.

The Duke of Markham.

Pale blue eyes regarded her coldly.

"I understand you seek an audience with me, but I fail to understand why you used the front entrance."

"I'm sorry?"

"You're Stanford's daughter, are you not?" he said, his mouth curled into a sneer. "Why did he send *you*?"

"He hasn't sent me."

"Then he should give you a bloody good thrashing for coming here unsolicited. What do you think you're about, girl? Barton said you sought an audience with me."

"No, Y-your Grace," she stammered. "I came to see Roderick."

The Duke sputtered and recoiled. "Roderick! How dare you address your betters in such a familiar manner!"

"Is he here?"

"No, he's not. Get out before I have Barton set the dogs on you. Barton!"

"But..."

"My son won't pay a penny," the duke said, "whether you've spread your legs for him or not."

She flinched under his crudeness. Anger boiled within her at the notion that the man in front of her thought nothing of violating young women and casting them aside.

"How dare you!" she cried.

"Get out," he snarled and pitched forward. The door burst open and the footman appeared.

"Your Grace! What's happened?"

"Get her out," Markham spat, "then set the dogs loose. Tell the bloody gamekeeper to earn his salary and run her off. I don't care how, but get rid of her!"

Markham reeled toward her, his face purple with hatred.

"Stay away from my son. And tell your father that's the last time I'll trade with him. A man too weak to control his slut-of-a-daughter is not one I wish to associate with." He lifted his cane and, with a surprisingly agile motion, swung at her.

She caught a glancing blow on her shoulder and staggered back. Before he could strike her again, she sidestepped him and ran out of the room, his words of hatred ringing in her ears.

Only when the main doors had closed behind her and she'd ran far enough down the drive for the building to be out of sight, did she slow down.

Grandpapa had been right. She was the daughter of a monster.

Chapter Sixteen

THE SWAN GLIDED along the Serpentine toward the piece of bread Frederica had thrown in the water. Unlike the birds which plagued her dreams with their dark feathers and beating wings, the swan posed no threat to her. Perhaps tomorrow, she would return to the park and sketch it, if Papa gave her leave to.

Papa wanted her to seek a wider acquaintance in London, and it was the least she could do after the damage she'd inflicted on his business. Only a few hours after Markham had thrown her out, a message had arrived for Papa declaring that His Grace would purchase his wine from another merchant from now on. Papa had merely patted her head and told her not to worry.

In turn, she'd resolved to accommodate his wishes, if that lessened his troubles.

The swan disappeared downriver. It would be disappointed, for few people were in the park at this hour. Which was why Frederica was there. She endured society parties for Papa's sake but needed solitude and fresh air to recuperate. Afternoons spent painting in the garden of Lady Axminster's townhouse only provided limited comfort. Even though the old woman still languished in Bath, which had reduced the number of calling cards being delivered, there was always the risk of visitors invading Frederica's peace.

Such as Hawthorne Stiles. Alice de Grecy had called for tea yesterday, full of tales of Hawthorne's success. Now an established magistrate, he presided over hearings, many in his home, and was gaining a reputation for justice.

Why did he have to be so honorable? The whole world admired him. Save, perhaps, Roderick Markham.

As if her thoughts conjured him out of thin air, Roderick's voice invaded her consciousness.

"Miss Stanford!"

She turned and looked into pale blue eyes and a smiling face.

"Lord Markham?"

"Miss Stanford, you don't look pleased to see me."

"Should you be seen with me?" she asked. "Your father…"

He snorted. "What the devil does that old miser have to do with it?"

"I doubt he'd want you to have anything to do with me."

"Nonsense!" he exclaimed. "Nobody could prevent me from seeing my little bird. We're good friends, are we not?"

"Friends?"

"Yes," he said more firmly. "The pater be damned."

He drew out his pocket watch, then snapped it shut with a sigh. "I must go, little bird. Permit me to call on you tomorrow."

"I don't know…"

"Don't break my heart." His face creased into an expression of hurt. "And your intelligence should be put to greater use than discussing the niceties of ribbons."

"Ribbons?"

"Whatever you ladies speak of when gentlemen are absent—lace, finery, or some such. But you're different, which makes you all the more interesting."

He was unlike any gentleman she'd met. Perhaps she might trust him enough to reveal the truth? Though he could never acknowledge her publicly as his relative, maybe privately he'd welcome her.

"Very well," she said. "You may visit me tomorrow."

He brushed his lips against her hand. His eyes glinted in the morning sun, a momentary darkness pulsing in their depths before he took his leave.

⤞⤞⤞⤝⤝⤝

"LORD STILES, YOUR intentions are well meant, but I know what's best for my daughter."

Hawthorne reached for the brandy and swirled the amber liquid in the glass. But the spiral motion failed to temper his frustration. "I'm sure you do, Stanford, but I must warn you against letting her run about London unfettered."

"You still see her as inferior?"

Hawthorne sighed. "No, Stanford, I value your daughter very highly. Which is why I urge you to ensure she takes care in the company of gentlemen. Think of her reputation."

Red blotches appeared on Stanford's cheeks. "My daughter would never act inappropriately."

"Then what is she playing at with Roderick Markham?"

"They enjoy a friendship, nothing more. Why should she be denied friends? The ladies hereabouts shun her, except that vapid de Grecy girl."

"If she wishes to secure a husband…"

Stanford raised his hand. "I'll not hear another word on the matter. I brought her to London to widen her acquaintance, not sell her off to the first man who wants her."

Stanford was completely ignorant of the danger she was in. That bastard Markham was sniffing round her again. Only yesterday, Hawthorne had overheard Markham in White's boasting of how he'd secured her attention after waiting up for her after a particularly vigorous night at Betty's bawdyhouse.

Betty's girls had catered to Hawthorne's own tastes when he was learning the art of seduction. But Markham was something else; he frittered away his fortune at whorehouses every night. Old Sir Benedict had been right when he'd asked Hawthorne to reduce Frederica's dowry. A large fortune led to misery and debauchery. Had Roderick Markham's fortune been less, his character might have been all the better for it.

But Markham's fortune only served to feed his cruelty. Since boyhood, his sadistic streak had governed his actions. Women shied from his more brutal form of lovemaking. Ever since Hawthorne had thrashed him at Eton for beating a first year, Markham seemed to view him as a challenge, their outward appearance of friendship purely for the benefit of nicety.

Hawthorne drained his glass. The brandy slipped down with ease, the smooth smokiness lingering on his tongue. No wonder Stanford was one of the most sought-after merchants. His liquor was manna from heaven compared to the astringency served up in most townhouses. Some of the best wines were to be found in Stanford's home.

And not just the best wine. The door opened, and the subject which had plagued Hawthorne's unconscious thoughts since Christmas entered the drawing room.

"Papa, I..."

Her voice faded into silence.

In the months since he last saw her, she'd gained back some of the weight she'd lost. As their eyes met, the color drained from her face.

He breathed in the aroma of lavender and rose. His body hardened, and he caught his breath with the force of it, crossing his legs to hide the bulge in his breeches. If he stood, his erection would be visible to both Frederica and her father.

"Rica, my love!" Stanford rose to greet his daughter. "Where have you been?"

"In Hyde Park, feeding the swans."

"You must take care. They're dangerous creatures. I heard one attacked Lady De Witt's dog."

"They're misunderstood," she replied. "Lady De Witt is an obnoxious woman with one of those high-pitched voices which cuts through your mind like a knife through butter. Her dog's just like her, round and vicious. She lets it run wild in the park. Any creature would seek to defend itself against such an onslaught." She glanced at Hawthorne. "But justice always defers to rank."

"I beg to differ," Hawthorne said. "True justice is above such matters."

"I have yet to see true justice accomplished, Lord Stiles."

"Rica, my love," Papa interjected, "I'm sure the earl dispenses justice fairly when in court." He nodded to Hawthorne. "I've heard great things of you, Stiles. I only wish there were more men like you in the magistracy."

"I encountered much opposition," Hawthorne said, "but my title secured my position."

"Which, itself, is unjust," Frederica said.

"Rica..." Stanford warned.

Hawthorne smiled inwardly. What joy to see her fighting spirit return, even if directed at him!

"Miss Stanford, I admit my position was secured as a result of my title, but I intend to capitalize on it for the good of the world rather than personal gain. Surely you wouldn't condemn me for my rank if I used it well?"

"Of course not," she replied. "But you must admit the inequity of your acquiring the position because of your birth. I dare say the clerks in your court, had they been born into the status you enjoy, might have performed equally well in the magistracy."

Stanford coughed, and she broke off, her cheeks flaming. The room fell silent save for the rhythmic ticking of the clock on the mantelshelf. The silence expanded, filled by unspoken words of abandonment and bastardry. Shame lingered in her eyes, and she looked away. Her background still pained her.

She'd spoken the truth about the swan. A misunderstood creature, seeking only to protect itself. But her vulnerability lay in her need to be valued and loved. It was that need which reprobates like Roderick Markham took advantage of.

He rose to his feet. "Stanford, may I have a word with your daughter in private?"

"Of course."

"Papa, Lord Stiles has nothing to say to me which you cannot hear."

"Let us indulge him nonetheless," Stanford said.

Before she could respond, her father slipped out of the room and closed the door.

She moved toward a desk beside the window where her sketchbook lay open and flicked through the pages. She ran her finger across the paper as if tracing an outline, then sighed, shut the book, and turned to face him.

"What do you want?" she asked. "Are you here to curtail my behavior again?"

He moved toward her. "Of course not, I—"

"Don't insult my intelligence, Lord Stiles," she interrupted. Her illness and the revelation about her past would have floored most ladies, but it seemed to have given her strength, as if the fever inside her had forged a backbone of steel.

She held her head high. "If you wish to instruct Papa on my reputation and my abilities to secure a husband, I suggest you do so more discreetly. Or did you think me hard of hearing?"

There was nothing for it but to tackle the issue head on.

"What are you playing at with Roderick Markham?" he asked. "He's your bro..."

"Don't say it!" she cried. "Papa doesn't know. I wouldn't want him finding out, least not from you."

"Then what are you doing? Carousing about London unchaperoned! You've been seen with him in Hyde Park, walking and laughing…"

"…activities I believe are acceptable for young ladies."

"Does Markham know who you are?"

"Not yet."

"Don't tell him." Hawthorne swallowed the fear in his voice. "He won't thank you for it."

"Oh, I see!" She fisted her hands. "You think I seek to ingratiate myself with him in order to secure recognition or a fortune? I only want friendship, something you cannot comprehend."

"I understand friendship," he said. "But Roderick Markham is *not* your friend."

Pain flashed in her eyes. "He was the only one who treated me as an equal at your house party, as opposed to a peasant invited in order to satisfy your need to bestow charity."

"You bloody fool!" he cried. "You think I invited you out of charity?"

He raised his hand to take her arm, and she shrank back as if she thought he'd strike her. Instead, he stepped close and gently took her hand, tugging her against him.

His manhood stiffened, nudging insistently against her body. Her eyes darkened, but a golden light pulsed from within, radiating fire. She parted her lips and gave a low cry of want.

He claimed her mouth, lips devouring her, tongue demanding entrance. Their tongues tangled, and the shackles binding them pulled tighter, invisible chains which spiraled around their bodies as he held her close. He reached for her hips, and a groan of need rumbled in his chest as his hands claimed her soft flesh.

"Hawthorne…" she whispered.

"Little changeling…"

He grasped her skirt and pulled the material up to expose her thighs. His fingers caressed the smooth creamy skin, moving toward the source of her heat.

Each encounter between them had led to this—the pinnacle of ecstasy when he finally claimed the one woman who could fully satisfy his hunger.

He dipped his finger into her heat, and his body almost burst with release. A whimper vibrated in her throat, and she opened her legs wider.

She belonged to him, *only him*. His body surged with the anticipation of having her, and he unbuttoned his breeches. One thrust and he would own her completely.

Three sharp knocks sounded on the door, and she stiffened in his arms.

What the devil was he doing? Lust and passion had obliterated his reason. He was known for his ability to keep a cool head, yet he was about to be caught tossing up a woman's skirts in broad daylight.

Not just any woman, his little changeling.

She jumped back, trembling, distress twisting her features.

"Miss Stanford?" A voice called from behind the door.

She wiped her forehead. "A moment!"

Hawthorne buttoned his breeches and smoothed down the front, his body tightening as his hand brushed over his groin.

"Dear God, Frederica," he said. "I'm sorry. Forgive me."

"Just go," she said, agony lacing her voice. "Please."

She swallowed and took a deep breath before composing herself.

"Come in, James. What is it?"

The door opened, and a footman entered, holding a silver salver with a card on it. She took the card and read it, and a smile crossed her lips.

"Thank you, James."

"He's in the morning room, miss."

"I'll be there directly."

"Who is it, Miss Stanford?"

She addressed the footman. "James, Lord Stiles is just leaving. Be so kind as to escort him out."

Hawthorne took her arm, and she stiffened. "Take care," he said quietly. She didn't answer, and he tightened his grip until she looked at him. "Please," he whispered, "please, Frederica." Her eyes widened at his familiar address, and he withdrew his hand.

She snatched her arm away. "James, show this gentleman out," she said. "If he refuses, fetch Papa."

Hawthorne raised his hands in surrender. "I can see myself out, Miss Stanford, but my warning is out of concern for your welfare."

"Since when have you cared for my welfare?"

"I'll leave you in peace," he said. "But I urge you to be cautious. I wouldn't want you hurt."

She nodded, the frost in her eyes melting a little. Perhaps a part of her understood he'd never stopped caring for her.

Loving her.

He bowed and left the room, waving away the footman's assistance. As he passed the morning room, he spotted the man inside, reclined in a chair, a brandy glass already in his hand. He looked up and raised the glass as if in a toast, then drained it, a smile of triumph on his lips.

Whatever Frederica believed, Roderick Markham had no intention of becoming her friend.

CHAPTER SEVENTEEN

"OH, I SAY, that's Felicia Long with her mama. Her gown has been made from the finest silk, but, I'm afraid, not even the attentions of the best modiste in town can make up for such a disturbing countenance."

The woman on Hawthorne's arm turned her face to him, malice glittering in her eyes. "You only need observe the length of Lady Long's nose to understand where her daughter acquired her somewhat extraordinary features."

"She seems a pleasant sort of girl, Miss Wilcott," Hawthorne said.

She let out a delicate laugh, the sort other ladies might describe as *tinkling*, designed to appeal to the opposite sex. Clearly, she sought to increase her appeal by undermining the worth of others in the eyes of the gentlemen she pursued, as if she would compare favorably either by virtue of their deficiencies or by her own demonstration of wit.

"My dear, Lord Stiles," she said, "when gentlemen use such words to describe a young woman, that's a sure indication that her tenure in the marriage mart is about to come to an end, and she's destined for the shelf." She curled her fingers around his forearm in a possessive grip. "Heaven help me if ever I find myself being described as 'pleasant' or 'kind'."

"On that count, at least, Miss Wilcott, you're safe from me."

Her lips curled in a smile of self-satisfaction, and indication that vanity, together with a lack of understanding, must be added to her list of attributes.

Dear Lord, was this what a man had to endure when he suffered the company of what society deemed to be an *eligible young lady*? By acquiescing to Lady Wilcott's public insistence that he call upon her daughter, Hawthorne had found himself manipulated into the position of her suitor. What he'd intended to be a simple stroll in the park to preserve the lady's pride had, instead, turned out to be the first step to courtship.

Perhaps a career in the army might have prepared him for such an onslaught. But no soldier could adequately prepare himself for such an assailant as an overbearing mama with an unmarried daughter in her fourth season.

He needed a wife, one of suitable birth, but why was it those desirable qualities seemed to go hand in hand with an absence of character? No wonder men of his station sought solace in the arms of courtesans. Had Adam lived, Hawthorne would have enjoyed more freedom in his choice of wife, like a spirited little changeling, a woman to warm the fire in his blood…

Miss Wilcott's voice cut through the image of *her* and returned him to the present.

"Some men might find themselves tempted by a large fortune," she said. "But, as Mama tells me, birth is everything."

"How so?" he asked.

"Society must be kept pure. If ancient bloodlines are to be tainted by those of no consequence, whatever their fortune may be, the world will degenerate. And as for these new titles…" She wrinkled her nose, as if a nasty smell lingered in the air. "The *nouveau riche* are tainting the streets of London," she said. "Why, only last week, Mama was forced into an introduction with the wife of a farmer! Fancied herself Mama's equal just because her husband is a baronet."

"There's no shame in a viscountess making the acquaintance of a baronet's wife, surely?"

"In my view, traders should remain belowstairs where they belong, rather than be given titles which give them ideas above their station. Any lady would agree with me, I assure you."

"But a man might not," Hawthorne said. "The civilized world is founded on commerce, Miss Wilcott, however invisible the participants may be among your acquaintance."

She gave an unladylike snort. "Clearly you spend too much of your time in the country, Lord Stiles." She cast him a furtive glance, a sly expression glittering in her eyes.

"Markham was speaking on the subject when he took tea with us yesterday. Now, there's an ancient family. They date back to the thirteenth century."

Hawthorne stiffened at the mention of that odious man's name, and he stopped walking.

"Are you well?" she asked.

"Quite so, I thank you."

Her smile broadened, and she gave a self-satisfied nod. She might lack wits, but her predatory observation of him could not have failed to notice his reaction.

"I trust you don't view him as a rival."

"I hardly think of him at all, Miss Wilcott."

She let out another laugh, the delicate bell-like tones grating on his senses. "I could never attach my affections to a man with such a public reputation for debauchery. A gentleman may be permitted a mistress in his youth, of course, but when he's courting, he must pay due respect to the wishes of the lady on his arm."

"The wishes," Hawthorne said, "or the demands?"

Her smile slipped for a moment before she laughed again.

"You do amuse me, Lord Stiles!" she said. "For all his attempts at conversation, Markham would struggle to rival you." She squeezed his arm. "Oh, look!" She pointed in front of her. "There's the subject of our conversation."

Ahead sat the lone figure of a woman on a bench, sketchbook in hand. Her hand moved across the paper while she watched a swan gliding across the water. Seemingly absorbed in her activity, she did not notice Hawthorne and his companion.

"I can't see Markham anywhere," Hawthorne said. The woman on the bench stiffened, but did not look toward him.

Miss Wilcott lowered her voice to a whisper. "I meant his mistress," she said. "Or, soon to be, from what Miss de Witt told me."

"His mistress?"

"Lizzie overheard one of her chambermaids talking about her. Apparently Markham had one of his servants dismissed when she became *enceinte*. The foolish little tart expected him to set her up as his mistress. When he evicted her, she had the audacity to think she could find employment elsewhere. Lizzie sent them both packing, but not before they told her about Mad Miss Stanford."

"Mad Miss Stanford?"

"The wine merchant's daughter," she said.

"Yes," Hawthorne said. "I am acquainted with her." Miss Wilcott continued, oblivious of the warning note in his voice. "She faints at parties and screams at birds, so Lizzie says. I cannot understand Markham's interest in her, but his valet told the girl..."

"Nothing but belowstairs tattle," Hawthorne interrupted, wanting to stem the flow of spite from her lips, "Miss de Witt should know better than to indulge in such gossip."

Miss Wilcott shrugged. "Lizzie wants Markham for herself," she said, "and she'll crush any rival underfoot before she strikes root in his bedchamber, respectable, or..." she glanced at Frederica, "...too *modern* to ever be considered respectable."

They drew nearer to the woman on the bench. Her hand stilled, and she looked up, her gaze meeting Hawthorne's.

A jolt of desire coursed through him. "Miss Stanford, I trust you're well," he said.

"Yes, thank you."

"Ahem." Miss Wilcott gave a little cough.

"Permit me, Miss Stanford," he said, "may I do you the honor of introducing Miss Wilcott."

"Charmed, I'm sure," Miss Wilcott said, her tone that of someone chewing on a lump of gristle. "Lord Stiles, we really must be going."

Ignoring her, he gestured toward the sketchbook.

"You've captured the swan perfectly, Miss Stanford. How can you manage to do so, when it moves across the water rather than remains still?"

"The trick is in not wishing to pursue an accurate likeness," she replied. "The essence of the subject can be captured in a few strokes without cluttering up the image with unnecessary detail, or being constrained by the rules of convention."

"I fail to see the purpose in drawing an object if you're not interested in producing a true likeness," Miss Wilcott said. "How else can the artist demonstrate their skill other than by following rules and traditions?"

"A painting has to be more than aesthetically pleasing for it to have value," Frederica said.

"That depends on your notion of value," Miss Wilcott said. "Traditions must be upheld to prevent society from descending into savagery. You'll find that ladies do not share your *modern* sensibilities, is that not right, Lord Stiles?"

"Quite so," he said.

Frederica said nothing. She closed her sketchbook as if to protect her drawing from Miss Wilcott's spite.

Miss Wilcott linked her arm through Hawthorne's. "We really must be going, Stiles," she said. "Mama will be expecting us for tea."

"I have not been invited, Miss Wilcott," he replied.

"Nevertheless, I believe she's expecting you."

Dear lord, was there no end to the woman's attempts at manipulation? But this time, he would not be hounded into a corner.

"Forgive me, Miss Wilcott, I'll escort you home, of course, but I have another appointment this afternoon."

"Whatever for?"

"I'm sitting for a portrait."

"Surely you can rearrange that? Mama was most insistent you attend."

"I'm afraid that's out of the question," he said. "The light in the afternoon is just right when it shines through my drawing room window, and today is the only day for some time which suits both the artist and myself. Is that not so, Miss Stanford?"

Frederica looked up, and he lifted his eyebrows in a silent plea. Understanding and compassion crossed her expression and she nodded.

"Of course."

He mouthed a silent thank you, and her mouth curved into a gentle smile.

"Oh, very well," Miss Wilcott said. She gestured toward her maid, who had been following them at the obligatory five paces. "Come on, Mary, stop dawdling!"

"Sorry, miss," the maid said. She approached the bench, dipped a curtsey to Frederica, who stood and curtseyed back, smiling.

"Well, *really!*" Miss Wilcott hissed.

Hawthorne bowed to Frederica. "My carriage will collect you at three, Miss Stanford. Don't forget your paint box."

She nodded and resumed her seat.

He may not be able to shield Frederica from Miss Wilcott's spite, but, at the very least, he must save her from Roderick Markham.

By any means necessary.

CHAPTER EIGHTEEN

THE CARRIAGE DREW to a halt, and a footman opened the door and helped her out. Clutching her paint box under her arm, Frederica followed him through the doors to Hawthorne's townhouse.

"The master awaits you in the drawing room."

"Very well." She followed him upstairs.

Her heart hammered in her chest at the prospect of seeing him again. When he'd come across her in the park that morning, she had fought to maintain her composure. With a viscount's daughter on his arm, he only served to widen the distinction of rank between them. Doubtless a woman such as Miss Wilcott was the type of creature deemed suitable for the position of a wife. With wealth, breeding, and a marked disdain for anyone lacking a title, she was the embodiment of the perfect lady.

Unlike Mad Miss Stanford, the bastard child of a duke.

Miss Wilcott was everything Frederica was not. To him, Frederica was nothing more than an object to aid him in subterfuge to avoid taking tea with the woman he courted. It seemed as if deception and disdain were prized among the aristocracy. There was no place in the ton for honesty or compassion.

The footman knocked on the drawing room door, and a deep voice answered. He opened it.

Hawthorne stood by the window, the evening sun illuminating his beautiful features, the intense, deep-set eyes, the straight nose, and strong mouth…

Her stomach flipped as he looked at her, and she caught her breath.

"That will be all, Harry," he said to the footman.

"Will you be needing anything, sir?"

"No, thank you," he replied. "We are not to be disturbed."

As soon as the footman closed the door, Hawthorne crossed the floor and took her hand. She snatched it free.

"Are you sure I should not have been admitted via the tradesmen's entrance," she said, "given that my modern sensibilities have rendered me a savage? Miss Wilcott wouldn't approve."

He sighed and gestured to the sofa by the fireplace.

"Won't you sit?"

She took a seat, and opened her paint box.

"There's no need for that," he said. "I didn't ask you here to take my portrait."

"Then why?"

He sat beside her. "Have you told Roderick Markham about your *relationship*?" He wrinkled his nose at the last word.

"It's none of your business if I have," she replied. "We move in different circles, Lord Stiles. What I do has no impact on your life."

He shook his head. "If only you knew…" he broke off and sighed. "If you're being gossiped about, then that is my concern as a friend. I promised your father I'd take care of your wellbeing. Don't you realize that if you continue to parade about London with Markham, unchaperoned I might add, it can only damage your reputation?"

"You think I care for my reputation?" she asked.

"You're a fool if you don't," he replied, "but, at the very least, consider the impact your behavior might have on the people you love, and who love you. Think of them, if you cannot think of yourself."

"Compassion should outrank proprietary."

"Not in the world in which we live, Frederica," he said. "I don't just speak out of concern for those around you, but out of concern for you, too. Please believe me when I say that Markham's designs on you are not honorable. He's the sort of man who will always have a mistress in tow, and will be quite content to brag about it."

"What about you?" she cried. "Or do you seek to persuade me that Lady Swainson is merely a friend?"

"This has nothing to do with Clara."

Her stomach clenched at the familiarity with which he used her name, and she rose from her seat.

"If my services are not required, I shall see myself out."

He took her hand and drew her to him. His eyes darkened and his nostrils flared; the anger which vibrated in his voice morphed into a flicker of desire.

"You need to listen to reason!"

"Why should you care?"

"Oh, Frederica," he said. "I do care. If only you knew how much!"

He lifted his hand to her forehead, then traced a light outline of her face with his fingertip. A pulse of need rippled through her at his touch on her skin, and the breath caught in her throat. He drew close, and his warm breath caressed her lips. Burning desire glowered in his deep-set eyes, inviting her to surrender.

But she would not be taken for a fool.

She jerked free, ignoring the sensation of loss.

"What about Clara?"

"I've not seen her since before Christmas," he said. "She's a clever enough woman to have long suspected I loved another, but I believe she only realized it during my house party."

He caressed the back of her head and gently pulled her close until their mouths almost touched.

"As did I," he whispered. "Only when I thought I was going to lose you forever, did I understand where my heart lay. I knew then, as I know now, that I will do everything in my power to keep you safe, my love."

"Hawthorne…"

He silenced her words with his lips, and her body dissolved into his embrace, surrendering to his declaration of love. Willingly, she opened to him. His tongue swept into her mouth, exploring, seeking owner-ship of her, and she joined him in a dance of courtship. A low groan rumbled in his chest as he fisted his hand in her hair and held her close.

A delicious warmth flared in her center, and she shifted her thighs to ease the ache building within her. He broke the kiss and held her face in his hands. Gold flecks pulsed in his brown eyes, drawing her in, as if his soul called to her.

"Frederica," he breathed. "My love."

He brushed his lips against her chin, and she tipped her head back, offering her throat to him. Hungry, open-mouthed kisses followed a path along her neck, then across her collarbone. Shivers rippled through her as he reached the top of her breasts. A low growl vibrated in his throat, and with one hand, he tugged at the front of her gown, exposing a breast. Her nipple tightened at the rush of cold air. A hot mouth claimed her breast, and she cried out as a shock rippled to her core.

"Let me love you, Frederica," he said. "Let me take care of you. I want nothing more than to hold you in my arms."

"Yes," she whispered. "Love me, Hawthorne. Love me as I love you."

He grasped the hem of her gown and lifted it, and she lay back on the couch. Gentle fingers caressed her ankle, then moved higher, toward the source of her need, the secret place which pulsed whenever she dreamed of him.

He drew in a deep breath, his body shuddering, and his hand stopped. His eyes showed uncertainty, asking for consent.

"Are you certain, Frederica?"

She nodded and parted her thighs. He closed his eyes, his nostrils flaring, then he opened them, their gazes locking.

"Do you trust me?"

"Yes," she whispered.

His body came down on top of her, a delicious weight, giving comfort and security.

"There may be discomfort your first time," he said, "but also pleasure. I'll be as gentle as I can. It pains me, the thought of hurting you, but it's only the once."

She lifted her hand and touched his cheek, brushing a lock of his hair aside.

"I trust you."

He fumbled at his breeches, and she looked away.

"No." His commanding tone held her captive. "Don't take your eyes from me, Frederica. You're safe as long as you stay with me."

She nodded, and a tear beaded in her eye. He shifted his body, and something hard brushed against her. Her body stiffened, but she held his gaze, her need to submit to him overcoming her fear.

His fingers slid across her flesh, and she fisted her hands in his hair. At the point of no return, she arched her back, offering herself.

"Hawthorne, please!"

He thrust forward, and she let out a cry at the sharp sting. He stopped moving, holding her close, never taking his eyes off her.

"Forgive me, my love," he whispered. "The worst is over, I promise. From now on, there's only pleasure."

She clung to him, reassured by his words and solid gaze. At length, the pain subsided as her body stretched to accommodate him. As she relaxed, he moved, withdrawing slowly, then plunged in again. She cried out, but this time, another sensation dwarfed the pain. Pleasure ignited deep within her, the promise of sweet release.

He moved again, and the pleasure glowed brighter with each thrust, until it exploded, and her body shattered.

A scream burst from her throat as pure pleasure tore through her.

His movements grew more frenzied until they culminated in a final, powerful thrust. He cried her name, surged forward, and collapsed on top of her, his body trembling. His heart thudded against her chest, and he moved weakly against her as little aftershocks shuddered through her body.

Eventually he stilled, his heartbeat slowing to a languorous rhythm, his breath hot against her cheek.

"You're mine, now," he whispered.

She did not know how long they lay there, their bodies fused together, joined as one. When he sat back and buttoned his breeches, the light had faded. He smoothed his hair and smiled down at her.

"My goddess," he said. "And I shall worship you forever. Here, let me help you."

He took her hand and pulled her up, then reached out to her, tracing the neckline of her gown.

"I'll have to buy you a new one," he said.

Her gown was torn at the front, exposing a breast. He ran his fingertip across the flesh, and a thrill ran through her as he flicked her nipple.

"I'll buy you a dozen," he said. "And a necklace to go with them. In fact, I have the very thing. A string of sapphires set in clusters of diamonds. They're the most extraordinary shade of blue, like a deep ocean. They shall be my gift to you. The first of many."

"We...we must speak to Papa, first," she said.

"Yes, of course." He planted a kiss on her lips. "I'll make the arrangements as swiftly as possible to prevent a scandal. I should have no trouble finding a house. I can speak to my lawyer tomorrow."

"A house?" she said. "For us?"

"For you," he replied. "Stockton can draw up the deed in your name."

"But..." She shook her head. "I don't want a house, Hawthorne."

"Your father will expect me to set you up, Frederica. We must be sensible over the arrangements."

Cold fingers of dread clutched at her insides, curling round her stomach.

"Arrangements?"

He took her hand, his touch possessive rather than tender. "Servants, a carriage. Nothing will be too much for you. I can find you a house lavish enough to provide all the comforts you should wish for, but discreet enough to ensure your privacy."

She shook her head, as if she could dispel the truth, but it remained, his words etched into her mind.

He was offering to establish her as his mistress. The man she had worshipped for as long as she could remember, viewed her as nothing more than an object to satisfy the needs of his body, to be hidden away while he courted another.

"Of course," he continued. "You'll have your independence. The income from your father's business will give you security."

"Income?"

"Has your father not told you?" he asked. "I invested in his business. When the time comes, you shall inherit a regular stipend. Of course, I shall furnish you with everything you need, but an income of your own will lend you respectability."

A rush of nausea flowed through her, and she leapt to her feet, swallowing the lump in her throat.

"My love?"

"Is this what this afternoon was about?" she asked. "You've bought the goods, so you wished to sample the wares? I thought you loved me, you *said* you loved me!"

Tears blurred her vision, and she wiped her eyes. "I thought…thought you wanted me."

He blinked, his expression full of sorrow. "Oh, Frederica! Forgive me, my love, I thought you understood. I do want you, and I'm offering you as much as I am able to. My protection. In my position, my choices are limited. Someone of your rank enjoys considerably more freedom than someone of mine."

His words could not have affirmed more clearly her inferiority. She reached for her shawl and wrapped it around her dress.

"I'm giving you freedom, Frederica," he said. "Is that not what you wanted? Forgive me, my love, I had no designs on seducing you. I asked you here to warn you again about Markham, to talk some sense into you. He's always hated me, ever since we were children. Because of my affection for you, he sees you as a pawn to be used against me in whatever manner he sees fit. But he won't touch you now. Can't you see that? What's happened is for the best."

"Why do you think so badly of him?"

"Because he's a debaucher of women!" Hawthorne said. "He's been heard boasting of his intention to set you up as his mistress. I couldn't allow that."

"And yet, I find myself in that position now!" she cried. "You have no objection to my being a whore, just as long as it's *your* whore, is that it?"

He flinched at her coarse expression "Frederica, I would never treat you like a whore."

"You just did."

She picked up her paint box and crossed the floor to the door. He rose to his feet and moved toward her, but she held up her hand.

"No," she said. "Whatever you think of me, I am not some harlot to be used in a battle of male prowess. I'm worth more than that."

"Take my carriage if you're going home," he said. "The streets are dangerous when it's dark."

"No more dangerous than a gentleman's drawing room."

"Then at least permit me to call on you tomorrow."

"Please don't," she said. "You have a lady to court."

Ignoring the regret in his eyes, she turned her back on him before the calling of her heart could stop her, and ran down the stairs, out of his house, and from his life.

CHAPTER NINETEEN

"Y OUR GUEST HAS arrived, miss. He's waiting for you in the parlor. Would you like me to send for Mrs. Brown?"

"No thank you, Harry," Frederica said.

The footman shifted uncomfortably in the doorway. "You need to be accompanied, miss. Your father's not at home."

Which was why she had sent for Roderick, but Frederica knew enough of proprietary not to tell Harry. Given what had happened the day before, she was already a fallen woman. But with luck, Roderick might be able to help her.

As she entered the parlor, relief flooded through her at the sight of her friend.

Not her friend, but her brother. And today she would tell him. She needed protection from Hawthorne Stiles and from her body's inability to withstand the assaults on her senses each time he drew near. Shame coursed through her at the memory of the day before, when she'd opened her legs like a wanton.

Papa thought highly of Hawthorne. Only Markham could protect her. Papa might love her, but would he understand her moment of weakness? Would he forgive her?

"Lord Markham!" Despite her efforts, her voice came out high-pitched and strained.

His eyes narrowed. "Miss Stanford! I trust you're well?"

"Quite well."

"I know when my little bird is indisposed." He took her hands and lowered his voice. "May I enquire as to the nature of your discomfort? I trust it bears no relation to our mutual friend, the esteemed earl?"

Her heart fluttered. Had Hawthorne been speaking about her? Was her fall from grace the subject of gossip already?

"Ah," he said. "I've strayed too close to the truth. Stiles is a rake, Miss Stanford. All the worse, for he thinks his position as magistrate elevates him above us mere mortals. Is that why you invited me here with such urgency?"

"I must speak to you. In private."

"We're alone—unless your father is here?"

"No," she said. "Papa's not in. But I don't want anyone to hear us, not even the servants. Would you care to take a turn about the garden?"

"It would be my pleasure."

Relief weakened her limbs, and she leaned against him.

"My little bird is trembling, but I'll take care of you."

Sunlight illuminated the corners of the garden. Summer was on its way, and soon the season would be in full swing.

Roderick steered her across the lawn. "Shall we find a secluded spot, Miss Stanford?"

She motioned toward the rear of the garden.

"Behind those bushes there's a secret spot, not visible from the house. I go there if I wish to be alone."

His smile broadened. "A secret spot?"

"Not even Papa invades my privacy there."

"Then I consider myself privileged to be invited into your—*secret garden*," he said, his tongue curling around the final words.

He squeezed her hand, and his body heat penetrated through her gloves. But unlike the searing inferno of need which had blazed through her at Hawthorne's touch, she felt nothing other than companionship.

She slipped through the bushes, and he followed. His breath echoed in the still air, hoarse exhalations as if he were exerting himself.

"Mind the leaves," she said. "They're prickly."

"Why doesn't the gardener clip them?"

"I prefer it that way. It means I'm less likely to be disturbed here."

"How clever you are!" he said. "You think of everything."

The bushes opened into a small area, completely concealed from above and from all sides, with a wooden bench in the center. The sun filtered through the leaves, casting dappled specks of light onto the ground.

A blackbird flew out of a nearby bush, and she leapt back with a cry as wings beat at her. Markham thrust his arm out and batted the bird away, and she closed her eyes and clung to him, focusing on her breathing to disperse childhood memories.

He pulled her to him. "My sweet, little bird."

"What are you doing?"

"Hush," he said. "There's no need to explain why you lured me here."

He kissed her fingers, one by one, then drew her index finger into his mouth and nipped it.

"You've no idea how long I've waited for this."

"No, Lord Markham…"

"Roderick, my name's Roderick."

"No, Roderick." She tried to snatch her hand away, but he took her wrist and held it firm and pulled her to him just as Hawthorne had done earlier. But this time panic, rather than need, ignited within her.

"Roderick, please!"

"Come, come, little bird," he said, his eyes hardening. "Why else would a woman invite a man into her secret place, if not for seduction?"

"No," she pleaded. "I didn't bring you here for this."

"That's enough!" he said, his voice hard. "I can tolerate a little unwillingness in a woman, even I relish it at times, but there's a time to stop teasing and that time is now."

He gripped the material of her gown.

"No!" She pulled free from his hold. "You can't! Roderick, you're my brother!"

He jerked back.

"What on earth are you saying?"

"It's true," she said. "I read a letter from my grandfather. My mother was one of your father's servants."

He threw back his head and laughed. "So that's why you came sniffing round my ancestral home! The pater told me of your little visit."

"You believe me?"

"You weren't the first, and I doubt you were the last," he said. "The old dog always had a fancy for redheads, and what else are maidservants good for? The countryside must be littered with his bastards."

He folded his arms and looked at her with hooded eyes. "So, not content with trying to extort a fortune out of a duke, you thought you'd seduce it out of his heir?"

"N-no," she stuttered. "I only wanted your help. It's Hawthorne. He...he..." she broke off, choking as her throat tightened with shame.

A lazy smile crept across his face.

"He fucked you?"

She winced at his crude words, and he let out another laugh.

"Did you offer yourself to him expecting marriage? Foolish little harlot! An earl would consider it a degradation to cleave himself to a common little country wench with a reputation for insanity! I suppose he rejected you after he'd sampled the goods. Does your father know?"

She shook her head, ashamed at her naiveté. Hawthorne had been right. Markham was not her friend.

"I'm still disposed to help you," Markham said. "Let it not be known that I'm uncharitable."

The cold expression in his eyes belied his words, and she took a step back. But he took her wrist and pulled her to him.

"I'm a generous patron, little bird," he said. "I'm willing to ignore the degradation of suffering Stiles's leavings, if you please me well."

Bile rose in her throat at his suggestion.

"You can't," she said. "Didn't you hear what I told you? You're my brother!"

"I only have your word for that, my dear," he said. "Who knows how many farm hands or stable boys your whore-of-a-mother spread her legs for? If Stiles has had you, why can I not take my share as well? Perhaps we could compare notes."

She struggled to break free, but his grip tightened, and she gasped in pain.

"The thrill is almost always to be found in the chase and in making the final kill."

He grasped the front of her gown, and she heard a tearing sound.

"I'd advise you to submit, little bird," he said, his voice smooth. "What would your dear papa think of you if he knew you lured me here? Or your precious Hawthorne? Offering yourself to another so quickly after whoring yourself out to him?"

She reached up and dug her fingernails into his cheek. He cursed and relaxed his grip. Then she punched him in the jaw. He fell back, and she rammed her knee into his groin. He collapsed on the ground, gasping for air.

Fear flickered in his eyes. The fear of a bully. She had seen it on the farm twins' expressions when they'd realized the folly in picking on someone with all the appearance of weakness.

"Have a care," she said. "A common country girl is not above giving a weakling a good kicking."

"Bitch!" He wiped his face and inspected the blood on his fingers. "You soiled whore! I ought to have you horsewhipped!"

"Try it," she said. "I've nothing to lose."

His face twisted with hatred, making his beautiful features quite ugly. How had she missed it? Had she been blinded by his gallantry, or by the hope that she had found a kindred spirit in a world where she'd always felt out of place?

He struggled to his feet, and she moved toward him, fists raised. Conquering the fear which boiled inside her, she forced her expression into a cold smile and locked gazes with him.

Papa's voice called out in the distance.

"Frederica! Are you there?"

"Shall I invite him to join us?" Markham asked. "I'm sure he'd be interested to know why you asked me here in his absence."

"Please do," she replied. "Did I ever tell you what an excellent shot he is?"

"Is that a threat?"

"A promise, *my lord*."

He blinked and lowered his gaze. With an air of nonchalance, he brushed the dust from his jacket and adjusted his necktie.

"Pleasant as your company has been today, Miss Stanford, I find I must be going."

He moved closer, and his expression hardened. "I'd advise you to be careful, my dear. London society is a dangerous place for a woman. And contrary to popular belief, even a *soiled whore* has something to lose, something she values above all else. It's just a matter of discovering what that is."

He clicked his heels together and bowed, then slipped between the bushes and disappeared, whistling. As soon as the merry tune faded into silence, the sickness churning inside her burst and she bent over, finally yielding to the fear which had almost conquered her. She retched and retched until there was nothing left except the bitter taste of betrayal.

CHAPTER TWENTY

A S HAWTHORNE ENTERED the clubroom at Whites, he spotted Ross who waved him over. He sat in the chair next to his friend, and a footman appeared with his favorite brandy. He drained the glass and brandished it at the servant, who nodded, took it back, and retreated to refill it.

Ross raised an eyebrow and sipped his drink with the measured action of a man who appreciated, rather than wasted, the comforts wealth afforded him. Society might think the worst of a man who acquired his fortune through trade. But hard work, though reviled, cultivated a self-control which most men of Hawthorne's class could only dream of.

Ross might envy Hawthorne for his title, which had eased his entry into establishments such as Whites, but, in turn, Hawthorne envied Ross his freedom—freedom to do what he liked with his fortune, being unshackled from entailments and the whims of trustees.

And freedom to marry whomsoever he chose, even if Ross had squandered that freedom on the colorless de Grecy girl.

If Hawthorne possessed such freedom, he'd have chosen someone far more worthy…

Frederica…

But instead, he'd taken her virtue like a hungry adolescent. Her view of the world had rendered her ignorant of the constraints of rank he suffered and the expectations placed upon him to marry well.

Selfishly, he'd taken what she had willingly offered without a thought to the consequences. Then, propelled by a need to possess her for himself, he'd insulted her with his crass offer, attempting to justify his motives by arguing that it was for her benefit.

Ashamed of his behavior, he'd attempted to call on her, but each time he'd arrived at her front door, the footman had informed him she was not at home. He couldn't blame her—she had every reason to hate him.

Had she told her father what he'd done? If Stanford had turned up on Hawthorne's doorstep, pistol in hand, demanding retribution, some of Hawthorne's guilt might have been spent. But instead, that guilt had festered.

For the past fortnight he'd looked for her in every drawing room and ballroom he entered, disappointment dousing his anticipation when he couldn't find her.

She didn't seem to be going out at all. Each morning, he rose early and ventured into Hyde Park, hoping to catch a glimpse of her. But, save for the occasional clandestine liaison between lovers or a furtive young boy up to no good, the park was empty. Not even that profligate Markham was about.

"You look out of sorts, my friend," Ross said. "If I were the sort of man to indulge in the bet book, I'd wager a hundred guineas your ill humor is to do with a woman."

"I'm in no mood to discuss women," Hawthorne said. "At least, not with a man who's soon to slip his neck through the parson's noose. Tell me, how does it feel? Are you a prisoner awaiting the gallows, or a witless fool blinded by the belief that wedded bliss awaits you?"

Ross snorted. "More a blessed release than wedded bliss," he said. The usual confident tone of his voice was conspicuous by its absence.

"How so?" Hawthorne asked.

"It seems as if I was deceived," Ross said. "Miss de Grecy has broken our engagement. In favor, as she so eloquently put it, of a man better suited to her rank."

"I'm sorry."

Ross let out a bitter laugh. "There's no need for such insincerities, Stiles. It seems you, and the majority of my acquaintance, were right about her. A colorless, soulless hunter of titles. I was foolish enough to believe she was different, that a heart existed within that cold shell of hers. But in the end, ladies of a certain disposition will always value the prospect of being a duchess over that of becoming the wife of a businessman."

"A duchess?"

"Yes," Ross said, "after evicting me so swiftly from her affections, she's accepted an offer from Markham."

Hawthorne's heart skipped with relief. Though he felt sorry for his friend who, for all his efforts at appearing indifferent, clearly suffered from his fiancée's change of heart, he couldn't help but rejoice. Markham must have lost interest in seducing Frederica and turned his attention to the pursuit of a wife and a dowry. Doubtless, the man's wastrel lifestyle had finally rendered him in need of cash.

His little changeling was safe. And Ross would recover. A woman such as Miss de Grecy, who valued material wealth and a listing in Debrett's, would only have made Ross miserable. She and Markham deserved each other.

"What will you do?" Hawthorne asked.

"I'll confine myself to more pleasurable business transactions in the future," Ross replied, "where the women who sell themselves prefer to deal with a man's cash, rather than his heart. I toast them both. He's welcome to her!"

He drained his glass and rose to his feet. "Till tomorrow, Stiles," he said. "I've better things to do than drink myself into a stupor over a harlot."

⇻⇻⇻≪≪≪

NOT TWENTY MINUTES after Ross left, the object of their discussion strolled into the clubroom, together with his friend, James Spencer. He stopped as he saw Hawthorne and gave a bow.

"Stiles, how pleasant!"

Hawthorne rose to his feet. "May I be the first to congratulate you, Markham?"

Markham narrowed his eyes, as if in thought, then a slow smile crept across his mouth.

"That's uncommonly generous of you, Stiles," he said. "I'd always taken you for a poor loser, but if you can be gracious in defeat, I'm prepared to overlook your incivility at your house party."

"Defeat?"

"Yes," Markham said. "You may have taken the first shot, as it were, but I'm the one who bagged the bird."

"The bird? I was speaking of Miss de Grecy."

"Oh, *her*," Markham said. "I thought you were referring to my little bird, or should that be *little changeling*?"

The skin crawled on the back of Hawthorne's neck.

Frederica...

Markham's smile broadened. "She invited me into her home so prettily," he said. "I believe she was anxious to make a direct comparison between us." He touched his face where three parallel scratches ran along one cheek. "A surprisingly vigorous partner." He nudged his friend's arm. "Was she not, Spencer? It must be the country upbringing."

Hawthorne tightened his grip on the glass, and his knuckles whitened.

"What have you done, Markham?"

"Nothing she didn't beg for," Markham said, "but you'd know all about that, wouldn't you? Though, in your eagerness to beat me to the chase, you forgot the basic rule, Stiles."

"Which is?"

"Prowess will always win in the end. Now that she's tasted better, I doubt she'll spread her legs for you again, unless out of desperation."

With an explosion, the glass in his hand shattered and pain tore through his flesh.

Markham's eyes glittered with triumph. "By rights, I'm the one who should be affronted, Stiles, being offered your leavings. She begged me to set her up as my mistress..."

"Stop there, Markham," Hawthorne said, gritting his teeth to stem the tide of anger swelling inside, "unless you wish to take this outside."

Markham laughed. "You have no need to view me as a rival, Stiles. You may take pleasure in indulging in soiled goods, but I don't find myself at such a loss."

The dam burst. Hawthorne swung at Markham's smiling face. His fist connected with Markham's nose. With an over-exaggerated howl, he dropped to the floor.

"How dare you!" Markham cried. "You've broken my nose! Someone help me!"

Two footmen approached and grasped Hawthorne by the arms.

"I'll do more than that," Hawthorne said. "I'll break your bloody neck!"

"That's quite enough of that, sir," the older footman said. "Perhaps you need to step outside to cool off."

"You should throw him out for ungentlemanly behavior," Markham growled.

"Ban him for life," Spencer added.

Hawthorne struggled against the restraining arms, but the footmen, evidently practiced in evicting members who'd indulged in too much liquor, held him firm and marched him to the door.

"Come along, Lord Stiles, you don't want any trouble."

"Have a care, Stiles," Markham called after him. "Your precious career hangs on your reputation. Society doesn't want to see justice dispensed by a magistrate with a reputation for brandy and brawling. The pater is a good friend of the Regent, and I'm sure he'd take a keen interest in the moral compass of those among his subjects who dispense justice on us lesser mortals."

Before they pushed him outside, Hawthorne glanced over his shoulder. Markham stood, brandy glass in hand, a smile of triumph on his lips.

>>><<<

"I'M SORRY, SIR, but Miss Stanford is not at home."

Despite having spotted her at one of the second-floor windows, Hawthorne wasn't surprised at the footman's response given that he'd uttered exactly the same words each time Hawthorne had tried to call on her. But this time, decorum took second place to the need to instill some sense into her head before she ruined her reputation completely.

"Pay me the courtesy of telling me the truth," he growled.

"In that case," the footman said, "she's not receiving visitors."

"Then I'll speak to Mr. Stanford."

"The master is out, sir. He's at the docks, overseeing a shipment of wine." The footman stared at Hawthorne, as if in challenge. Perhaps he thought the provision of detail regarding Stanford's errand might disarm further accusations of falsehood.

"I'll wait until he returns," Hawthorne said. "Let me in."

"I'm afraid, I cannot…Sir!" The footman exclaimed as Hawthorne pushed past him.

But the young man lacked the confidence and brutishness of the footmen at Whites. Most Mayfair homes rarely suffered from the need to evict unwelcome earls.

Hawthorne marched across the hall and into the morning room, while the footman followed, protesting loudly.

"Don't trouble yourself to bring any tea," Hawthorne said. "Just tell your master, as soon as he arrives, to attend me here. I shall not move from this room until he does. Close the door behind."

The footman flinched at Hawthorne's tone but complied with his orders. The arrogant demands of an earl would always yield the desired result, to a greater effect than the polite request of a family friend.

After the footman had closed the door, Hawthorne heard male voices in the hall outside. Doubtless, the poor young man was explaining to the butler his inability to keep out intruders.

He crossed the floor and took a seat. It was the same seat he'd spotted Markham sitting on the day Hawthorne had almost made love to Frederica. If only he could return to that day! He would have chased Markham out of the building and tried harder to make Frederica see reason. The jealousy which had burned within him at the thought of Markham seducing her had led her to the very ruination he'd tried to prevent.

And it had been at his hands, his inability to resist her.

The acrid smell of paint stung his nostrils. The table beside the window was laden with jars containing brushes, a palette, and a canvass, still bright with wet paint, mounted on an easel.

He cast his eyes over the painting, and his heart tightened at the dark, twisted images. Gnarled trees, their branches stretching outward, giant claws tearing across a blood-red sky.

Never before had he believed colors could be combined on a canvas to portray such pain.

Had he hurt her that much? Or was her pain due to Markham's rejection of her?

A whisper of air caressed his skin, and he looked round.

She stood in the doorway, a fistful of brushes in one hand, a jar of water in the other.

"What are you doing here?" she asked. "I'm not receiving visitors."

"Yet you invited Markham, did you not?"

She stiffened but made no response, then she took a brush and swirled it in the water. But this time, her silence would not prevent him from finding out the truth.

"Well?" he demanded.

She sighed and set the brush down.

"Yes," she said. "I invited him. Now you've had your answer, please go."

"Not until I have satisfaction, Miss Stanford."

She turned to face him, her eyes glistening with distress. "You've already had your *satisfaction*, if I recall," she said. "In one matter, at least, Roderick was right about you."

"Oh, *Roderick*, is it?" he said. "I might have guessed. Though I'm astonished at how quickly you've entered into such familiarity with him. Did my warning mean nothing to you? I told you, he's always sought to have what's mine. Or were you eager to compare us?"

"How dare you!" she cried. She swept the jar off the table, and it landed with an explosion of splintering glass and water. "I thought you better than him, but you're as bad as each other, vying for supremacy in the art of seduction! Was I nothing more than a prize to be fought over and claimed by the victor? Did the two of you set out to ruin me?"

"Frederica, I never had any intention of ruining you."

"But you did, didn't you?" she asked. "The only difference between you was the manner of your assault. You might consider yourself the better man because you used words rather than physical force, but your objective was the same."

"Don't be a fool!" he cried. "I would never enter into anything so sordid, and certainly not with him."

"Then why are you here?"

"To warn you to keep away from him before your reputation is ruined irrevocably. You're already the subject of gossip. Markham has been boasting about your offer."

"My offer?"

"Yes," he said. "You think he'd be a better patron than I?"

Her face twisted in horror. "You *believed* him?"

"He'll toss you aside within a week of setting you up," he said, "however eagerly you spread your legs for him."

"I did no such thing!" she cried. "I fought him off."

"Did you?"

"He forced himself on me!"

"And you let him?"

She slapped him across the face. "Get out!" she screamed.

A low cry rose up from behind.

Stanford stood in the doorway. The anger which had strengthened her drained from her body, to be replaced by horror and shame.

"P-papa..."

"Frederica!" Stanford shook his head. "Is it true? Have you lain with a man?"

"How long have you been standing there?" Hawthorne asked.

"Long enough," Stanford replied. "Answer my question, daughter."

Frederica cast a glance at Hawthorne. Her chest rose and fell in a deep sigh, and she nodded.

"Forgive me, Papa."

Stanford opened his arms to her. "There's nothing to forgive, Rica. Come here."

She rushed toward her father, and he took her in his arms, giving her the comfort she needed, the comfort Hawthorne should have given her.

"It's my fault," Stanford said. "I should never have brought you to London. Society here is too degenerate."

"Sir," Hawthorne said. "Let me help. Her reputation..."

Stanford raised his hand. "Stop there!" he said. "Her reputation is nothing compared to her happiness. I believe my daughter asked you to leave."

"But…"

"Please respect her wishes and go," Stanford said. "I'll be damned if see my child distressed any further."

"Very well," Hawthorne said. "But at least let me call on you to-morrow."

"As you wish. I care not."

She was safe in her father's arms. Stanford was the one creature in the world who truly loved her and who had never let her down. And in doing so, he shone a light on Hawthorne's own inadequacy.

Hawthorne clicked his heels together, issued a bow, and left.

CHAPTER TWENTY-ONE

A FTER EVICTING HAWTHORNE, Papa ushered Frederica to a chair. Trembling with shame, she sat, waiting for his accusation.

But none came. The ticking of the clock on the mantelshelf filled the silence, the flat notes beating out a rhythm of disdain and contempt.

Her secret was out.

She closed her eyes but it made no difference; she couldn't will him away. She heard the sound of liquid being poured, and a glass was pushed into her hand.

"Drink this, daughter," he said. "Then tell me what's happened."

She took a sip. The liquid caught at the back of her throat, but lessened the nausea which had been plaguing her, and she took another taste.

A warm hand covered hers.

"Oh, Rica, my love, what have you done?"

She shook her head, her body too engulfed by shame to move. Dearest Papa had done so much for her—the changeling child who was not even his. And she had repaid his kindness with disgrace.

"I–I'm sorry, Papa."

"My darling child, why didn't you tell me?"

She bit her lip, choking back a cry of shame.

"Can you not look at me, Frederica? Don't you owe me that at least?"

She opened her eyes, and a spike of pain ripped through her heart. Moisture glistened in her father's eyes, their expression dark with pain. Love still shone in face, but it was now overwhelmed by another emotion.

Disappointment.

He drew her into his arms, but she took no comfort from it.

"I didn't want to bring any more shame on you."

"Has he offered marriage?"

"No," she said. "Nor is he ever likely to."

"Good Lord, he's not married, is he?"

"No, Papa," she said. "He...he's too far above me in station. I was a fool to think otherwise."

Papa shook his head, and his voice cracked. "Frederica, how could you? My child, my precious child. What did I do wrong?"

"I'm sorry, Papa!" she cried. "You have every right to hate me."

He placed a kiss on her head. "I'll always love my darling girl, whatever you've done. It's him I hate."

He tightened his hold on her. "Damned blackguard. Bloody aristocrats are all the same, thinking their lineage entitles them to take advantage of innocents."

"No, Papa, it wasn't like that..."

"Don't make excuses for him, Frederica. Perhaps an encounter at dawn would teach him that debauching an innocent has consequences."

"No, Papa!" she cried. "I just want to forget, please!"

He sighed. "Very well, if that's what you wish. But you must tell me his name."

She shook her head.

"Was it Stiles?"

Her stomach clenched at his name, and she drained her glass to temper the nausea swirling inside her. Hawthorne deserved Papa's wrath, deserved to be punished for breaking her heart. But a piece of her heart still belonged to him. Her love for him was ingrained in her very being, carved into her soul. No matter what he'd done, she could not live with herself if she caused him harm. And she owed it to Papa, who admired and liked him. She would not let her folly cost Papa a good friend.

She had already sinned. A small falsehood to protect those she loved was nothing in comparison.

"No, Papa," she said. "It wasn't him."

"Very well," he said. "Let us speak no more on the matter."

"What will you do?"

He kissed the top of her head.

"I'll return you to Hampshire."

His reassurance released the tears, and he stroked her head, murmuring words of comfort. The only creature in the world who cared for her. Dearest Papa.

"I'm so sorry, Papa," she said.

"No matter, child. Go to your chamber and rest, now. I have a few business arrangements to conclude, then we shall take tea and discuss our future. Together. I promise, you'll never have to see *him* again."

THE CLOCK STRUCK seven, and Frederica opened her eyes. The light was fading, but nobody had come to wake her.

Where was Papa?

She pulled back the blanket, sat up, and smoothed down her dress.

Our future. That's what Papa had said. And it stretched before her like a golden glow, no longer bleak. Perhaps he'd permit her to help with his business. Or let her keep house for him and paint for a living. Her prospects of making a match on the London marriage mart were now over, but she would never have been happy surrendering her freedom to a man.

With renewed hope, she made her way to the morning room. Her footsteps echoed into silence, warring with the ticking of the longcase clock in the hall.

Papa was not there.

She crossed the hall to the study, but there was no sign of Papa. A nagging doubt propelled her toward the mahogany desk, and she pulled open the bottom drawer where Papa kept his pistol.

The drawer was empty.

She ran out into the hall.

"Papa! Papa!"

Hurried footsteps approached from behind the servants' door, and the footman appeared, wig askew, his body heaving with exertion.

"Yes, miss?"

"Where's Papa, James?"

"He's gone out, miss."

"How long has he been gone?"

"He left shortly after you retired to your chamber."

"That was hours ago! Did he say anything?"

"No, miss, but he was in such a temper!"

"Did he take his pistol?"

"I–I can't say," the footman replied, "but he was in a rare hurry to see him."

"Who?" Frederica asked. "Lord Stiles?"

"No, miss. He went to Hackton House."

A cold fist clutched at her heart.

The residence of the duke. Papa had gone to confront Markham.

Her body jerked to life, and she rushed toward the door. James caught her arm.

"Miss, you cannot be seen running about London unaccompanied."

She pushed him aside. "No, James, I have to!"

Before he could stop her, she dashed outside. The sun had yet to slip below the horizon. Orange fingers spread out across the buildings, giving the bricks a sinister glow. Uttering a silent prayer, she broke into a run.

⇛⫸⫷⇚

HACKTON HOUSE, MARKHAM'S London residence, was set back from the street, separated from the rest of the world.

The façade of the house threw sharp shadows across the drive, and she walked into darkness as she approached the building. She knocked on the door.

It opened to reveal the stark, white face of a footman, and cold soulless eyes staring down at her.

"His Grace is not receiving visitors."

"Is Mr. Stanford here?"

He looked over his shoulder.

"Let her in," a low voice spoke from inside. She stepped inside, and her blood froze at the sight before her.

Two men stood near the door, wearing the unmistakable uniform of the Bow Street Runners. The duke and his son stood at the far wall. Side by side, the family likeness was striking, though the duke's hair was thinner and grayer than Roderick's.

At their feet lay the body of a man.

Legs twisted, arm thrown out, he lay on his back, sightless eyes staring upward. A pool of dark liquid spread out from beneath his form, glistening in the candlelight. His shirt, once white, bore a single mark, a gaping hole.

"Papa…"

"I wondered when you'd come." Roderick drained his glass.

"You bastard!" She rushed toward him, but one of the runners darted toward her and caught her arm.

"Steady as you go, miss."

Roderick cocked his head to one side. "I rather think *you're* the bastard, my dear."

"Y-you killed him…"

"My son acted in self-defense." The duke's mouth twisted into a curve of contempt, mirroring his son's. "Stanford tried to murder me, look!" He pointed to a bullet hole in the wall. "Narrowly missed my head. If my son hadn't stopped him, your father would be facing the gallows like the common criminal he is."

"You mean *was.*" Roderick grinned.

Papa…

It couldn't be true. This was a civilized world where gentlemen didn't murder each other. Papa must be jesting. If she could only reach him, touch him, he'd wake up and hold her; call her his precious Rica again. They were going to live together in the country.

She struggled to break free, but the runner tightened his grip.

"Please! Let me go to him."

"Eject this *female*," the duke said. "I've endured enough distress at the hands of that man's family."

"Come on, miss," the runner said. "We'll take you home."

"No!" she cried. "Papa, you promised! Wake up!"

The runner pulled her toward the door. "Now, miss, that's quite enough of that."

"He's killed Papa!"

"That's for the law to decide, miss," he said. "Now, you need to go home. His Grace has had a shock."

The Duke turned his back on her and disappeared as the runners dragged her toward the doors.

"Wait!" At Roderick's command, they stopped, and Roderick advanced on her.

"You can still be mine, little bird," he whispered. "Who will take care of you? I'm willing to be generous. With my protection, you'll want for nothing." He reached up to caress her face, but as his fingertips touched her skin, she spat at him.

"I'd rather die than have you touch me again!"

He recoiled and wiped his face.

"You'll regret that, little bird." He nodded to the runners. "Get her out of my sight."

"Papa!" she screamed, but her words echoed into silence. He would never hear her again.

CHAPTER TWENTY-TWO

A S HAWTHORNE FINISHED his fourth brandy, the harsh lines of guilt at the thought of his little changeling and what he'd done, had softened. By the time he'd drained the seventh, the constraints of reason had shattered to expose the calling of his heart.

Frederica.

She deserved so much better than what he'd offered—the life and world of a mistress. The word *protector* implied a relationship of security and benevolence. But in reality, it existed only to serve the base needs of wealthy men.

Some women enjoyed the occupation, but what happened when their protectors moved on? What happened when the woman mistook mere fucking for love? If a man fell in love with his mistress, he could perpetuate the union with gifts and turn a blind eye to her indifference. But heartbreak was the only reward for the mistress who had the misfortune to fall in love with her patron.

Even Clara, with all her *joie de vivre* and financial independence, was often caught staring into the distance when she thought herself unobserved, regret etched into her brow. She had a comfortable home, a stipend for life, courtesy of her late husband, and lovers aplenty. She illuminated every room she entered. Yet beneath her vivacity, lay the knowledge that her chances of securing a mate for life, a family, and children of her own, diminished as each year passed.

How could Frederica, who lacked Clara's predatory sophistication, hope to survive in such a world?

What did he value most? Was it his footing in society, his reputation, and career as a magistrate—the fulfilment of his lifelong ambition to right the wrongs of the world?

Or was it the woman he loved?

The world meant nothing to him if it were a world in which she suffered.

"Forgive me, sir," a voice spoke. "There's a gentleman to see you." The butler stood in the doorway.

Hawthorne waved his empty glass at him. "Send him packing, Giles, then get me another."

"I'm unable to do that, sir."

"If the bottle is empty, open a new one."

"No, sir, I mean I'm unable to send him away. He was most insistent. I took the liberty of escorting him to your study."

Muttering a curse, Hawthorne stood. "If it's not a matter of life and death, I'll have you dismissed for this."

The butler's expression remained stoic. Either he cared little for his master's threats, or his abilities to remain poker-faced were unmatched. Or... *A matter of life and death...*

He brushed past Giles and strode into the study.

His lawyer stood beside the desk, leaning on a cane.

Hawthorne motioned to him to sit, then took the seat opposite. "What do you want, Stockton? It's past ten o'clock. Couldn't it wait until tomorrow?"

"I'm afraid not," the lawyer said. "There's been an accident, a shooting."

"Which is my business because?"

"You're Stanford's executor."

Fear clawed at him, and he gasped for breath.

"Frederica..."

Stockton raised an eyebrow, then shook his head. "No, it's her father. He's been killed."

"How?"

"Markham shot him."

Rage exploded inside him, and he leapt to his feet. "That bastard! What has he done?"

Stockton held his hand up in warning. "By all accounts, Markham acted in self-defense. Several witness accounts testify to the fact that Stanford was the aggressor. He threatened to kill Markham and fired the first shot."

"Who witnessed it?"

"Two footmen in Markham's employ," Stanford said. "And before you refute their testimonies, we already have witnesses who saw Stanford running toward Markham's home, brandishing a pistol. A courting couple. It appears that Stanford collided with them and almost knocked the lady to the ground."

"Dear, God!" Hawthorne cried. "It's my fault."

"How so?" Stockton replied. "Was Stanford acting under your direction?"

"No, no, of course not. But Frederica..." he broke off as the lawyer leaned forward at the mention of her name. "Why are you here, Stockton?"

"Mr. Stanford named you in the will as his daughter's guardian. It seemed simpler to send her to you tonight."

"Tonight?"

The lawyer shifted uncomfortably. "You may be unaware that one of my partners, Mr. Allardice, is lawyer to Lady Axminster, whose London residence Mr. Stanford had been occupying. Allardice has insisted his client would view the presence of the daughter of a murderer in her house as an unnecessary inconvenience and that she be evicted forthwith."

"How can Stanford be a murderer if he was killed?"

"The evidence points to his intentions," Stockton said. "Allardice insists on her being removed from the house before midnight." He hesitated. "Of course, if you're unwilling to take her in, I can make temporary arrangements for her to be housed elsewhere."

"No...I couldn't allow that."

"I understand if you're unwilling to be associated with a scandal," the lawyer said. "I'm not here to judge you, but to carry out your instructions."

"In that case, you can send a message to Mr. Allardice."

"And tell him what?"

"That his *unnecessary inconvenience* will be dealt with. And that he has my leave to rot in hell."

Stockton had the grace to look ashamed.

"How is she?" Hawthorne asked. "Have you spoken with her?"

"Only a little," Stockton replied. "The runners said she'd grown violent by the time they brought her back."

"Is it any wonder?" Hawthorne interrupted. "Her father had just been killed!"

"The housekeeper managed to give her a dose of laudanum," Stockton continued. "When I saw her, she was subdued and unresponsive, so I doubt she'll give you any trouble, at least for tonight. Tomorrow, of course, might be another matter."

"Tomorrow will be no concern of yours, Mr. Stockton."

The lawyer picked up his cane and eased himself out of his chair as Hawthorne strode out of the study.

The butler stood in the hallway, almost exactly where he'd left him.

"Giles, I need the carriage."

"I've already taken the liberty, sir. It's waiting outside."

"Good. Now, send for Doctor McIver. Tell him to come here directly."

"At this hour?"

"Don't argue!" Hawthorne roared. "Tell him he can name his

price, and if he doesn't come, I'll hunt him down and bloody well shoot him."

"As you wish."

The butler exchanged a glance with the lawyer, then opened the front door. Hawthorne stepped out and climbed into the carriage.

He should have listened to the voices which had whispered of a tragedy surrounding Frederica. With her state of mind, he prayed he would not be too late to prevent further misfortune.

THE COLORS WHICH had inspired Frederica on her arrival in London had faded. No longer bright, the world around her was a mass of gray. Papa was the only person, save, Grandpapa, who'd ever truly loved her. Now he was gone, and there was no longer any need for color.

After the runners had taken her home, they asked her endless questions about Papa, his pistol, and state of mind. Judgmental eyes watched her while she tried to form answers, but the words would not come.

What did it matter? Everything she loved was lost.

This wasn't even her home. It was Lady Axminster's, and Frederica was no longer welcome in it. While the questions continued to flow, another man had appeared. At first, she wondered whether he'd come to protect her from the questions. But his benign appearance was merely a cloak to conceal his predatory nature. In a smooth voice, he'd informed her that she was to be evicted.

"POOR WEE SOUL. Is it any wonder she almost lost her mind? But she'll make a full recovery, provided she's looked after."

A soft Highland burr penetrated Frederica's consciousness.

"Thank you, Doctor McIver."

Her body responded to the familiarity of the second voice—skin tingling, blood warming. Soft colors swirled in her mind, gentle greens and a rich, comforting chocolate.

"Ye gave me little choice, Lord Stiles," the first voice said.

Warm fingers grasped her hand.

"Where..." The word stuck in her throat.

"You're at my home." His hand solidified and pulled her into consciousness.

She opened her eyes.

She blinked to dissipate the fog muffling her senses and focused on the world around her: an ornately carved table, a candlestick which glinted in the light, a washstand, and bowl. At the far end of the room, a fire burned. The fireplace, a pale marble, was shot with pale, brown streaks, spreading vein-like through the stone.

Two men were in the room. One, so familiar, sat on the bed, holding her hand, grounding her body which yearned to drift back into nothingness. The other sat more formally in a chair, back stiff with the demeanor of a paid professional, a neat black bag on the table beside him.

"Doc...doctor..."

"Hush." Hawthorne squeezed her hand. "Doctor McIver's been tending to you."

He leaned over and brushed his lips against her forehead.

"When..."

"You've been here two days."

Something dark lurked in the back of her mind. A memory of tears and pain, just out of reach.

She pushed herself into a sitting position, and a wave of nausea rippled through her.

"I feel sick..."

The doctor leapt to his feet. "It's to be expected under the circumstances," he said. "I have a tonic for you."

"Frederica," Hawthorne said. "May I be the first to say how sorry I am?"

The memory sharpened into clarity. A broken body lying on the floor of a cold, soulless house, while his assailant had looked on in triumph.

Papa...

He pulled her to him, and she stiffened. She had given herself to him, and it had been the first step to her ruination, and to Papa's death.

"Let me go!" she cried.

"No, Frederica, I..."

"I think ye'd best do as the lass asks," the doctor interrupted. "Give her some space."

Hawthorne sat back, and the doctor approached, a glass in hand.

"Will ye drink this?"

"What is it?"

"A tonic to settle your stomach," he said. "Nothing more, I promise."

His eyes showed kindness, but she hesitated.

"Let me," Hawthorne said. He moved toward her, and she shrank back.

"Leave her be!" the doctor said, his voice sharp.

"But..."

"Miss Stanford might be your ward now, but, first and foremost, she is my patient and as such, her welfare comes before your wishes. Stand aside."

The doctor sat beside the bed and held out the glass. She took it and drained the contents.

"That's better," he said. "Would you permit me to continue to call on you until you're recovered?"

His demeanor reminded her of Papa, and she nodded. He leaned forward and lowered his voice. "Your host has employed me to tend to your every wish until you've made a full recovery. Send for me if you have need of anything."

"I wouldn't want you, or Lord Stiles, to go to any trouble, sir."

"It's no trouble, lass." He glanced at Hawthorne. "You could always visit my premises, if you prefer privacy. When in town, I share a small practice with a colleague, on Harley Street." He rose to his feet. "And now, I must be going. Take care of her, Stiles, won't ye?"

Not long after showing the doctor out, Hawthorne returned.

"Little changeling, I…"

"It's Miss Stanford," she said.

He sighed and sat on the bed, which dipped under his weight. "I'm sorry about your father."

"It's my fault," she said.

"No," he said. "It's mine. I should never have taken advantage of your naiveté."

"My naiveté?" she asked. "You see me as a child?"

"No, of course not."

"What, then? An object of seduction? You and Markham thought nothing of Papa when you devised your little game, did you? Do you consider yourself the victor because you were the one to succeed? Did you never think how I might have felt? Or Papa? Were we worth so little to you?"

"Of course not," he said. "We played no game, Frederica. I despise Markham. Your father was a good friend. I admired him very much. As for you…"

He took her hand and drew her to him. "You mean a lot to me, Frederica. It pains me to see you hurt."

"What shall I do without him?" she said.

"I'm responsible for you now. Your father was very particular about that in his will."

"Can't I return home? To Hampshire?"

"I'm afraid not," he replied. "You must remain here with me."

He wrapped his arms around her. For a brief moment, she dreamed that he loved her. But he only wanted her for his own gratification.

The man who loved her was dead.

"No!" She struggled to break free. "Let me go home. You can't want me here."

"Yes, I do," he said. "Very much."

"Why?" she whispered. "Why can't you let me go and be rid of me?"

His voice rumbled in her ear, his breath a warm caress. "Because you're precious, Frederica. And my world would be poorer without you in it. You must promise me not to leave."

"But I'm nothing to you," she said, shaking her head.

He remained firm, his hold both unyielding and protective. "Frederica, a bond was forged between us the moment you entered the world. Did you think I never noticed the little red-headed sprite who followed me everywhere and darted into the depths of the forest when she thought I'd spotted her? You were like the magical faerie who'd grant a mortal man his dearest wish if he could capture her. I have you in my arms now, and hope you will grant my dearest wish."

"And what is that?"

"To have you trust me."

"Then I promise, I'll not leave you," she said.

"You swear?"

"On my father's life."

"Then," he said, "in turn, I promise to do everything in my power to earn your trust."

Her soul swelled with hope at his words, but her heart cautioned her not to fall prey to them again.

CHAPTER TWENTY-THREE

"WILL WE BE meeting your new ward today, Stiles?"

Ross drained his teacup and placed it on the saucer, his nose wrinkling. Gentlemen rarely enjoyed tea. Ross, like Hawthorne's other visitors of late, had one purpose for today's visit. At least he didn't bother to conceal his curiosity. It had been a fortnight since Hawthorne had taken Frederica in, and a week since he'd buried her father in a quiet ceremony where he'd held her in his arms while she sobbed. Since then, she'd shown a marked improvement, even venturing out into the garden of his townhouse.

On returning from her father's funeral, she had asked for her watercolors and began to paint again, not the dark images he'd last seen on her canvasses, but rich, warm colors to match the blooms in his garden. Her work grew brighter with each piece she produced. Perhaps, in time, the girl he had fallen in love with would come back to him.

Her nightmares had returned, though. Every morning the housekeeper gave him reports of her waking during the night, with tales of black wings, ropes, and her father's body. But, according to the young chambermaid Hawthorne had sent for from Radley Hall to tend to her, they were growing less, both in frequency and intensity.

All he need do now, was keep her from reading the newspapers until the gossipmongers had better stories to share, and her recovery would be complete.

The worst of the reports had told of a murderer's daughter, prone to madness. The gutter press may not have mentioned her name, but society gossips were all too willing to fill in the missing pieces. Hawthorne had managed to limit some of the damage by persuading Markham to publish a second report of an accident. But, for all that had cost him, the rumors of murder still circulated.

He set his cup down, untouched, and addressed his friend. "Are you here to beat your rivals in the race for the first glimpse of the subject of so many salacious stories?"

"So, you've read the papers, Stiles."

"Read and discarded," Hawthorne said. "And I'll thank you not to mention them in my presence. The last report was over a week ago, and the gossip is already lessening. Miss Stanford must never know what they've been saying. It's the last thing she needs."

"And the last thing you need, my friend, is to be known for harboring the daughter of an attempted murderer in your home. It can only damage your reputation as a magistrate."

Hawthorne sighed. "What would you have me do, Ross? I'm partly to blame for what happened."

"How so?" Ross asked. "By all accounts, Stanford turned up at Hackton House with intent to kill, and Markham's been sporting a bandage on his arm ever since. Is it true Markham raised a lawsuit against Stanford's estate before he changed his story and said it was an accident?"

Hawthorne looked away, lest his expression reveal his anger. "I persuaded him against it."

Understanding crossed Ross's expression.

"The report in the papers about it being an accident, that was your doing? How did you get him to comply?"

"With cash, of course," Hawthorne said. "He agreed to it for five thousand."

"So large a sum?"

"A small price to pay for her peace of mind."

"Not to mention your career prospects."

Hawthorne picked up his teacup and drained it, wishing it contained brandy instead. Never had he felt so impotent. The magistrate's objective was to uphold the law and further the cause of justice. But this was the first time where the two were in direct opposition to each other. Society would always side with one of their own. In their view, Stanford was the aggressor by virtue of his birth, even though he died at Markham's hand.

"However much it cost," Ross said, "you did the right thing, relating the story about an accident."

"How so?"

"An accident provides little entertainment for society compared to anything more salacious. Interest in the events at Hackton House has already diminished. I'm sure their curiosity in your guest will fade also, once you've settled the more delicate matter of courtship."

"Courtship?"

Ross smiled. "I saw Miss Wilcott on your arm in Hyde Park yesterday."

"What of it?"

"Ravenwell told me she was overly forward in displaying her dance card at the Strathdean's ball last week, and he couldn't fail to notice you were engaged to her for two sets." Ross let out a laugh. "Yet another lady seeks to incite jealousy in prospective suitors in order to further her marriage prospects. I should pity her. It's her fourth season, and rumor has it her father's desperate to get her off his hands because he cannot afford a fifth."

"Then why don't *you* offer for her?" Hawthorne said bitterly. The last thing he wanted was a spurned heiress parading her indignation around London in an attempt to coerce him into matrimony. Dear God, with that materialistic, characterless creature in his home and bed, even with his renowned prowess, he'd struggle to produce an heir.

Not that he wanted any woman in his bed except…

His body hardened as the faint scent of her drifted into the air and the door opened.

"He's in here, miss…" A young girl in a maid's uniform recoiled as she caught sight of the two men.

"Begging your pardon, my Lord, I didn't know you had company."

"No matter, Jenny," Hawthorne said. "Bring Miss Stanford in."

The maid moved aside to reveal the young woman standing behind her.

Though clad in a simple white muslin gown, vivid colors assaulted Hawthorne's senses. Expressive eyes widened, tones of blue and green glittering as the sunlight from the window caught her face. Coppery hair contrasted with the color of her eyes.

Jenny had learned much since Hawthorne had brought her here to tend to his charge. Her skilled hands had piled Frederica's hair into a becoming shape, which emphasized the length of her neck. A cascade of tresses curled either side of her face, giving her the air of a Grecian goddess.

A goddess to worship. Had she been wealthy and titled, she'd have been the triumph of the season, a prize among the dull heiresses who swam in the seas of society—mere minnows compared to such an exotic creature.

Hawthorne stood, as did his friend.

"F–forgive me." She shrank back as her gaze fell upon Ross.

"Frederica, come here."

Her body stilled as his command reverberated around the room. Even Ross raised his eyebrows at the dominant tone. But a firm hand was the only way to control her, an untamed filly who needed the security of her master's hand.

She drifted toward his outstretched hand, and cold little fingers entwined with his.

"There's someone I particularly want you to meet, Miss Stanford. My best friend, Ross Trelawney." Hawthorne turned to Ross and issued a silent plea with his eyes. "Ross, may I present, Miss Frederica Stanford?"

Ross bowed and took her free hand, lifting it to his lips, but not quite touching.

"It gives me great pleasure to see you again, Miss Stanford."

"Likewise." Her fingers tightened on Hawthorne's hand, and Ross glanced at him.

"I trust you're well," Ross said warmly. "I cannot begin to understand how you must feel since losing your father, so I'll not insult your intelligence by offering the condolences society seems to think are adequate. But I hope my friend is taking good care of you."

"Thank you."

"Miss Stanford and I are to take the air in Hyde Park," Hawthorne said, giving Frederica's fingers a reassuring squeeze. "Perhaps you'd care to join us, Ross?"

She shrank away, but he held her firm. If she were to overcome her fear, she needed to face it.

"Ross is my friend, Miss Stanford," he said. "I'd trust him with my life. Wouldn't you prefer two champions escorting you today?"

Ross held out his arm. "I'm at your disposal, Miss Stanford."

Her lips curled in a quick, tight smile, and she took his proffered arm. Perhaps there was hope for her recovery after all.

THE RIPPLE OF laughter caught Hawthorne unawares. He'd lagged behind Ross and Frederica, on the lookout for the one man who must be avoided at all costs. It wouldn't do for her to come face to face with Markham.

Ross proved an adept champion, a knight in armor who'd understood Hawthorne's plea and drawn her into conversation. Not the vapid remarks between soulless members of society, but a discussion among equals of intellect.

Ross's heart might still be broken from Miss de Grecy's rejection, but he was better off without her. Perhaps Ross and Frederica might heal each other. They were of the same social class, and he seemed enraptured with her explanation of how she painted landscapes when there was insufficient time to sit outdoors before the light disappeared.

"Tell me, Miss Stanford," Ross said. "If you are unable to paint an exact likeness, what is the purpose of art?"

"To capture the *essence* of the subject."

"You mean its soul?"

"If you like."

Hawthorne joined them, and her face colored, as if she knew she'd revealed too much of herself.

"I would like to view some of your paintings, Miss Stanford," Ross said. "Too long have I been subjected to the accomplishments of ladies who consider themselves artists simply because they present a tree in perfect proportion as if it's been forced to conform to the aesthetics of society."

"You prefer flaws to perfection, Mr. Trelawney?"

"What is a flaw, if not a mark of experience as we travel through life? That which society deems to be perfect, I find rather dull."

Such as Miss de Grecy.

As they rounded a corner, the lone figure of a woman came into view, staring at the Serpentine. Golden hair shone in the sunlight and pale blue eyes widened as they approached.

"Alice?" Frederica's smile broadened as she spotted her friend.

"Perhaps we should turn back," Ross said. "I wouldn't want you catching cold so soon after your recovery. Miss de Grecy will be much occupied with her betrothed, and I'm sure they'd prefer not to be disturbed."

Frederica stiffened. "She's engaged?"

"Mr. Trelawney is right," Hawthorne said. "If you wish to see Miss de Grecy, I'll issue an invitation."

He took hold of her arm and pulled her toward him. "Trust me, little changeling." Ross arched an eyebrow but said nothing.

"Miss de Grecy, I'm so sorry I kept you waiting!"

Frederica's body stiffened at the familiar voice.

"Oh, I say, it's Lord Stiles. What a *pleasure* to see you!"

In a few quick strides, Roderick Markham was upon them.

"I trust there are no hard feelings between us, Trelawney," Markham said. "Miss de Grecy is perfectly happy in her new situation. I believe it turned out for the best."

Ross's body stiffened. "I beg your..."

"Come, come, Trelawney," Markham said. "Let's shake hands. I'd be honored if you attended our wedding next week."

"Of course." Ross bowed. "It's a pleasure to see you so happily settled at last, Miss de Grecy."

The vapid creature cast a quick glance at Markham, then nodded.

"And you, of course, Stiles," Roderick said smoothly, turning his gaze to Hawthorne. His smile had broadened, but his eyes glittered with ice.

"And your new ward! I wish you success in finding a suitable husband for *her*, given her status."

She dug her fingers into Hawthorne's arm. "My status?"

"Of course," Markham said, "I understand why your guardian was keen to protect his reputation by circulating stories of an accident, but we know different, do we not?"

"I don't understand," she said.

Hawthorne met Markham's gaze, and the blackguard had the nerve to smile. "That's enough, Markham," he growled.

"Come now, Stiles," Markham said. "Our little bird deserves the truth." He lowered his voice. "You have my sympathies, Miss

Stanford, on the occasion of your father being declared a murderer. I cannot begin to understand the effect that must have on your reputation, fragile as it is already."

A small gasp left Alice's lips, and Markham squeezed her hand. "Quite so, my dear," he said. "I believe it's time we moved on. It's most ungentlemanly for a man to make the woman on his arm stand while engaging in conversation, when that woman is a *lady*." He wrinkled his nose and looked at Frederica. "Of course, Stiles, you're in no such danger, given the company you keep."

"Why, you..." Frederica raised her arm, and Hawthorne caught her wrist. It was thin and bony under his fingers. She struggled against him, her eyes blazing with anger, but he held firm.

Beyond Markham and his fiancée, a small crowd had begun to form.

"Temperamental fillies should be placed in a halter, don't you know, Stiles?" Markham said mildly.

"How dare you!" Frederica hissed. "I hate you for what you've done!"

Markham laughed. "It was at your hand, my dear," he said. "After all, you invited me so *prettily*."

"I did not!"

"You must remember," Markham said. "You took such pains to summon me when your father was not at home. You were so eager to show me your *secret place* in the garden, weren't you?"

The color left Frederica's face.

Markham issued a bow. "Alice, it's time we left. Stiles, Trelawney—*Miss Stanford*—I bid you good day."

As the couple disappeared round a corner, Hawthorne pulled the trembling Frederica to him. Guilt and horror pulsed through her expression.

"Frederica, what did Markham mean?"

"Stiles," Ross said, "We should continue this conversation somewhere private."

The crowd had grown in size, their whispers filling the air. Hawthorne tightened his hold on Frederica's wrist and marched back toward the waiting carriage. She made no attempt to resist, and he bundled her inside, then climbed in after her.

"Are you coming, Ross?"

Ross shook his head. "I'll make my own way home." He leaned through the carriage window and lowered his voice. "Be kind."

The carriage set off with a jerk, but she made no attempt to move.

"Tell me the truth, Frederica. Did you invite him?"

She nodded. "I–I wanted to tell him…" Her voice tailed off as she looked directly at Hawthorne. Whatever she saw in his expression froze her speech. She lowered her gaze to the door handle but before she could move, he took her wrist.

"You're not going anywhere until you tell me the truth."

"When were you going to tell *me* the truth?" she cried.

"I don't know what you mean."

"About Papa. Does the world think him a murderer? Don't they know the man parading around Hyde Park with my friend on his arm murdered Papa?"

"There's no proof your father was murdered!" Hawthorne cried. "He entered the duke's home, in full view of his son and servants, with one intent. To kill him!"

"But you know different!" she cried. "Surely you can do something? Aren't you supposed to dispense justice?"

"Not in the face of such overwhelming evidence," he said. "Think about it, Frederica. You issue an invitation to Markham while unaccompanied, and a few days later, your father turns up at his doorstep brandishing a pistol. Any fool in possession of the facts would draw the same conclusion."

"Nothing happened!" she cried. "I fought him, and he left me alone!"

"Sadly, there is no one to corroborate your side of the story."

She grew still, and her stricken expression clawed at his heart. He pulled her toward him.

"Forgive me, Frederica, I wanted to protect you from the truth. I was going to tell you when you were ready."

"What, ready to learn that the world sees Papa as a murderer?" she snarled. "I'll never be ready for that, but I could have borne it had I not realized you believed it also."

"Frederica," he said. "I..."

"Don't," she interrupted, withdrawing her hand. "If you didn't believe it, you would have defended him just now."

"You must pay no attention to what I say in public, Frederica," he said. "Listen instead to what I say to you now."

He moved to take her hand again, and she folded her arms and turned her head away.

"How silly of me," she said, "to believe you valued integrity over your position in society."

"Forgive me," he said. "I only want you to be happy."

She turned her head, and he was assaulted by her green gaze, sadness and resignation gleaming in her soulful eyes.

"Nothing you do or say will achieve that," she said. "Just take me home."

He nodded and issued an order to the driver. The carriage set off. Perhaps he'd ventured out with her too soon. She was not ready for the world just yet. But he owed it to her to try again.

And the perfect occasion would come as soon as Markham was married and safely out of the country on his honeymoon.

CHAPTER TWENTY-FOUR

"WOULD YOU PREFER the yellow or the blue, Miss?" Jenny placed two dresses on the bed. "If you don't mind my being so bold, the blue shows off the color of your hair better."

"Then I'll wear the yellow. I've no wish to attract attention to-night."

"But Miss…"

"The yellow, Jenny. Do as I say."

The maid recoiled at Frederica's tone. Poor Jenny had worked so hard to make her feel comfortable and had grown adept at taking care of Frederica, despite her lack of training as a lady's maid.

And Frederica repaid her with harsh words.

She took Jenny's hand. "Forgive me, I spoke out of turn."

"No, miss, I forget my place," Jenny said. "But you look so lovely in the blue."

Jenny was a romantic fool. Her obvious infatuation for Harry, as pleasant as the footman might be, clouded her judgement. But Frederica did not have the heart to admonish her further.

"Would it please you if I wore it, Jenny?"

"Oh, yes!" the maid said. "And it would please the master. Harry told me he'd overheard him telling Mr. Trelawney that blue is his favorite color on you."

The master.

Hawthorne.

Since their altercation in Hyde Park, Hawthorne had resumed his enjoyment of London society, disappearing to balls and parties, often returning with his friends while Frederica lay in her bedchamber, cold and alone, listening to laughter downstairs. She had promised she'd never leave him, yet he abandoned her to enjoy the company of others.

But tonight, at Mr. Trelawney's insistence, Hawthorne was taking her to a ball. Mr. Trelawney had visited her on a number of occasions. He'd admired her paintings, even insisting he purchase some. Perhaps some men existed who sought only friendship from the opposite sex.

Hawthorne waited for her by the bottom step. A dark green jacket fitted his form perfectly, and his breeches clung to his legs like a second skin. Polished black boots completed the look. As if he sensed her, he turned slowly and lifted his gaze. The buttons on his waistcoat glinted in the candlelight, mirroring the flecks of gold in his eyes.

He looked magnificent. No wonder he had hadn't wanted her to accompany him before. He outshone her as the sun dwarfed a candle.

He held out his hand, and she drifted down the stairs, a falcon gliding toward her master's hand.

"Frederica." His eyes crinkled into a smile. The sharp scent of desire thickened in the air, and his nostrils flared.

"I'm glad I chose to take you with me tonight."

She tipped her head up to meet his gaze, and he lowered his mouth over hers. A fire ignited in the pit of her belly.

"Ahem."

He pulled away and smoothed down his waistcoat.

"Of course, Giles, we mustn't be late. Lord Wilcott is expecting us. Come, Miss Stanford, the carriage awaits."

FREDERICA LIFTED HER glass to her lips. She wrinkled her nose at the sickly-sweet taste of the punch, so unlike the rich depth of Papa's port, but it helped to soothe her nausea.

After finding her a seat, Hawthorne had joined the dancers. His initial disappointment at her refusal to dance was replaced by gallant enthusiasm as ladies surrounded him, brandishing their dance cards. Mr. Trelawney had approached her several times, trying to involve her in conversation, but while she appreciated his kindness, she had no wish to draw attention to herself by speaking.

Their hosts had made their hostility plain. Lord Wilcott seemed gentlemanly enough when Hawthorne introduced them to Frederica. But Lady Wilcott had stared at her as if she were an insect, saving her smiles for Hawthorne as he complimented her on the string of pearls decorating her headdress.

And now he'd abandoned her to bestow compliments on others, elegant women who lived colorless, pampered existences, women whose idea of suffering was the absence of sufficient sugar in their tea or the wrong shaped fork in a place setting.

They lived in a world in which Frederica didn't belong, and had no wish to.

The mass of people shifted to form an even pattern of couples running the length of the ballroom. One couple stood out from the rest. A tall figure moved with the easy fluidity of one born to live in the privileged world of the rich and titled. His partner, though taller than some of the men, could not match him in height. As the dancers moved along the rows, she caught a glimpse of his face. But Hawthorne had eyes for none but his companion, the honorable Louisa Wilcott.

Her hair shone like gold and curled around her face in soft waves. As she moved her head, the diamonds studding her hair twinkled in the light. Pale blue eyes hardened as they focused on Frederica before she resumed her attention on her partner. A perfect, heart-shaped mouth smiled graciously at him, and she parted her lips to speak. He glanced in Frederica's direction and laughed.

No amount of schooling would give Frederica a fraction of Miss Wilcott's accomplishments. She was, without doubt, the most beautiful creature Frederica had ever seen.

"That she is, my dear."

She started at the voice. An elderly woman sat on her right.

"I'm sorry?"

"You said she was beautiful." The woman nodded toward Hawthorne's companion. "If any woman can secure Earl Stiles, she can."

Frederica tightened her grip on her glass as the woman rattled on, evidently relishing the opportunity to gossip.

"Everyone's expecting him to offer for her soon," she continued, her voice lifting with the pleasure of having someone to talk at.

The ground shifted beneath Frederica's feet. The colors dissolved around her, turning the world gray, and the music morphed into muffled, discordant sounds, the faint beating of wings in the background. The nausea which had been plaguing her for almost a month, threatened to overcome her, and she drew in a deep breath.

"My dear, are you all right?"

"I think I've had too much punch."

"May I fetch someone? Your mother, perhaps?"

Frederica shook her head.

"Your father?"

With a word of apology, she leapt to her feet, and crossed the floor to the balcony doors in search of fresh air.

A pair of ladies stood near the doors, heads bent together, deep in conversation.

As Frederica passed them, she heard a name.

"Stanford..."

Reason told her to keep moving. What good came of eavesdropping?

"Yes, that's it! Frederica Stanford," the second woman said. "Her father was the wine merchant."

"The one who died under suspicious circumstances?"

"I heard it was an accident."

"That's what the papers said, but I heard he tried to murder Markham!"

"Over what, an unpaid bill?"

"Whatever it was, it's left Stiles with an unexpected houseguest."

"Louisa won't want her in the house when she enters it."

"Of course not, Maria," the first woman lowered her voice. "Not even Stiles, with his sensibilities toward the lower classes, would insult his fiancée by letting his harlot remain under her nose."

"Is she here tonight?"

"Yes, poor Louisa told me she was forced to greet her. Finish your punch, and I'll point her out."

Frederica moved away, her heart thumping. She grasped a glass of punch from a nearby footman and drained the contents. But rather than steady her nerves, it only made her body shiver more violently.

It was only a matter of time before Hawthorne tossed her out.

CHAPTER TWENTY-FIVE

A S SOON AS Hawthorne helped Frederica into the carriage, she fell
asleep, most likely due to an overindulgence of punch. She'd
spent the whole evening avoiding company, drinking, and refusing to
dance or even take a turn with him round the room. Only Ross had
been able to lift her spirits, albeit, only a little. She smiled for him, at
least, if nobody else.

When the carriage stopped outside his townhouse, she jerked
awake. A momentary flash of terror crossed her expression, and he
took her hand, her fingers ice cold against his. She turned her gaze to
him, and his stomach knotted.

The trust in her eyes had gone.

She let him lead her inside, but when he moved toward the stairs,
she froze in the middle of the hall.

"Miss Stanford?"

"I want to leave."

"I beg your pardon?"

She withdrew her hand. "I've no wish to stay here anymore. Take
me home."

"This is your home, Frederica," he said.

"No, it's not. Take me to my real home. I have the income from
Papa's business. I can support myself."

"You're not ready."

"Who are you to tell me whether I'm ready or not?"

He reached for her, but she backed away, hostility in her expression.

"Frederica, what's happened?"

"I wish to make room, *my lord.*"

The formal tone of her voice belied the turmoil boiling in her expression.

"Make room?"

"For your bride," she said. "I have no wish to put you, or the honorable Louisa, to the trouble of having to turn me out."

"Foolish creature!" he said. "You think I'd be tempted by that peacock?"

"I saw you with her, all smiles and charm. You looked so happy with her, so animated, as if she breathed life into you. As if I'm nothing compared to her. I may have lost everything, but I will never yield my dignity. And I refuse to be an unwelcome guest here."

"Good God, Frederica!" he cried. "You think my natural disposition is to titter with laughter every time a lady makes a vacuous comment on the cut of another's gown?"

"Are you not driven by the need to court a lady, something I shall never be?"

Bitter laughter burst from his chest at the preposterousness of her words. "Do you wish me to bestow such niceties on you, when you are worth so much more? If I wanted you less, I'd be able to flatter you as I do those vapid creatures."

A stray curl tumbled over her forehead. He brushed it aside, and her lips trembled at his touch.

"I want none of them, little changeling. I have only ever wanted one woman, to the exclusion of all others."

He caught her hand and pulled her into an embrace. "I have that woman in my arms now."

He lowered his mouth to hers, and a whimper bubbled in her throat. She parted her lips, and her body softened in his arms. He brushed her breast with his hand, and beneath the soft muslin of her gown, her nipple hardened against his palm.

She arched her back against him in offering.

A groan burst from his chest, and he devoured her mouth, unable to control the need simmering in his body.

"You're mine, Frederica," he whispered. "You've always been mine."

Her body stiffened in his arms. She grasped his shoulders as if to push him away, but remained still for a moment. Then she pulled him toward her and claimed his lips. One hand fisted in his hair while she thrust her tongue into his mouth, her teeth grazing against his lips. Her other hand traced a path down his chest, then slipped inside his breeches. His manhood jerked at her touch. As he grew hard, she curled her fingers round him and squeezed, tightening her grip.

She sunk her teeth into his lip, and he tasted blood.

"What will I earn if I perform to your satisfaction?" she asked. "I confess I do not yet possess the experience to effect a proper negotiation, but when you first enjoyed my services, I believe a necklace was mentioned."

He fisted his hand in her hair and yanked her head back. Tear-stained eyes stared back at him.

"What on earth are you doing?"

"What you want!" she cried. "I know what they call me, I heard it tonight. At least have the compassion not to parade me in front of them so I'm forced to hear it from their lips."

"Hear what?"

"That I'm your harlot!"

"Oh, Frederica!" he said. "Is this what I've brought you to? Never think of yourself in such a manner. You are worth more to me than the world itself."

"But, what you said before..."

"I was mistaken," he said. "You'll never know how deeply I regret saying those things to you. You think I want to hide you away from the world? Tonight was about showing the world that your place is by my side. And I intend to do that in every drawing room in Mayfair."

She broke free and stepped back. "I think you'll find your mistress would not be welcome in the drawing rooms of London, however many necklaces you indulge her with."

Dear Lord, he was making such a hash of this! Trelawney would laugh himself silly.

He brushed his hand across his eyes.

"My love for you cannot be measured in jewelry or gifts," he said. "Though I hope you'll permit me to indulge in adorning you with tokens. Forgive me for my inability to articulate my love better."

He took her hands and caressed the skin of her wrists, running his thumbs along the scars, then dipped his head, and brushed his lips against them. Then he lowered himself onto his knees and wrapped his arms around her waist.

"My love," he whispered. "Make me the happiest of men."

"A mistress is no different than a whore."

He tightened his grip at her last word and groaned.

"Even now, you think the worst of me! I'm offering you my hand. You complete me. Without you, I'm only half a man, half a soul. Everything I am and have is nothing compared to you."

He turned his face to her stomach, fearful of her reaction. "Marry me, Frederica. I'm not ashamed to say I need you. Say the word, and you'll make me the happiest man alive. But if you wish it, I'll release you from my guardianship."

He waited, uncertain for the first time in his life. She remained silent, the only sound the ticking of a clock in the distance, as if the whole house waited for her response.

At length she lowered herself to her knees and cupped his chin.

"Yes." She blinked, and a tear splashed onto her cheeks. "Yes, I'll marry you."

He leaned forward, and his forehead touched hers.

"I never want to let you go," he whispered. "If you left, it would destroy me. Promise me, little changeling. Swear you'll never leave."

"On my life, I swear."

"I'll make the announcement in the newspapers tomorrow," he said. "I want us to be married as soon as possible, but I won't petition the archbishop for a special license."

"Why not?"

He stroked her hair, tracing an outline of her face until his fingers touched her lips. "I wish to do this properly," he said. "We'll announce the engagement and have the banns read, to show the world there's no shame in our union. We shall be married in a month, in front of all society, so they may bear witness to my becoming the luckiest man alive."

He leaned forward to kiss her, then hesitated.

"I must leave you be until our wedding night, until you are completely mine."

She took his hand and kissed his knuckles.

"I'm already yours, Hawthorne. I never want to be parted from you, not for a single moment."

He lifted her into his arms. "Then come, little one," he said. "I'm going to spend the rest of the night making love to you, and the rest of my life loving you."

⋙✕⋘

THE LIGHT OF a solitary candle flickered as Hawthorne opened his chamber door. He would willingly drown in her beautiful eyes. His body had hardened the moment she'd accepted him. But to hold her in his arms again, to feel that soft flesh, his body had almost burst with desire.

Nothing mattered, save the need to satisfy the deep craving to own her completely. Forever. If he had to lock her up so no other man would touch her, then he would.

Like a devotee ready to worship her, he placed her on the bed and peeled off her gown. His expert fingers unlaced her corset. She surpassed any woman, for no one could touch his soul like she did. Her skin glowed in the candlelight, accentuating the shape of her body, her slim hips, those lush breasts which had been fashioned just for him, with their little peaks standing erect, beckoning to him.

He pulled off his shirt and threw it behind him, not once taking his gaze away from her. Her eyes showed such trust in him. And he would never betray her again.

He stepped out of his breeches and climbed on the bed. His manhood was rigid with pain, begging to be buried among those red curls. She lowered her gaze and drew in a sharp breath.

"Don't take your eyes from me, Frederica. You're safe as long as you stay with me."

She nodded, and a tear beaded in her eyes. He shifted his body, and his manhood brushed against her, moving against her belly. The musky scent of his own need thickened in the air. She shifted her legs, and he almost exploded with release at the sweet scent of her desire.

He settled himself on top of her and nudged her knees apart.

"Trust me," he whispered.

He traced the outline of her breasts with his fingertips, then moved his hand lower, caressing her stomach, until he reached her curls. His body surged forward as if pulled by an invisible chain, and he fought the primal urge to claim her.

"I can't hold on much longer..."

"Hawthorne." Though quiet, her voice reached into his soul.

With a cry, he thrust forward. Her body shuddered against him, but she kept her eyes open, not hiding from him, but giving herself to him. The trust in her gaze was his undoing, and he withdrew and plunged into her again. The raw pain of sweet release tore through him as he shattered against her, a wave against a rock, surrendering.

He was nothing without her. She completed him, made him whole.

"Oh, Frederica!" He cried her name. He had found his mate.

Still inside her, he wrapped his arms around her, tightening his grip as if expecting her to slip away. Her body stiffened.

"No, Frederica," he said. "Be still. You're mine, now."

She closed her eyes but not before he caught a flash of something in them—fear or mistrust? But it didn't matter. She was now his, wholly his. And nobody would take her from him.

CHAPTER TWENTY-SIX

W HEN FREDERICA WOKE, the chamber was already bright. The
sunlight stretched across the room, highlighting dust motes
which swirled in the air. Until this morning, she'd always woken
before the dawn, her mind unwilling to remain in the land of dreams
where predators lurked in the shadowy recesses.

But last night, her nightmares had been driven away by Hawthorne. After taking her the first time, he had drifted into a fitful sleep,
her name on his lips. But during the night, he'd claimed her again, as if
driven by desperation.

But now he had gone, the only evidence he'd been there a delicious soreness between her legs and an imprint of his form in the bed
which bore traces of warmth and the scent of him.

She yawned and stretched, then sat up. A wave of nausea rippled
through her, and she took a deep breath.

The door opened, and he entered the bedchamber, holding a flat,
square box. Fully dressed in a dark blue jacket, cream waistcoat,
breeches, and polished leather boots, he looked every bit her superior
compared to her disheveled, naked form. Heat rose in her cheeks, and
she lifted the bedsheet to cover her nudity.

He approached the bed and opened the box. A flash of light caught
her eyes. Nestled among smooth, blue satin lay a necklace. A row of
sapphires surrounded by tiny diamonds winked at her, the sunlight
reflecting off the facets, diffracting into tiny rainbows.

"To mark our engagement," he said. "It was my mother's. Do you like it?"

He moved to the sofa beside the fireplace and beckoned to her. "Come here so I can put it on you."

She reached for her undergarments.

"No!"

Her body froze at his ability to control her with a single word.

"Let me savor the sight of you."

She drew back the coverlet and stepped off the bed. He cast his gaze over her naked body, and the heat rose within her at his scrutiny. The need which had consumed him last night gleamed in his eyes. He pulled her onto his lap and placed the necklace around her throat.

"Beautiful…" he breathed.

He set her on the sofa beside him and gently, but firmly, pushed her back. Strong hands teased her thighs apart, and long, lean fingers caressed her skin. He kissed the inside of her thigh, his breath warm against her flesh.

"Trust me," he whispered. "I only want your pleasure."

His lips moved toward her center where the ache screamed to be eased. Stubble chafed her skin, igniting shockwaves of pleasure through her.

"Let me taste you."

Slow, rhythmic pulses rippled deep within her, and she squirmed under his exquisite touch.

"So responsive, my darling," he said, his voice hoarse. He traced a line across her stomach, following a path up her body and between her breasts, until he came to the necklace, which he hooked under his fingers and lifted.

"It looks beautiful on you, Frederica," he said softly. "You were born to be a countess. And I shall worship you until my dying day."

She reached toward him, but he caught her hand.

"I'm afraid there's no time," he said. "I'm overseeing a hearing today."

"Is it important?"

"Yes," he said. "A young woman accused of assaulting her husband."

"And did she?"

He sighed. "The evidence suggests she did. She claimed she acted in self-defense, but the law permits a husband to correct his wife." He shook his head. "Sometimes I wish I were in a position to change the law rather than administer it."

"Is there nothing you can do?"

"Even if I have no choice but to declare a guilty verdict, I have the means to ensure her protection," he said, smiling. "There are many sanctuaries for the lost and dispossessed. One only needs to know where to find them."

"You're a good man, Hawthorne."

"That's all I have ever wanted," he said. "To further the cause of true justice. And to have the woman I love in my arms. If I have nothing else, I'll die a happy man."

He reached inside his waistcoat and pulled out a pocket watch, then snapped it shut.

"I must go," he said. "Will you be all right in my absence?"

She smiled. "You've been absent before, Hawthorne."

"Ah, but not while betrothed to my elusive faerie. I fear if I blink, she may disappear."

"I wondered if I might venture out, to pay a call?"

His smile disappeared. "Do you think that's wise?"

"I can take Jenny, if you think I need a chaperone."

"It's not that..." he hesitated. "I just want you to be safe. We can take a walk together when I return. Who do you wish to visit?"

"Just a friend."

His eyes showed uncertainty, and she took his hand and kissed it.

"Hawthorne, I won't leave you. You have my word."

"Of course," he said. "I'm merely being foolish. I'll send Jenny to help you dress."

He pulled her to him and gave her a long, lingering kiss, then released her.

"Until later, my love."

⧽⧽⧽⧼⧼⧼

"DO YOU KNOW what's wrong with me, Doctor McIver?"

Frederica sat opposite the doctor's desk and took a sip from the glass of water he'd offered her. After congratulating her on her engagement, he swiftly dispensed with niceties, exercising the brisk efficiency of a medical practitioner in performing an examination.

He finished rinsing his hands and wiped them with a towel, then took the seat at his desk.

"There's nothing wrong with you, Miss Stanford. I'm pleased to say you're fully recovered from when I last saw you."

"Then why have I been sick?"

He smiled. "The most natural reason in the world, my dear. I'm afraid you're pregnant."

Her stomach gave a little jolt, and she placed her hand over it.

Dear Lord...

The doctor leaned forward, his forehead creased into a frown. "I understand it's a delicate matter, but may I be permitted to enquire as to the..." he gave a nervous cough, "...the circumstances?"

She opened her mouth to speak, then closed it again, and lowered her gaze, her cheeks warming with shame.

The silence stretched and, at length, he sighed. "I ask only out of your welfare, Miss Stanford. It will help me determine when you are expected to enter your confinement. Of course, that's assuming you wish for me to attend you."

Her hand shook as she set the glass on the desk. "It was a month ago."

"I see," he said. "That explains the sickness you were suffering when I treated you before. And…" he hesitated, "…the other party?"

She closed her eyes. "It was Hawth… Lord Stiles."

"Forgive me for asking, my dear," McIver said. "When are you to be married?"

"Next month."

"I take it you don't want him to know about your condition?"

"I–I would rather he didn't," she said. "I've caused him enough scandal." She blinked, and a tear splashed onto her cheek.

McIver rose from his seat and circled the desk to stand beside her. A warm hand engulfed hers.

"I quite understand, lass," he said. "Society is a world of many rules, some of which exist to perpetuate the distinction of rank. Where one's livelihood and wellbeing are too often dependent on reputation and adherence to such rules, the smallest indiscretion can change the course of lives."

"But the child," she said, "when it's born, Hawthorne will know I've deceived him."

"Your child will be born seven months after your marriage," McIver said. "A seven-month baby is not so unusual as to raise suspicion."

"I cannot let you be party to a deception."

"My primary concern is your health and wellbeing," he said. "You're not the first young woman to experience such a predicament, and you won't be the last. I understand your desire for discretion, and I swear I will not breach your trust or divulge a single word of what passes between us. I would be breaking my oath to my profession if I did. But I would advise you to tell Stiles the truth. I'm sure he would understand. It takes two to make a child, after all."

"I cannot risk anyone else finding out," she said. "Society already looks on him unfavorably for his association with me."

"Then tell him once you're married," McIver said. "The whole of society could overhear and it wouldn't matter. It's not unusual for a wedding night union to bear fruit."

In her mind, she saw Hawthorne taking her hand and kneeling before her while she told him he was to be a father—the love in his expression as he drew her to him and claimed her with hungry lips and loving hands...

"Very well," she said. "I'll tell him once we're married."

The doctor gave her a smile and patted her hand. "When I send his lordship my account, I will, with your permission, say I treated you for a mild sickness—which, I'll add, is the truth."

She rose from her seat. "Thank you, Doctor McIver. I won't take up any more of your time."

"May I summon a hackney carriage?" he asked.

"No, thank you. I'd rather walk."

"Take care of yourself, my dear."

He took her hand and bowed, then escorted her down to the hall where Jenny stood waiting.

As she stepped out onto the street, she collided with a man and dropped her reticule.

"Begging your pardon, miss!"

He stooped to retrieve it and handed it to her.

"Thank you," she said.

"No harm done, miss." His eyes, a pale blue, looked almost color-less in the sunlight as he gazed at her with a thoughtful expression. Then his mouth curled into a smile, showing white, even teeth. "Mind how you go, now."

She crossed the street, Jenny following. As she reached the junction with New Cavendish Street, she glanced over her shoulder. The man stood beside McIver's doorstep, watching her. He thrust his hands into his pockets, headed along Harley Street in the opposite direction and disappeared.

CHAPTER TWENTY-SEVEN

A MONTH AFTER she'd agreed to make him the happiest of men, Hawthorne stood beside his fiancée, ready to greet their guests on the eve of their wedding. She glowed with health and happiness, though their engagement had proven to be something of an ordeal for her.

Since the announcement of their betrothal in the Times, he'd protected her from the worst of the gossip, but he could not miss the disapproving glances cast their way when they walked out together. Once they were married, his title would protect her from any overt incivility.

And there was Markham. They'd managed to avoid that bastard until tonight. Tongues would have wagged if he'd been excluded from Hawthorne's party, now he'd married Alice de Grecy, who was known to be Frederica's friend.

As if fate heard his thoughts, the footman announced Markham and his wife. The hand engulfed in Hawthorne's tightened, her grip on his fingers the only sign of Frederica's distress. They had argued about his invitation, the first sign of discord between them. But he'd be damned if Markham caused a rift between them.

When they were alone, his skittish little changeling abandoned her protective layers and released her true self—a wild, wanton creature. The passion he'd seen in her eyes manifested itself into a goddess who gave herself to him night after night, her warm, welcoming body drawing him to previously unknown heights of pleasure.

He gave her hand a reassuring squeeze, and she looked up and smiled. Her lips glowed pink in the candlelight, as they had done only the night before when she'd taken him into her mouth. Her craving to please him surpassed her own need for pleasure. He'd never believed such a woman existed, but his little changeling was unique. Perhaps that was why he craved to be near her constantly, for fear she'd be spirited away.

Markham approached him and bowed, his colorless wife on his arm.

"We're honored you could come," Hawthorne said.

"The pleasure is all mine," Markham replied, his gaze focused on Frederica. "Wouldn't you agree, Miss Stanford?"

Frederica dipped a curtsey but said nothing. She addressed Lady Markham, but Alice only gave her a curt nod.

Markham smiled indulgently. "Permit my wife some liberties, Miss Stanford. Her standards of proprietary are unsurpassed. She was as surprised as I to hear of your engagement. But we wish you the best. May you be bestowed with the fate you deserve."

Frederica's body stiffened against Hawthorne, and he squeezed her fingers.

"Thank you, Markham," he said coldly, gesturing toward the ballroom. "Please go in, we've no wish to detain you further."

Frederica's body relaxed, and a small sigh escaped her lips.

"Good girl," Hawthorne whispered. She colored and looked down; they were the very same words he used as praise when she pleasured him.

The footman announced the next guest, Henry Drayton, Lord Ravenwell.

Ravenwell, with hair as black as a raven's wing and the ability to seduce a woman with a single look of his brilliant blue eyes, was considered one of London's most eligible bachelors. Were Hawthorne interested in that sort of thing, he'd have marked him as his chief rival. But Frederica, after accepting his congratulations, withdrew her hand before he could kiss it. Ravenwell recognized defeat when he saw it, and swept past Hawthorne with a nod of recognition.

Hawthorne, indeed, was the luckiest man alive. He was engaged to the most alluring creature in the room who had eyes for none but him and gave herself wholly to him in his bed. He felt a familiar stirring in his breeches and drew in a sharp breath. Would his craving for her ever cease?

This time tomorrow, she would be his wife.

FREDERICA WATCHED THE guests move around the ballroom, lords and ladies far above her in station who stared at the commoner who'd snared an earl. She could weather their ire, but her resolve almost crumbled at the sight of the man who'd murdered Papa.

Why had Hawthorne insisted they invite him? It had been their only argument. Doubt crossed Hawthorne's eyes every time he uttered Markham's name. Would he never stop seeing him as a rival?

Hawthorne already risked his reputation and career as a magistrate by an association with her. He paraded her around the parks and the streets of London, as if to exorcise the demon of distrust sitting on his shoulder. Did he strive to convince himself, as much as society, that she was worth it?

Only when they were alone did he shed the cloak of the society gentleman to reveal the lover within. As she submitted to him at night, the demon disappeared. But it always returned in the morning. She'd wake to find him staring at her, a flicker of doubt in his expression. Was his invitation to Markham tonight a test of her resolve as well as his?

He lifted her hand and kissed it, his lips warm through the soft material of her gloves.

"I am so proud of you," he whispered. "My beautiful wife."

"I'm not your wife yet," she said. His eyes narrowed, and he tightened his grip. "Tomorrow," he said. "You'll be mine, tomorrow."

>>><<<

AS THE NIGHT wore on, the heat of the room grew oppressive. Frederica made her way toward the terrace doors. Her wrists itched, but she was reluctant to remove her gloves and reveal her scars which society gossiped about.

A thin, pale woman stood in her way, her gown shimmering in the candlelight. A deep crimson silk trimmed with scarlet lace, it outshone every dress in the room. As she turned her head, the tiny diamonds in her hair glittered. The bright colors drained her complexion. Dark rings circled her eyes, and as Frederica approached, she set her mouth into a hard line.

"Alice." Frederica held her hand out. "Are you well? You look dreadfully pale. May I fetch you something to drink?"

For a moment, Alice's eyes glistened, then she blinked and shook her head. "I'm quite well, Miss Stanford."

The formal tone could not disguise the pain in Alice's voice. Frederica took her hand. Her skin was almost translucent, veins protruding beneath the flesh.

"Alice, I can see you're ill. Let me help you, as a friend."

"We're not friends."

"Yes, we are," Frederica lowered her voice and squeezed Alice's hand. "You can trust me. If you're suffering, if anyone is giving you cause for pain, you must tell someone before it's too late."

Alice opened her mouth to speak, her lips trembling. Then she cast a glance sideways and snatched her hand away.

"Who are you to judge me?" Alice asked. "It's Lord Stiles who suffers. You'll find society doesn't take kindly to scandal. Wedded to a murderer's daughter? It'll destroy his reputation." She turned her back and strode away.

It was worse than Frederica had feared. For herself, she cared little. But could Hawthorne, a man who'd commanded respect all his life, withstand the contempt of his peers?

The voices in the room fluttered around her, harsh whispers, the caws and cackles of predators. Black feathers danced across her vision, and she pushed through the doors and ran out onto the terrace and drew in a lungful of the cool night air.

She leaned back against the wall and closed her eyes. The aroma of roses grew stronger until she could almost taste their color, the hot reds and soft pinks.

"Well, well, well, what do we have here?"

A smooth voice cut through her dreams, and the colors turned to black. She snapped her eyes open in an attempt to quell the nightmare, only to find it standing before her.

"Hush, little bird," he said. "You wouldn't want to draw attention to yourself, at least no more than you've already done."

He ran a fingertip across her cheek. Her flesh tightened, sending ripples of revulsion through her.

"Careful, my sweet," he said, "or I might believe your desire for me has waned."

"I never desired you!" The words came out in a snarl, but he merely smiled.

"We both know you invited me into your home and your *secret place.*"

"What do you want, Roderick?"

"Roderick, is it? How terribly familiar!" he laughed. "Almost as if you wished our relationship were more *intimate.*"

He cupped her chin. "I want you, little bird."

"What about Alice?"

"Her dowry services a need," he said. "But you..." He closed his eyes and his nostrils flared "...you'd satisfy a different need altogether."

He drew close, and her body froze—the instinctive action of an animal caught in a trap from which it has no escape.

"Leave me alone," she hissed, but he merely chuckled.

"Foolish little slut! You think Stiles cares for you? He values you only as the bird he bagged before me."

"He loves me."

Roderick's smile broadened, showing big, even teeth which seemed to sharpen in the evening light. "We both know he'll tire of you eventually. If you go ahead with this ridiculous charade-of-a-marriage, I'll ruin you both."

"You can't do that."

"Oh, can't I?" His voice grew quiet, the calm tone freezing her blood. "What do you think will happen when it becomes known that his wife is nothing but a doxy who spread her legs for half of London and offered herself to her own brother?"

"I did no such thing!" she cried. "I'll expose you for a liar. I remember our encounter well, even if you don't. I'm not above bruising your jaw a second time."

"And I'm not above telling the whole company tonight that you tricked my learned friend into marriage in order to give your bastard a name. The pedigree of a child born seven months into a marriage will always be in doubt, whatever the good doctor might say."

Icy fingers crawled over her skin, and she stumbled back, the breath forced from her lungs.

He let out a soft laugh and took her wrist. "Who did you spread your legs for, little bird?"

"Say what you like about me," she said, "I care not. My love for Hawthorne is the only defense I need against your threats."

"What about his love for you?" Markham asked. "Is it enough that he'd be willing to sacrifice everything that matters to him? He's an ambitious man, little bird. A word or two in the right place can further his aspirations or crush them, especially when one has the ear of the Regent himself."

"The-the Regent?"

Roderick smiled. "We're old friends, my dear. He's terribly enamored with Alice. He's a discerning man and recognizes quality when he sees it. The word of a duke will always carry more weight than that of an earl. Hawthorne would agree with me."

The memory of Hawthorne's expression flitted across her mind, the doubt and the pain which often bled through unguarded moments when he thought she wasn't looking.

"He won't withstand society's derision forever," Roderick said. "Do you think he'll welcome seeing everything he's worked for slip through his fingers for the sake of a harlot? Like gilt, the sheen of your marriage will soon wear off to reveal the base metal beneath."

His words transfixed her, conjuring the image in her mind of Hawthorne's face, his strong features filled with love, before it was replaced by bitter resentment and hatred, leaving him a broken man.

"He'll convince himself at first that he can weather the scandal." Roderick's voice burrowed into her mind. "He may be kind to you, as anyone might bestow charity on an *orphan*." She flinched, but he continued. "You'll see it in his eyes at first. Little creases will appear, then they'll grow dull until his heart withers. Is that what you want for the man you profess to love?"

"It's a risk I'm willing to take," she said.

"But are you willing to risk his life?"

Tendrils of dread tangled inside her, and her stomach knotted. He gave her a lazy smile and drew an object out of his waistcoat pocket. He held it up, between his thumb and forefinger, and it glistened in the moonlight.

A brass button. An unremarkable object save for the familiar crisscross pattern etched into the metal. How many times had she studied that pattern, before replicating it with a few strokes of her pencil?

"Is that...?"

"My latest trophy," he said. "As an accomplished dueler, I have amassed a very pretty collection from the coats of my opponents. After all, they have no further need of them, do they?"

She reached out to touch it, but he slipped it back into his pocket.

"I daresay, if I were to reveal your sordid little secret tonight, Stiles would wish to settle the matter like a gentleman. His coat button would make an interesting addition to my little collection, would it not? Did I not say the *soiled whore* would always have something to lose, which she valued above all else?"

"No!" she cried. "Leave him alone!"

"Only you have the power to stop it."

She shriveled under his gaze. "What must I do?"

"Leave him. Come to me."

"I can't leave him," she choked. "He'll follow me, he'll think I've been taken..."

"Then write to him. Tell him you've changed your mind."

"He won't believe me."

He gripped her chin and forced her head up until she looked directly into his eyes. They had grown pale, the color of ice, pupils forming tiny pinpricks of hate.

"Then you'd better make it convincing."

Defeated, she nodded. He pulled her close for a brutal kiss, then relaxed his grip.

"Tell him you wish to retire. Write the note, then go to Hackton House, and wait for me there. Do it quickly before I change my mind and tell the whole company tonight what a whore you are."

A shadow moved near the glass doors, and Ross Trelawney appeared.

"Markham, your wife is looking for you," he said. He cast a glance at Frederica. "Miss Stanford, are you all right?"

Markham interrupted her before she could reply. "She nearly fainted, so I escorted her outside. But she's quite well now, aren't you, my dear? I trust you understand what you must do to preserve your health and that of those around you."

Ross's brow furrowed, but he made no attempt to seek an explanation. Roderick took her hand and kissed it. Fighting her revulsion, she returned inside.

"Frederica!" A warm hand circled her arm, and her body melted at the familiar touch. His scent caressed her nostrils, and she looked up into the soft eyes of the man she loved, the man she was about to betray for his own sake.

"Forgive me, Hawthorne," she said. "I beg to be excused."

"Has something happened?"

She shook her head and forced a smile. "No. I'm just a little unwell. Nothing a night's rest can't cure."

Doubt clouded his expression, and she lifted her hand and touched his cheek, relishing the smooth skin and soft downy hair on his chin, the beginnings of a beard which, by tomorrow, would be gone.

As would she. This would be the last time she set eyes on him.

"I'll bid you goodnight, my love." His eyes crinkled into a smile.

"I love you, Hawthorne," she said, "and will always love you, until I draw my last breath." Her throat constricted, and she blinked back the tears which stung her eyes. "Never forget that."

"Until later," he said. "Tomorrow our future begins."

She nodded, and he rejoined the company. Memorizing every curve of his body, every feature, she watched him, his straight back, broad shoulders, and fine profile until the guests obscured him from view, then she slipped upstairs to her chamber. As she pulled her travelling cloak from the closet, she spotted a piece of cloth on the floor. Hawthorne's necktie. Not one for dandyism, he preferred plain adornments. It was an unremarkable piece of cloth except for one feature. It belonged to him. She lifted it to her lips and inhaled, breathing in the warm, masculine scent. It was a piece of him she could take with her, a token to remind her in the years to come that, for a brief moment, she had thought her dreams fulfilled.

ROSS APPROACHED HAWTHORNE, a look of concern in his eyes.

"Where's Miss Stanford?"

"She's retired. She was feeling unwell."

The party was drawing to a close, and Hawthorne was anxious to see her. He cursed himself for subjecting her to the party, but he had to show society she was worthy of being Countess Stiles.

Frederica had acted admirably tonight. Once they were married, they could enjoy the rest of their lives. She was stronger than everyone gave her credit for. They called her insane, weak-minded, but none could match her resilience.

And she was his. All his.

Ross gave him a knowing smile. But he was too much of a gentle-man to voice his suspicions that Frederica already warmed Hawthorne's bed.

"She seemed well enough when she was with Markham," Ross said.

"Markham?" A cold fist clawed at Hawthorne's stomach. "She was with him?"

"Outside, on the terrace. I thought she disliked him, but I must have been mistaken as she kissed him."

"Markham..." Hawthorne's throat constricted as he strained to pronounce the name.

"Markham's always gallant to the ladies when he wants to be." The bitter note of rejection hung on Ross' lips.

Was he still pining over that insipid de Grecy creature?

At that moment, Markham and his wife moved into Hawthorne's eyeline. Lady Markham looked anything but happy, her eyes bearing the expression of a cow in the slaughterhouse. Markham's gaze met Hawthorne's, and he lifted his lips in a smile of triumph.

A cold hand of dread draped itself around Hawthorne's neck.

Something was wrong.

"Frederica..."

He pushed past Ross and ran into the hallway. Taking the stairs two at a time, he dashed up to her chamber, and flung the door open.

It was empty.

It seemed untouched since he'd left it that morning. Except for her dressing table. The sapphire necklace was gone, replaced by an envelope bearing a single word, written in her hand.

Stiles.

He tore it open and unfolded the note inside. The ink had long since dried, but smudges blurred some of the words. His legs gave way beneath him, and he collapsed into the chair as he read the words, each line driving a stake through his heart.

Sir,

I find myself no longer able to maintain this charade. I don't expect you to forgive me, nor will I attempt to insult your intelligence by giving you an explanation. By the time you read this, I will be gone. Please do not make any attempt to find me. I believe you are better suited to another. For myself, I have only ever wanted one man, and nothing you say or do will change my mind. If I cannot be with him, I would rather be alone.

Yours,

FS

He crumpled the note in his fist and rushed out of the chamber, roaring at the footmen by the main door.

"Where is she? Where's Miss Stanford?"

The younger of the two cringed under the force of his voice, while the older stepped forward.

"She left about an hour ago. She wouldn't tell me where."

A hand caught his sleeve. "Hawthorne, are you all right?"

"Ross," he choked. "She's gone."

"Gone?"

"She loves another."

"Oh, I say!" a familiar voice cried. "Stiles looks somewhat put out! What's the matter, old chap?"

Roderick Markham stood before him, a knowing smile on his face. His wife stood a pace behind, her eyes fixed on the floor.

A deep pain bled through his body as ivy chokes a tree, squeezing the life out of it until it withered.

She had abandoned him for another.

"Dear, God!" Ross cried. "I can't believe she's jilted you."

"Oh, I can," Markham said smoothly. "Perhaps the better man did win in the end, after all?"

Acid burned in Hawthorne's gut, and he doubled over in pain. The seed of doubt which had festered deep within his mind began to grow, nurtured by his mistrust, and the assured tone of Markham's words.

"Hawthorne." Ross clasped his shoulder. "Don't let them see your distress."

The guests closed in on him, a pack of dogs cornering their victim.

Was this how it felt to have one's heart broken?

"Are we to commiserate you on some ill fortune, Stiles?" Markham asked, mock sympathy in his voice.

Gritting his teeth, Hawthorne faced his enemy. Markham's eyes widened with the fear a bully experiences when challenged.

Hawthorne fisted his hands, digging the nails into his palms, the sweet pain deflecting his mind from the agony in his heart. It was all he could do to fight the urge to wrap his fingers around Markham's neck and squeeze the life out of him.

"I am to be congratulated on making a lucky escape," he said quietly. "You're welcome to her. Now leave, and never come near me again."

Markham's lip twitched, and he blinked. "I'm not sure I understand your meaning."

"Get out, you bastard."

Markham's smile broadened. "I rather think *she's* the bastard."

"I said, get out!" Hawthorne cried. A murmur rippled through the onlookers, and he whirled round to face them, the cream of society who would no doubt relish the opportunity for gossip. Vultures and scavengers the lot of them.

"Leave!" he roared. "All of you! There'll be no wedding tomorrow. Now, get the fuck out of my house!"

Cries of shock burst from the ladies' lips. Ross pulled him aside and barked orders to the footmen who scurried about the hallway, fetching coats and cloaks in their desperation to dispatch the guests as quickly as possible.

Ravenwell took charge, ushering the others out. Before the door closed behind him, he cast a quick, concerned glance over his shoulder, nodded at Ross, then followed the rest outside.

The footmen needed no instruction. As soon as the door shut, they disappeared.

Bitter tears stung Hawthorne's eyelids, but he wouldn't succumb.

Ross touched his arm. "Would you like me to stay?"

"No." he said coldly. "Forgive my outburst, but I'm well now. It was for the best."

"You can't mean that, Hawthorne. I know how much you love…"

"Don't say it, Ross, or I'll throw you out as well." Hawthorne forced a grim smile. "I would have been miserable had I shackled myself to her. I should thank her for releasing me from the obligation at so little cost to myself. She only took a necklace. Other than that, I've lost nothing of any real value."

"You can't mean that." Ross offered his hand.

Hawthorne slapped him away. "Get out."

Ross sighed. "I'll return in the morning."

"If you intend to mention her name again, don't bother to return at all."

After the door slammed behind Ross, Hawthorne crossed the hall to his study. Hands trembling, he picked up the decanter and filled a glass, the amber liquid splashing over the desk. He tipped the glass and drained the contents, spluttering as the liquid burned his throat.

"Curse her!"

He threw the glass against the door, and it shattered on impact. But the whisky served its purpose. The pain had lessened. With luck, it would disappear completely, deaden his heart, and obliterate the memory of her. He took another glass, emptied the decanter into it, drained it, then rang the bell for Giles. His cellar was well stocked. It was going to be a long night.

CHAPTER TWENTY-EIGHT

Airth, Scotland
1819

"M**RS. FORD!**"
The innkeeper stood at the end of the corridor, waving a note in his hand.

"Good news," he said. "Another painting sold."

Frederica wiped her hands on her apron. "Who bought it, Mr. Campbell?"

"Mr. MacDonald, the merchant who wouldn't stop talking about his children. He said it was a present for his wife. That's five this month. You're getting quite the reputation."

"Thank you, Mr. Campbell."

"No," he said, smiling. "Thank *you*. My fortunes changed for the better the day I hired you. Not even my Morag, God rest her soul, worked as hard."

He wiped his eyes, and a rush of sympathy blew through Frederica's veins. Mr. Campbell had given her employment when nobody else would, mainly out of fondness for old Mrs. Beecham. But nonetheless, a woman with no background was a risk for anyone to take on. Frederica owed him her livelihood. As for Mrs. Beecham, she owed the woman her life.

"Och, forgive me, Mrs. Ford," he said. "The melancholy threatens to overcome me, particularly when I've enjoyed too much of our wine." He nodded. "Which reminds me, I wondered if you could help us tonight? We've two gentleman guests having a private dinner. They're returning to London after a shooting party and have broken their journey here. They'd appreciate someone a little more ladylike than wee Isla. With your knowledge of wine, you're the best person to serve their burgundy."

"I don't know…"

"But I do," he said, his tone kind, but insistent. "I'd like to give them a good impression in case they come here again. You're good with the patrons, Mrs. Ford. The men who stay spend their days talking to their colleagues and their nights being talked at by their wives. They appreciate a little quiet attention, not the idle chitter-chatter of girls like Isla. I'll pay double."

"You pay me enough as it is."

"Then consider it a little extra for Mrs. Beecham, or wee Georgia."

"Very well."

"Good, lass!" he said. "And I have something for you. Yesterday's copy of the Times. Mr. MacDonald left it in his room. You can read it while you have your tea. It's waiting for you in the parlor. Isla's had hers, so you'll have a bit of peace."

After pouring her tea, Federica slipped off her shoes to ease her aching feet. She dropped a spoonful of sugar in her tea and sipped it. Though she wrinkled her nose at the sweet taste, the sugar provided much-needed energy. As did the cake. Isla might be a gossip, but she baked an excellent fruitcake.

She opened the paper, drawn, as usual, to the society pages. The accounts of balls and parties had thinned now the London season was coming to an end, but births, marriages, and deaths still filled the page. Last year, she'd read of the death of the old Duke of Markham but had felt nothing. Over the years, her fear of discovery had dwindled.

As for Hawthorne, her heart tightened every time her eyes lingered on the account of the marriages. Had he married? Not Louisa

Wilcott, she'd married a duke less than a month after Frederica had settled in Scotland. He must be married by now. Perhaps she'd missed the notification. Mr. Campbell didn't always manage to procure a copy of the Times.

Elsewhere, she'd read accounts of his success as a magistrate and his reputation for fairness. The Regent had commended him on his prowess. Revered and admired, he had achieved his heart's desire.

But was he loved?

She folded the newspaper and set it aside. Work was the best remedy for memories. She had others to live for now, and once she'd served the dinner guests, she could return home to them.

FREDERICA STOOD OUTSIDE the dining room door, holding a tray laden with two portions of steak and a bottle of wine. She nodded to Isla, and the girl knocked on the door, then opened it after a voice hailed from within.

Two men were in the room. One stood by the window, almost hidden in shadow. The other stood facing the wall, where a number of her paintings hung. Perhaps she'd make a sale tonight.

She placed the tray on the table and picked up the bottle.

"Your supper is ready, sirs. Shall I open the wine?"

The man admiring the paintings turned, and their eyes locked. A jolt of recognition coursed through her, and the bottle slipped from her grasp. He darted toward her and caught it.

"I thought I recognized the paintings."

"Mr. Trelawney…"

"I'd know your style anywhere," he addressed his companion. "Didn't I say so?"

The other man stepped out of the shadows, and her chest tightened, forcing the breath from her lungs. Eyes focused on her, eyes which had once been full of warmth and love, were now black and cold.

"Hawthorne…"

He advanced on her.

"Ross, get out," he spoke so quietly, she almost thought she'd imagined it.

"No," she said. "*I'll* go. I mustn't keep you from your dinner." She moved toward the door.

"I've not given you leave to go, madam."

"Hawthorne, please…" Ross said. "Surely this can wait."

Frederica twisted the door handle.

"Stop!"

Her body froze at the force of his voice.

"Are you employed here?" Hawthorne asked.

She nodded.

"In which case, you must do as you're bid." He grasped her wrist and pulled her toward him. "Where's your lover?" he hissed. "Did you tire of him, too?"

The door opened behind her.

"Gentlemen, is everything to your…" Mr. Campbell's voice trailed away. "Is anything wrong, sir?" he said. "Is the meal not to your liking?"

"The meal is satisfactory, I'm sure," Hawthorne said, "but I find the service somewhat lacking. I didn't know you were in the business of employing harlots."

Mr. Campbell's eyes narrowed. "Unhand Mrs. Ford, if you please."

"*Mrs.* Ford?" Hawthorne eyed the innkeeper with a sneer. "Are you her husband?"

"She's a respectable widow, and I'll thank you to take your hands off her."

"Hawthorne, for pity's sake!" Ross cried.

Hawthorne winced and relaxed his grip.

"Come along, my dear," Mr. Campbell said. "Let's leave these gentlemen to their meal."

"I'd like a word with Mrs. Ford," Hawthorne growled.

"I think not."

"It's all right, Mr. Campbell," Frederica said. "He can't hurt me."

"If you're sure?"

She nodded, and the innkeeper slipped outside. "Call me if you need anything, my dear."

Hawthorne waited until the door closed.

"So, you're a widow?"

"I…"

"Did you drive him into his grave?"

She shook her head, and he moved closer, body vibrating with anger. "Perhaps you're spreading your legs for the innkeeper? Is that how you earn your keep?"

The force of his hatred sliced through her heart. Is this what she'd done to him? By setting him free, had she turned him into a monster, a man without compassion?

"No," she whispered.

He shrugged, gesturing with casual indifference.

"I was merely curious. It matters not who you're fucking."

Bitter pain burst within her at his words, and she flew out of the room.

Mr. Campbell looked up as she raced into the kitchen.

"Is everything all right, Mrs. Ford?"

"It's time I went home."

"Are you in trouble, my dear?"

"No," she said. "But I must go."

"Of course," he said. "I'll see to the guests. I'm sorry you had to deal with their rudeness. Sometimes I wonder what state our country is in if that's how gentlemen behave. Och, perhaps it's why London is so degenerate. But dinnae worry. They're leaving tomorrow and need never bother you again."

"Thank you."

"Here." He held out a slice of cake wrapped in paper. "Take this."

She bade him goodnight and slipped outside, praying Hawthorne wouldn't follow her. At all costs, the one she loved most in the world must be protected.

⟫⟫⟫⟪⟪⟪

"ARE YOU SURE you know what you're doing, Hawthorne?" Ross reached for a slice of toast and spread marmalade on it. He bit into it and sighed with relish.

"Don't lecture me." Hawthorne pushed his teacup aside, the liquid long since having turned cold. He motioned to the manservant to clear his place. Other than lifting his eyebrows at Hawthorne's untouched breakfast plate, the man complied in silence.

How could Ross take such enjoyment in his food? Last night's supper had tasted like dust, the wine turning to acid on his tongue. Fate had delivered a cruel blow, reopening wounds she'd inflicted, wounds which refused to heal.

And he'd tried. Weeks of searching had proved fruitless. Months of drinking had lessened the pain at first, but it always returned tenfold. Were it not for Ross and Ravenwell, he would have descended into oblivion—another nameless sot who lived only for drink and opiates. But his career had given him a purpose. With the magistracy to satisfy his ambition, he was able to muffle the cries of his heart and soul.

But the sight of her eyes widening in recognition and fear had threatened to pierce the armor he'd fashioned around himself.

Reason told him he should forget her and continue his journey to London with Ross. But he needed to confront her, to understand why she'd abandoned him. The truth would set him free, rid him of her once and for all.

Ross set his cup aside. "Do you wish me to wait while you conduct your *business?*"

"No. You go ahead. I'll follow once I'm done." Hawthorne reached into his pocket and drew out a handful of coins. "This should be enough for a mail coach."

Ross pushed the money across the table. "Keep it."

A young woman, barely out of childhood, entered and began clear the table.

"You there," Hawthorne said. "Do you know Mrs. Ford, the woman who works here?"

"Aye." The girl's Scottish burr almost obscured the words. "But ye'll no see her today."

"I wish to speak with her," Hawthorne said. The girl's eyes widened, and he softened his voice, "to purchase one of her paintings."

"Oh!" the girl said. "Mr. Campbell can arrange it. I'll fetch him."

"I'd rather speak to Mrs. Ford directly," Hawthorne said. "I wish to offer her a commission."

He avoided Ross's gaze. The knowledge that he lied was only partly tempered by the knowledge that his deception paled into nothing compared to *hers.*

"She'll be delighted," the girl said. "She's in the cottage at the edge of the village, just beyond the smithy. You can't miss it, there's roses lining the front door. Old Mrs. Beecham keeps them ever so bonny." Doubt crossed her features. "Perhaps I shouldn't be telling you."

"You're a good and clever girl," Hawthorne said, and the girl blushed. "But don't tell Mr. Campbell. I wouldn't want to cause trouble for Mrs. Ford, or you, with your employer."

The girl bobbed a curtsey and slipped out of the room. Ross rose and picked up his gloves. "I hope you know what you're doing."

"I won't fall for her wiles again, Ross."

"Be careful, my friend," Ross said, a tone of warning in his voice. "I've no wish to see you in the state you'd fallen into after she left." He hesitated and looked away, as if contemplating something before resuming. "I'd also suggest you listen to what she has to say."

"You can't expect me to forgive her."

"Five years is a long time to remain angry," Ross said. "Her circumstances have been reduced to servitude. Is that not punishment enough?"

"Punishment!" Hawthorne scoffed. "The bastard daughter of a servant cannot be reduced further."

A pang of guilt twisted in his gut even before he finished uttering the words. Try as he might, his hatred never burned as fiercely as he wished.

"You go, Ross. I'll settle the account here. With luck, I'll overtake you on the road, and we can spend the rest of the journey together."

As soon as Ross left, Hawthorne went in search of the innkeeper to secure his room for another night.

Frederica would not escape justice this time.

CHAPTER TWENTY-NINE

THE COTTAGE, THOUGH tiny, looked well-kept and loved. The roses surrounding the door were neatly trimmed.

As Hawthorne climbed out of the carriage, he spotted movement at one of the widows. He'd barely knocked on the door when it opened to reveal a dark-haired girl in a servant's uniform.

"Are ye lost, sir?"

"I'm come to see Mrs. Ford."

"Is she expecting ye?"

"I rather believe so."

The girl hesitated, then stepped aside.

"Let me take you to the parlor while I fetch the mistress."

The furnishings in the parlor were threadbare, the wood stained and blemished, but it looked clean and tidy. He took an armchair beside the empty fireplace and waited.

A table beside the window was laden with art materials, an earthenware pot full of brushes, smaller jars and boxes, and a threadbare sketchbook. A landscape hung over the fireplace. It depicted a lake with an expanse of heather in the foreground, the land beyond dotted with deer. In the background, a large mountain stood over the land like a giant sentinel, its jagged edge pointing toward the sky.

He stood to inspect it, his eyes drawn to the detail in the foreground. The flowers had been portrayed with sensitivity, their delicate purple hue mirroring that of the lake. His gaze moved to the left where a small creature foraged among the grasses, bright blue-black eyes peering out, a soft brown face and a rotund body covered in prickly spines.

Despite himself, his lips curled into a smile at the memory of the little woodland creature he had once picked up, the creature she'd defended with such courage.

The door opened, and he jumped back, guilt warming his cheeks as if he were a young lad caught with his fingers in the sweetmeats.

"Madam, your guest is…"

The girl's voice was cut short by a cry, and he came face to face with the woman who'd almost destroyed him.

Her face was paler than he remembered, perhaps due to the shock of seeing him in her home. Small lines creased the skin around her eyes. He recognized the air of a prisoner standing in the dock through no fault of their own, the unfairly accused, the dispossessed, prisoners of their own suffering. He'd seen that look too many times. But he brushed it aside.

"Earl Stiles," she addressed him quietly. The girl at her side gasped and dipped another curtsey.

"*Mrs. Ford,*" he replied, saying the false name.

"Anna," she said, "would you be kind enough to fetch some tea?"

"Yes, ma'am." The girl scuttled out of the room as if being chased by wolves.

Frederica gestured toward an armchair.

"Please, sit."

Despite her calm exterior, he noted the way her hands shook, his ear registering the tremor in her voice. She moved toward a chair and into direct sunlight. Her beauty still captivated him. She turned her head toward him, her pupils contracted to pinpricks in the light, and the green of her eyes vibrated against the color of her hair.

"Are you, are you well?" The musical notes of her voice threatened to deceive him once more.

He leaned forward, and she shrank back, as if aware of the inanity of her question.

"Is it any business of yours if I am?"

A spark of pain crossed her expression.

He sighed. "I must apologize for what I said last night, what I called you." What the devil was he doing placating her?

"Given that you'd run off with a lover," he added, "I had good reason."

She shriveled under his words.

"I'm sorry."

Her lips barely moved, but her quiet whisper penetrated his mind as surely as it had penetrated his dreams for the past five years—dreams which always ended with him waking in a cold, empty bed.

He opened his mouth to respond, then thought better of it. An apology was almost always followed by a statement of absolution. But she deserved no such consideration.

He gestured around the room. "This is a very pleasant parlor. The windows let in plenty of sunlight. It must get very warm in the summer."

Ye gods, was this what he'd been reduced to? Small talk? The devil on his shoulder propelled him forward. "Your patron must be very generous."

Her eyes had darkened with anger, and she set her mouth into a hard line.

"It may astonish you to know, I'm able to support myself. Every penny I earn is through honest work."

"And what's your definition of *honest work?*" His conscience twitched, but he had to know who she offered herself to, who she desired more than him.

"Cooking and cleaning, serving dinner," she said. "Lately, I've earned a little money from my paintings."

"Is it enough?"

"The winter months can be hard, but we set a little aside in the more prosperous months."

"And that's enough for *you*?"

"Yes," she said. "Though I wouldn't expect you to understand."

"What about the money you inherited from your father? You left it untouched."

The chink in her armor widened, and she looked away. "I don't want it. You keep it, in lieu of the necklace I took."

"The necklace?"

"Aye," she said softly. "It's plagued my conscience ever since I took it."

"The necklace?" he growled, rising from the chair. "Is that your only regret?"

The door opened and he sat back, fighting to control the anger vibrating through his bones. The servant girl set out the teacups while Frederica closed her eyes.

"Will that be all, ma'am?"

"Yes, Anna," she said quietly. "But tell me if Mrs. Beecham wakes…" she hesitated, "…or Georgia."

"Yes, ma'am." The girl disappeared again. Frederica opened her eyes as soon as the door closed. For a moment, he saw nothing but raw pain reflected in them before she blinked and looked away.

"I care nothing for the necklace," he said. "It was a gift to you. But I'll make arrangements to have your fortune released. At least it would elevate you from your current situation."

"You don't understand, do you?" she said, passion coloring her voice. "A fortune would leave me prey to suitors who'd squander it and seek to own me. I have no desire to be a prisoner again. Here, I have independence. I'm free."

"Free? In a hovel, working as a servant?"

"You'll never understand the value of freedom, until it's been taken from you."

Before he could respond, the door opened. A child burst into the room in a whirlwind of excited chatter, followed by the maid.

"Little mistress! You shouldn't be here. Your mama has a guest."

"I want to see him!"

The child crossed the room and leapt onto Frederica's lap. Frederica wrapped her arms around her and kissed her on the forehead.

"Little angel."

The child turned her gaze on Hawthorne. Warm brown eyes captured him with frank, honest appraisal. As if she sensed his hostility, she shrank back against Frederica.

"You have a child," he said quietly.

Frederica tightened her hold on her, and the angry resolve in her expression dissolved, replaced by a crippling fear.

Hawthorne held out his hand.

"Come here, child," he said, using the tone which elicited testimonies from the most frightened witnesses. The truly innocent had every reason to trust him, for he was a champion of their plights.

The girl wriggled in her mother's lap.

"Be still, angel," Frederica whispered.

"No," the child said petulantly, "I want to see him!"

"Let her come," he said. "I won't harm her. You should know that of me, if nothing else."

She released the child who surged toward him, and he lifted her onto his lap. She turned her gaze to him, and a shock of familiarity coursed through his body.

"Do you live here alone with your mama?"

"And Mrs. Beecham," she replied "Mrs. Beecham is teaching me my letters. Would you like me to show you?"

"Angel, Mrs. Beecham is resting," Frederica interjected. "We mustn't disturb her."

The girl's smile disappeared. Hawthorne bounced his knee, and the smile returned.

"What about your papa?" he asked.

Frederica gave a sharp intake of breath.

The child wiped her nose. "Papa is gone."

Frederica gave a low cry. "Please…"

Ignoring her, he bounced his knee again. "Do you miss him?"

The child leaned toward him. "I never knew him, but Mama misses him."

"How do you know?"

"She cries for him at night."

Frederica leapt to her feet. "Leave her alone! You have no quarrel with her."

Whatever sins Frederica had committed, the child was innocent. He stroked her hair and gave her a reassuring smile. She rewarded him with a smile of her own.

"Such a pretty child," he said softly. "What's your name?"

"Georgia."

"An unusual name. Did your mama choose it?"

"She named me after Papa," the child said proudly, sitting upright as if proclaiming herself to the world. "Georgia Hawthorne Ford."

Frederica let out a cry. The child turned her gaze on him once more, and recognition slid into place. The deep-set, brown eyes which looked at him so thoughtfully. It was as if he were looking at himself.

The child in his arms was his daughter.

CHAPTER THIRTY

ICY FINGERS CLAWED at Frederica's insides. Hawthorne had grown still, his forehead creasing as he studied the child on his lap. He lifted a hand to Georgia's face and stroked her cheek.

"Georgia…"

Doubt glittered in his eyes while he scrutinized her as he must have examined countless witnesses over the years. At length, he dipped his chin and buried his face in her hair. His chest rose and fell in a sigh, then he composed himself, lifted his head, and looked directly at Frederica.

The frost in his expression tore into her heart.

"Hawthorne…" she croaked, her throat dry with guilt.

"Did you know?" he asked quietly.

"I don't understand."

"Did you know you were carrying my child when you…" he hesitated before his expression hardened further "…when you betrayed me?"

"I-I'm sorry," she stuttered, but he raised a hand.

"Spare your words, madam." He took Georgia's chin in his hands and tipped her head up. His expression softened from betrayed suitor into loving parent.

Georgia took his hand, and tears pooled in Frederica's eyes at the love in his eyes.

"Are you my papa?"

He kissed Georgia's forehead and glared at Frederica in challenge.

"Yes, angel," she whispered. "He's your father."

The child wrapped her arms around Hawthorne's chest. "I prayed you'd come!"

He held her tight as if his life depended on it. Years of grieving for a child he'd never known vibrated throughout his frame.

Guilt ripped through Frederica at the sight of what her abandonment had done to him. She'd run away to protect him, so he could fulfill his ambition. But, instead, she had broken him.

She crossed the room, unable to bear his pain any more. She placed a hand on his shoulder and he stiffened.

"Hawthorne…"

He jerked away.

"Leave me be."

Georgia clung to him while he caressed her hair, telling her he loved her more than the world, that his life was empty without her. He spoke of his joy on finding her. Settling his gaze on Frederica, he told the child he would not abandon her, that he would do everything in his power to ensure he was never parted from her again.

His words of love and comfort to the child were, to Frederica, a warning.

The door opened, and Anna appeared.

"Is everything all right, ma'am? The noise has woken Mrs. Beecham."

"Yes, Anna," Frederica said. "Leave us."

"No!" Hawthorne commanded, the force of his voice making Anna stop. "Go to my carriage, girl, and tell my man to come in."

Anna hesitated and glanced at Frederica.

"Now!"

She jumped and rushed out of the room. Not long afterward, she returned with a liveried footman.

"You wanted me, sir?"

Hawthorne nodded. "See if you can find a trunk in this house. I want their belongings packed and ready to leave by this evening."

Panic rose within Frederica, and she took a step toward him. "What are you doing?"

"Giving my child the life you denied her."

"No, you can't!"

"I think you'll find I can," he said. "This child is mine, and the law is on my side."

"What should I pack, sir?" the footman asked.

"Whatever you deem of most value," Hawthorne said. "I doubt it will take long. I would rather my daughter forget the squalor she's lived in."

Fury boiled in Frederica's blood.

"How dare you, my daughter's had love!"

"I'm capable of loving, as well you know," he said, "but I am more discerning now."

"A child needs a mother's love," she pleaded. "Don't take her from me."

"She needs a father," he growled, "and she has one. One you denied her. Given that Stanford took you in despite your origins, you, of all people, should understand your cruelty when you abandoned me."

"I thought only of you," Frederica said.

Still in his arms, Georgia looked from one to the other, perhaps unhappy with the way they talked to each other.

"No, madam," he hissed. "You thought only of yourself and continue to do so by trying to deny what's mine by right. But I'm not so cruel as to deny the child her mother. You shall remain with us while the child has need of you."

Relief rippled through her, fighting the fear of returning to London.

"Thank you."

Ignoring her, he addressed the footman.

"Start packing immediately. If she tries to run, you're at liberty to restrain her. Use any force you deem necessary."

"What's all this, lass?"

Frederica froze at the voice from behind.

Mrs. Beecham stood in the doorway, leaning on her cane. Her intelligent eyes flicked between Frederica, Georgia, and Hawthorne. Years of almost constant pain had taken their toll on her, and she looked more tired than usual. There was little the doctor could do for her, though he was kind enough not to charge Frederica the full amount for his services.

"It's him, isn't it, lass? I see the likeness with your bairn."

Hawthorne scrutinized the old woman with his piercing stare.

Georgia leapt off his lap.

"Mrs. Beecham, Papa's come! We can all be together, now."

"No, child," Hawthorne said. "You'll need to say your goodbyes to this woman."

"Hawthorne, please…" Frederica whispered, "I cannot leave Mrs. Beecham here alone with just Anna to care for her. She's ill and has no money."

"You seek to manipulate me by inciting sympathy?" he scoffed. "In the interest of my child, I'll suffer the company of the woman who bore her, but I'll not waste my resources on every ragtag stray in Scotland."

"Papa, please!" Georgia wrapped her arms around his leg. "I love Mrs. Beecham! She has nobody else to take care of her."

He heaved a sigh. "Very well."

"Thank you," Frederica said. "Please, don't concern yourself about money. I have a little put by I can use for her…"

He cut her off with an angry word. "Don't thank me. I'm doing this for my daughter."

He took Georgia's hand and bent to kiss her forehead.

"Papa will return soon, sweet one, then we'll go home." Her lip wobbled, and he stroked her face. "I promise, you'll be happy with me. Nobody loves you more than your Papa."

The child sniffed. "You're leaving?"

"I have a few arrangements to make, then I'll come straight back. I want to make sure your room at home is all ready for you. Do you like dolls?"

"Oh, yes!" A broad smile illuminated Georgia's face, the smile which, over the years, had given Frederica jolts of recognition, as if it were Hawthorne himself. But he would never smile at her again.

"I will have the finest doll in London ready and waiting for you.

Georgia's eyes widened. "London?"

"You'll love it," he said. "You can ride in a carriage every day and wear the most beautiful dresses a loving Papa can give his daughter."

Georgia clapped her hands with excitement.

Hawthorne nodded to the footman. "Get on with it. I want to be away from here as quickly as possible."

Without another glance at Frederica, he swept out of the room, the front door banging behind him.

"YE ALWAYS KNEW he'd find you sooner or later, lass."

Mrs. Beecham was right. She was the only soul in the village who knew Frederica's history. The childless widow of a parson, she'd taken Frederica in when she was nothing but a homeless, pregnant woman fresh off the coach from London. She had comforted Frederica when her nightmares plagued her and nursed her through her confinement. It was out of respect to Mrs. Beecham that Mr. Campbell had given Frederica employment. Mrs. Beecham had come to fulfil the role of the mother she'd never known. The small stipend afforded to her by the church had dwindled to nothing, and both she and Frederica needed each other.

Georgia lay curled up in the armchair. Across the room, sat the silent footman. True to his word, he'd watched Frederica constantly while she packed her trunk. But it wasn't his presence that compelled her to do as Hawthorne bid. The agony in Hawthorne's eyes had clawed at her heart. She owed it to him to ease his pain and give him what he demanded, no matter how much he hated her.

"I can stay here, ye know," Mrs. Beecham said. *"He's* your family."

"I couldn't bear to leave you, Mrs. Beecham," Frederica said, "and Georgia loves you as much as I."

"Mr. Campbell would take me in. You know I'm not long for this world. You need to get to know him again, lass, and a sick old woman would only get in the way."

Frederica choked back the tears. "He hates me, Mrs. Beecham. It's Georgia he wants."

Thin, bony fingers interlocked with hers. "How many times have you told me of his kindness, his devotion to justice? Such a man could not harbor hatred forever."

Frederica sighed and looked at the trunk in which she'd packed her most precious possessions—her art materials, sketchbook, and Georgia's favorite dress and doll. Hawthorne would likely discard Georgia's things in favor of something more befitting an earl's daughter. But to Frederica, they were worth more than anything his money could buy. She had worked hard to afford them. She reached into her reticule and fingered the frayed piece of cloth inside, rubbing her fingertips along the fibers. His necktie had given her comfort over the years. His masculine scent had long since dispersed, but if she closed her eyes for long enough, the memory of it always softened her pain.

The main door rattled, and Hawthorne strode into the parlor, magnificent in a dark coat, cream breeches, and polished black boots. A top hat and cane under his arm, he looked every part the aristocrat, a world above Frederica.

He barked an order at the footman, who leapt to his feet and dragged the trunk outside, then he approached Georgia and gently woke her. The child rubbed the sleep from her eyes, and a smile brightened her face.

"Papa!"

He kissed her hand. "Come, little angel. Your new life awaits."

He carried Georgia outside, not bothering to check whether Frederica followed.

⟫⟫⟫⟪⟪⟪

THE CARRIAGE HAD only been moving for a few minutes when it stopped. Hawthorne climbed out and motioned to Frederica.

"Get out."

Georgia's eyes widened at his harsh tone.

"Papa?"

"Sweeting, stay here while your Mama and I conclude our business."

He pulled Frederica out of the carriage, and her stomach churned with fear.

"Are you to abandon me on the road?"

He said nothing, but tightened his grip, and pulled her toward the nearest building, the village church.

The creak of wood on metal echoed through the church as he pushed the door open. The afternoon light shone through the windows, leaving a trail of colors on the floor of the aisle. At the end stood the parson, accompanied by two men, Mr. Campbell and the village blacksmith.

She tried to break free, but his grip was too strong.

"Be still!" he hissed. "Do you want the witnesses to think you unwilling?"

"I can't marry you!"

243

"Are you already married?"

"No, but don't you have to secure a license?"

"We're in Scotland, my dear, where one has no need to wait."

"But…"

"Enough!" he said. "If we return to London unwed, society will call our daughter a bastard. Do you want that on your conscience?"

Her resolve crumbled. He knew he had her cornered. However, much she disliked the idea, she must put Georgia's needs first.

"Very well, I'll do as you ask."

She turned her gaze on him, but he kept his eyes forward, jaw firm.

"Please, Hawthorne. Can't we begin again?"

For a moment, the pain in her heart was reflected in his expression, then his eyes hardened.

"It's too late for that."

CHAPTER THIRTY-ONE

HAWTHORNE JOLTED AWAKE as the carriage hit a rut.

They were nearing London. Beside him, his daughter lay asleep, her hair fanned out over his lap. In the light of the setting sun, he could discern traces of red. Her features were delicate, with high cheekbones and a heart-shaped mouth. The image of her mother, except for her eyes.

He relaxed back and watched his wife. She sat opposite him, eyes closed, the old woman next to her. Though she had grown thin, her body hummed with resolve, as if years of hardship had strengthened her will to survive. His little changeling had undergone a transformation. Doubtless she'd resist him at every turn. But he had the one thing that would defeat her.

Her child.

How often had he wanted her at his mercy? But instead of triumph, he only felt regret.

The old woman let out a moan. Frederica opened her eyes, took the woman's hand, and spoke to her in a low voice. He held his breath while she knelt at the woman's feet and adjusted the blanket around her legs, the act of tender devotion touching his heart.

"Are you in pain, Mrs. Beecham?" he asked.

The woman nodded.

"Forgive me," Frederica said. "The laudanum ran out yesterday. When we reach London, I'll…" She glanced in Hawthorne's direction, then lowered her voice. "I'll ask permission to buy some. I've enough money to keep you comfortable until…"

"Until I'm gone?" the old woman said. "Dear, sweet child." She took Frederica's hand and sank back, her face twisted with pain.

The child stirred, and Frederica returned to her seat. Holding the old woman's hand, she stared out the window and kept still, as she had done all those years ago in an attempt to appear invisible.

As the journey wore on, she rubbed her wrists, the precursor to her nightmares. But each time the old woman whispered to her until she grew calm. Memories of her screams swirled in his mind along with another memory—her unconscious form abandoned on her father's doorsteps while he'd slunk away like a coward.

Had she told the old woman the part Hawthorne had played in her childhood nightmare?

The sound of the hooves changed to the familiar clatter over stones as they reached London's streets. Georgia woke, and he lifted her to a sitting position. Frederica grew quiet. By the time the carriage drew to a halt outside his townhouse, her knuckles were white as she gripped her companion's hand.

He fisted his own hand, fighting the instinct to protect her. The carriage door opened, and he climbed out, the child in his arms.

"Mama!" she said excitedly, "are you coming?"

Frederica followed him out.

The servants had lined up to greet their master. Though he'd sent word ahead, only the upper servants knew who he brought with him. Whispers rippled down the line until a sharp word from Giles silenced them. Several pairs of eyes focused on the child. They couldn't fail to recognize who she was; the likeness was unmistakable.

The woman behind him attracted more than mere curiosity. A bolt of shame threaded through him. His servants had witnessed his disintegration after his search for Frederica had proven fruitless. Many of them had tended to him while he'd lain ill from the effects of drink and afterward, when he'd fallen into the Thames amid rumors that he wanted to end his life.

Dark days and painful memories. He could withstand her company, but not his servants' pity.

Near the end of the line, a young woman leapt forward and took Frederica's hand. The compassion in her eyes threatened to melt his heart, but it was Frederica's soft cry which clutched at his soul.

"Oh, Miss! I was so worried about you!"

"Forgive me, Jenny," Frederica said, her voice thick with pain. "I never meant to harm anyone."

Giles cleared his throat, his meaning plain. The wife of an earl shouldn't be seen acting in such a familiar manner with her servants.

"Jenny, that's enough," the housekeeper snapped.

Frederica straightened and glared at her. Hawthorne recognized her act of defiance for what it was. His little changeling would always champion the cause of the disadvantaged, those with nobody to fight for them.

His conscience stirred, but his resolve crushed it. The servants needed to know her betrayal would not go unpunished. Handing his daughter to the governess Giles had hastily employed, he took Frederica's arm and hissed in her ear.

"You must show proper decorum now you're a countess."

She let him lead her into the house where he dropped his hand as if she burned him.

He nodded to the footman. "Harry, take the old woman to her chamber, then see my wife's belongings are unpacked."

"I want to go with Georgia," Frederica said. "Please."

His instincts yearned to grant her request, to ease the pain in her voice. But he must be strong. "Our daughter is tired. You may see her in the morning."

"But…"

"Enough!"

She flinched at the force of his voice.

"As my wife, you pledged to obey me. She is tired, and we must place her needs before our own."

Silently, she let him lead her toward his study. He stopped at the entrance to the room next door.

"You're at liberty to move around the house, with one exception. You are not permitted to enter this room."

"What is it?"

"It's where I conduct my business as a magistrate and preside over some of my cases."

"You think my presence would taint the course of justice?"

"Nobody in my household or in my employ is permitted to enter other than those directly involved in each case."

"Then I pray I never fall foul of the law," she said. "I would prefer not to find myself on the receiving end of your justice."

Ignoring the brief flare of rebellion, he led her into his study and gestured toward a chair. She sank into it, her body crumpling under fatigue.

"Before I permit you to take your rest, I feel it appropriate to clarify what I expect of you."

She lifted her gaze.

"The gossips have long since exhausted their tales of your flight, but you must nevertheless behave appropriately, both privately and publicly."

He'd expected her to react, but she remained still.

"Your behavior around men will come under particular scrutiny."

She straightened her back. "And your behavior around women?"

"You question my behavior when you've spent the past five years indulging in your own selfish desires?"

"You have no idea how I spent the past five years."

"Whose fault is that?" he asked.

Her eyes glistened with tears, and he fought the knot of anger unfurling in his gut. If he wasn't careful, he'd succumb to the need for her which he'd spent years battling. But he had a weapon to use against her.

"I trust you'll stay away from Roderick Markham."

The blade hit home, and she gave a low hiss and closed her eyes. He ignored the guilt in his need to hurt her as much as she'd hurt him.

"We may come across both him and the duchess on social occasions. I trust you'll behave as befits a countess and not…"

"…his bastard sister?"

Had he blinked, he would have missed the brief flash of fury in her eyes.

"I'm thinking of our daughter," he said. "In the eyes of the law, she's illegitimate because we were unmarried when she was born."

"Then why marry me at all?"

"It gives her some respectability, though not as much as she deserves."

He moved to sit beside her, then thought better of it. The invisible bond between them couldn't be severed, no matter how hard he'd tried. His body quivered with the need to be near her.

"I will not demand much of you," he said. "I presume you'll take responsibility for the old woman. I'll grant you a small stipend to care for her needs if she requires medicine.

Gratitude flickered in her eyes.

"You'll have no other duties," he said. "You only need present yourself in public as befits my wife when the occasion demands."

"I understand," she said, her voice cold. "May I be excused now?"

"Yes. Go."

She rose and turned away from him. After the door closed behind her, soft footsteps faded into the distance.

CHAPTER THIRTY-TWO

"I'M GLAD TO be doing this again for you, ma'am."

Nimble fingers set Frederica's hair in place, and Jenny placed a hand on her shoulder.

Since her return to London, she had never been lonelier. Georgia had a governess to occupy her, and Mrs. Beecham, her health failing, spent much of her time asleep.

It almost broke her to see the man she loved reduced to a cold shell. But he treated their daughter with love and reverence. Each time he looked at Georgia, it was as if he struggled to believe she existed. He'd lift her into his arms and call her his precious child while she squealed in delight.

With all the love he indulged on his daughter, there was none left for his wife.

Jenny helped her to stand and led her to the staircase where Hawthorne waited at the bottom.

He looked up, and his eyes widened. For a moment, she caught a glimpse of the kind of expression he'd once bestowed on her, then he blinked, and the frost returned. Her hopes of an ally at the ball tonight died as he led her into the carriage, then remained silent for the entire journey.

VOICES WHISPERED AROUND Frederica as she crossed the ballroom. She clung to Hawthorne's arm, drawing comfort from his presence, though he remained unresponsive.

Ladylike titters accompanied the harsh notes of the violinists tuning their instruments. Hawthorne's fingers tightened their grip on her as Ross Trelawney approached.

In the weeks since her return to London, she'd grown to like Mr. Trelawney. A faithful friend to Hawthorne which, in itself, recommended him, he was also the one person of Hawthorne's acquaintance who viewed her with compassion. During her five-year absence, he'd endured his own share of heartbreak. He'd married shortly after Frederica left, but lost his wife in childbirth a year later. Widowed with a young daughter, he'd told Frederica his history without a shred of bitterness.

"Countess, how delightful to see you." Mr. Trelawney proffered his arm. "Would you do me the pleasure of joining me on the dancefloor?"

"I don't intend to dance," she said.

"Let me persuade you otherwise, if your husband permits it."

Hawthorne, who relinquished his grip, bent his head as if to kiss her cheek, but whispered harshly in her ear. "Do not disgrace yourself tonight."

"I'll take care of her," Ross said, coldly.

Hawthorne shrugged and crossed the room where he was soon joined by a tall woman dressed in dark blue silk, her honey-blonde hair shimmering in the light of the chandelier.

"That's Lady Holmestead," Ross said. "She's not averse to a dalliance, but I have it on good authority she avoids married men."

He nodded toward a couple joining the line of dancers. Frederica recognized the man. Lord Ravenwell, now the Duke of Westbury, and his wife. The duchess looked out of place among the stone-faced ladies in the ballroom. Her natural smile was as outlandish as the curves of her body, emphasized by the cut of her gown. "Westbury's a case in point," Ross continued. "He was well acquainted with Lady Holmestead, but as soon as he married, she turned her eyes elsewhere. Of course, nobody watching them could question whether Westbury loves his wife."

"Are you making idle conversation, Mr. Trelawney?" she asked. "Or do you seek to assure me of my husband's fidelity?"

His expression grew serious as he watched Hawthorne cross the floor.

"Forgive me, Countess," he said. "Let us discuss something more pleasant. Is your painting complete yet?"

"Almost. There's some finishing touches to make to the foreground."

"I must call on you tomorrow to encourage its completion," he said. "Amelia is anxious to see Georgia again. I can't say how grateful I am to you for permitting my daughter to play with Georgia. Amelia needs companions her own age."

"And I'm grateful for Georgia's sake," Frederica said. "For too long she's had only myself and Mrs. Beecham for company..." She broke off, a needle of guilt stabbing at her.

Ross gave her hand a gentle squeeze. She may have been the cause for her daughter's isolation, but Ross was too kind to mention it.

A group of ladies nearby let out a laugh, their eyes on her.

"Pay no attention to them," Ross said.

"Is my husband the laughing stock of society?"

"You ask for him, but not for yourself?"

"I brought about my situation."

"I'm sure you had good reason," he said, "and it's time my friend honored you as you deserve."

"Please..." She tried to release herself from his hold, but he only held her more firmly.

"It must be said, Frederica. Someone must teach Hawthorne the folly of his ways."

"You're in no position to judge."

"Am I not?" he asked. "A man should savor every waking moment he has with the woman he loves. He never knows whether it will be the last."

The woman he loves...

How could Ross be so mistaken? Every time she looked into Hawthorne's eyes, she saw the expression of a man no longer capable of any feeling toward her but the bitterest hatred.

Yet, still she loved him.

She wrenched herself free. "Forgive me, Mr. Trelawney. I cannot..."

"Frederica?"

"Leave me be!"

She crossed the dancefloor toward the balcony doors and slipped outside, only then succumbing to despair. Hawthorne would never forgive her. Tonight had not been about introducing her into society; it was about Hawthorne publicly affirming his contempt of her.

Had she hurt him that badly?

Music filtered through the doors, punctuated by an owl hooting. A dark shape circled the garden. Images of wings beating at her swirled in her mind, and she shut her eyes against the night.

"My dear, are you all right?"

A woman stood before her, head to one side as if scrutinizing her. At such close quarter, the bright orange color of her gown looked even more outlandish.

"Leave me alone," Frederica said. "I've endured enough for one night."

"Which is why I'm asking." The woman held out her hand. "You're Countess Stiles, aren't you?"

"And you're the Duchess of Westbury," Frederica retorted. "I detest titles."

The woman laughed. "So do I, which makes us both contradictions, considering we both married titles." She lowered her hand. "Please, call me Jeanette. Your reputation precedes you."

"My reputation?" Frederica asked.

"As an artist, which is the only reputation I'm interested in." She folded her arms. "Ladies who indulge in gossip can go to the devil."

"Should you say such things?"

"If a woman seeks gratification from venting her spite at others, she must accept the consequences. I prefer to evaluate each case on its own merit. I've heard much of your skill as an artist."

"You flatter me."

Jeanette laughed. "If you knew me, you'd realize I have no talent for flattery. My husband often admonishes me for my directness. I had the pleasure of seeing one of your paintings in Mr. Trelawney's morning room. I found it a refreshing change from the bland efforts of society ladies who deem painting a mere accomplishment. A work, whether portrayed by the medium of paint or music, only has value if it speaks to the observer."

"And what did my painting say to you?"

"It spoke of pain and loss." The duchess turned her gaze on Frederica. Her eyes were a similar shade of green to Frederica's own but deeper and punctuated by gold flecks. They were the eyes of a woman who'd known pain herself. "It also spoke of redemption," she continued. "The longer I looked at it, the more detail I could see, glimmers of hope dotted about the landscape."

"Do you paint?"

Jeanette laughed. "I have a singular lack of talent for it. But that doesn't mean I can't appreciate talent in others. I've tried in vain to draw a likeness of my youngest son."

She paused as if in thought, then a broad smile crossed her face.

"Would you be so kind as to draw his likeness? My husband is indulgent enough to praise my efforts, but my son possesses the delectable honesty of a child and is my severest critic. I believe he's a similar age to your daughter. You could bring her with you when you come."

"I don't know…"

"Please say yes. I'm sure your daughter would enjoy making a new friend." She took Frederica's hand. "Perhaps you might appreciate a friend also. London might be full of people, but it's the loneliest place in the world. I would very much like to further our acquaintance."

Frederica shook her head. "If you knew my history."

"I know a great deal," Jeanette said. "As I said before, I value only that which deserves to be valued."

Unable to speak, Frederica wiped her eyes.

"That's settled, then," Jeanette said brightly.

The door opened, and a tall figure stepped into the moonlight. Cold eyes focused on Frederica before he turned to Jeanette.

"My love, I've been looking for you. The next dance is about to start, and Oakville's waiting inside to partner you."

"Henry, I…"

"Now, Jeanette."

"Oh, very well." Jeanette dipped a curtsey to Frederica and slipped back inside.

Before Frederica could follow, a hand circled her arm.

"A word if you please, *Countess*."

"What do you want?" she asked.

"Stay away from my wife."

"Is she not permitted to choose who she acquaints herself with?"

"On certain matters, I believe my perception is clearer than hers."

"Is a countess not an acceptable acquaintance for your wife?"

"Don't take me for a fool, madam," he said. "I know what you did to your husband. You betrayed him after he'd already damaged his reputation by offering you marriage."

"That's no concern of yours."

"No concern?" he said, gritting his teeth. "You weren't there when he almost destroyed himself. While you were indulging in lord knows what, he was ripping London apart trying to find you. You didn't have to watch him descend into madness. You weren't there to pick him up every time he was found unconscious on the floor, stinking of whisky. You weren't there when he threw himself into the Thames to end it all."

Her blood turned to ice, knives of pain slicing through her as if she had been the one in the water.

"Dear God," she whispered. "Did you not seek help?"

"Foolish woman!" he scoffed. "Do you know what they would have done to him? He'd lost his wits. They would have confined him to Bedlam. Don't you know how society treats those it does not understand?"

"Yes, I do," she said quietly.

"You know nothing!" he spat. "Play the dutiful wife, and leave *my* wife alone."

Guilt gnawed at her. To think she'd fled to save him, to give him the future he wanted. But instead, her flight had almost destroyed him.

"I must thank you, sir," she said.

"What for?"

"For taking care of him. For saving his life."

"I didn't do it for you," he said coldly. "I did it for him."

"I know," she said. "It may be worth nothing to you, but you'll always have my gratitude, respect, and admiration."

He said nothing but gave her a curt nod and returned inside.

The music struck up once more as the next dance began. But nothing could compel her to return inside where everyone would be laughing at her. As for Hawthorne, how could she face him, finally knowing what her abandonment had done to him?

The door opened again.

"Leave me alone!" she cried.

"I beg your pardon?" A rotund man stepped onto the balcony. "I'm here for some air, that's all. It's Countess Stiles, is it not?"

"Yes."

"I thought so. I'd heard much of your beauty. Your husband's a damn lucky man."

He clicked his boots together and bowed. "Viscount De Blanchard, at your service." He held out his hand, and she took it. He grinned at her, showing a row of large, uneven teeth.

"I should return inside," she said. "My husband will wonder where I am.

"What, the moment I've introduced myself?" he said with mock hurt. "You impugn my gallantry. I've been anxious to make your acquaintance, and I believe I can do so more easily without your husband's presence."

He took her shoulder and pulled her close. A wave of panic rose within her, and she pushed him back.

"I like spirit in a woman." He brought his mouth close to hers, and she twisted her face away.

"Get off me!"

"Come, come," he said. "You think I don't know your reputation? All of London knows it! Why else would you be servicing the guests on the balcony?"

"That's not true!"

"What's Westbury got that I haven't?" he asked. "I was bedding fillies while he was still in the schoolroom. Why shouldn't I sample what's been handed out to so many?"

A large fleshy hand grasped the front of her gown, and she pushed him away.

"Leave me be!"

"What the devil's going on?" a voice roared.

Hawthorne stood in the doorway, shaking with fury. Behind him, Mr. Trelawney's concerned face came into view.

De Blanchard composed himself and spoke amiably. "Isn't it obvious, old chap? Your wife's been offering her services, and I joined the queue."

"The queue?"

"You're to be commended on your generosity in sharing her."

"Is this true, Frederica?" Hawthorne asked.

Bitter shame and hurt stabbed at her insides, but she would not give him the satisfaction of an answer.

He raised his eyebrows. "Well?"

She shook her head. "Why waste my effort denying what you already believe to be true?"

A smile of triumph crossed De Blanchard's face. "You must forgive a man for succumbing to temptation when it's so prettily placed before him."

"And I suppose you wish to continue?" Hawthorne asked.

"That's enough!" Ross cried. "De Blanchard, get back inside before I kick your arse across the floor. Hawthorne, take your wife home. Can't you see she's distressed?"

A flicker of guilt crossed Hawthorne's eyes, then it passed.

He took her arm and led her back inside the ballroom. Several pairs of eyes followed them as they crossed the room. The chatter increased, forming a cloud of contempt which swirled inside Frederica's head. It swirled around her mind during the carriage ride home, only ceasing when Hawthorne pushed her through the front door.

"Go to your chamber," he said. "I'll deal with you in the morning."

"Hawthorne, please…"

"Please what?" he asked. "Is that why you abandoned me? Was I not enough for you?"

"You were everything to me!" she cried. "There was never anyone else but you."

"What about Markham?"

She drew a hand back to strike him, but he caught her wrist and pulled her against him, his body hard and ready.

"How dare you speak of him!" she screamed. "I hate him! But you, you I love! I only ever wanted one man my whole life, and that was you. I'll never want or love another man again!"

"Oh, I wish to God it were true!" His mouth crashed against hers, and he groaned with need.

Years of yearning drove her forward, and she opened her mouth to invite him in. Their tongues met and clashed in a battle of desire. He moved his body against hers, and she shifted her legs to accommodate him. Desire flared in her center, threading heat throughout her body.

Eager, desperate hands clawed at her gown, and she pressed herself against him, offering her body. He dipped his hand into her bodice, and her nipples beaded to painful little points. Material tore against her skin, and the rush of cold air was met with a blistering heat as hot, hungry lips covered her breast. His whole body rumbled with need, a deep growl vibrating in his chest as he devoured her. He grazed her nipple with his teeth, and she arched her back at the sharp sting. He pushed her back, and their bodies crashed against the morning room door. It flew open, and they fell onto the floor.

Hands tore at the hem of her gown, lifting it to expose her thighs, and he teased her legs apart.

"God forgive me, you're as beautiful as I remember," he said, his voice hoarse. "You're mine. This body is mine. Too long have I been denied it."

He ran his fingertip along her leg, stopping where her thighs met, and his lips twitched in a smile.

"I can smell your need, little changeling," he said. He ran his finger along her center in a smooth motion, and her body pulsed in response. He lowered his head and kissed her curls.

She thrust her hips toward him, chasing the nugget of pleasure, and he lifted his head and withdrew. The wave receded, and she whimpered in frustration, and he smiled. He knew her body better than she knew it herself. He dipped his head again. Skilled in delivering a firm hand, he played with her body, drawing her to the brink of pleasure until his own vibrated with the effort to maintain control.

He finally plunged himself into her, and her body shattered. She screamed his name, lifting her hips to meet each hard thrust. His mouth claimed her cries, thrusting his tongue in to mirror the movement of their bodies. His movements grew more frenzied until she felt the familiar sensation of his body rippling inside her. He lifted his head and roared out her name, crying out the words she had yearned to hear, that he loved her and would never let her go again.

With a final thrust, he collapsed on top of her and lay still, utterly spent, his heart hammering against her chest, hot, salty tears spilling onto her face.

He shifted, and she clung to him. For five long years she had longed to feel his weight on top of her once more, to feel loved, claimed, and completely owned by him.

"Please, Hawthorne, stay inside me."

He nodded, and she buried her hands in his hair, relishing the softness.

"Forgive me, my love," she whispered.

His breathing grew steady, and a single whispered word crawled inside her head.

"Always."

CHAPTER THIRTY-THREE

As the fog of bliss dissipated, Hawthorne clung to the soft, welcoming body beneath him, as if he'd finally come home after years of wandering in a barren wasteland.

"My little changeling…"

She lay still, her chest rising and falling softly. Her skin was pale except for her breasts, which were flushed a delicate shade of rose. His mouth watered at the sight of the dark nipples he'd devoured earlier.

A twitch of guilt rippled through him. In his desperate need for her, he had lost control, yet she'd welcomed it. Since he'd brought her home, she had accepted his boorish behavior with fortitude. Not once had she said a word against him, not even when he'd overheard Georgia complaining in the midst of a childish tantrum that Papa had no right to tell her what to do. Frederica had merely taken the child into her arms and said he was the kindest man she knew, and the best way to honor him was do as he wished.

Did she deceive him? Perhaps, now she looked at peace, she might reveal her true form. But the closer he looked at her, all he could see was innocence and purity.

She stirred, her body splayed before him as if in offering.

How many others had she offered herself to?

The words she'd written the night she abandoned him still burned in his mind.

I have only ever wanted one man, and nothing you say or do will change my mind. If I cannot be with him, I would rather be alone.

She opened her eyes. Their intensity struck him like a thunderbolt, and his chest tightened at the love in their expression. He looked away, closing his eyes to bring forth the memory of the pain she'd caused him, the nights where he'd lain alone, not knowing whether she lived or died, exhausted from searching for her.

She reached out, and he jerked back. Her eyes narrowed as he stood and pulled his breeches on. The sparkle in her eyes died.

"Hawthorne…"

"It's late," he interrupted. "You should go to your chamber." He turned his back on her and left the room, but not before he heard her soft voice.

"I'm sorry."

Giles waited in the hall, a sliver of anger in his expression. Hawthorne gestured toward the morning room.

"Send Jenny to tend to the countess."

"Very good, sir." The butler's usual flat tone displayed an undercurrent of disapproval. "And for yourself?"

"I want a brandy."

"I'll bring it to your study, sir."

Giles bowed and disappeared. A small voice whispered in Hawthorne's ear; his conscience reminding him that a man should be given what he needs, not what he wants. And what he needed was the woman he had left alone in the morning room.

As HAWTHORNE ENTERED the breakfast room the following morning, he heard bright voices.

Frederica sat at one end of the table, Georgia on one side, the old woman on the other. The child ate her breakfast with gusto, chatting animatedly, and he smiled to himself. She was a bright little thing. All fathers most likely said the same of their children, but even her governess remarked on how the little girl devoured her lessons. Yet another thing her mother had deprived her of in that hovel.

But Frederica's love for Georgia was obvious in the way she tended to her. Small gestures barely noticeable, but to his eye, spoke more than words, tucking a stray hair behind the child's ear or a gentle hand on her arm as she reached for the eggs.

Her love for the old woman was just as obvious, though of a different kind. Doctor McIver had already told Hawthorne Mrs. Beecham didn't have long. The laudanum kept her pain at bay, but her condition would only deteriorate.

Frederica never spoke of it, but occasionally when she turned her gaze on the old woman, a deep sadness darkened her eyes.

Georgia made a remark, and the women laughed. For a moment, Frederica's face lit up with joy. How many years had he longed to see her smile?

He scraped back his chair, and the laughter stopped. Three pairs of eyes looked up, one joyous, another suspicious, the third fearful.

"The child is late for her lessons."

"But Hawthorne, she has yet to finish…"

"Miss Jones is waiting, Frederica. I pay good money for my daughter's education. If she's to be taught any form of moral compass, she must learn punctuality."

"Moral compass?" Rebellion flared in her eyes and she stood, taking Georgia's hand.

"Of course," he said. "The child not only needs an education to stimulate her intellect, but her lack of moral education must be redressed."

Frederica opened her mouth as if to speak, but after glancing at the child, she closed it, then left the room, taking the child with her.

He settled into his seat and waved Giles over. The old woman remained at the table, her black eyes focused on him as if she were issuing a curse. Perhaps Frederica had insisted she bring her to London because she wanted a witch for company.

He set his fork down.

"What do you want, old woman?"

"How long do you intend to torment that child?"

"I'm giving my daughter the life she was denied," he said. "In what way is that a torment?"

"I meant your wife," she said. "You dote on the child, but you treat Frederica with contempt. I thought you better than that."

"You don't know me at all."

"Don't I?"

"I don't know what my wife has told you, but she abandoned me the night before our wedding, in front of a houseful of guests. She denied my child her birthright. My daughter was born a bastard, into poverty and obscurity."

"I know what your wife did," the old woman said, "and she suffered for it! She turned up on my doorstep, penniless, lost, and alone. I took her in. She never told me her full history, but I could see she'd been mistreated by the men in her life. For five years she has toiled to secure her independence, so she would never have to rely on a man again. She's worked hard to give Georgia the best in life."

"The best in life?" Hawthorne slapped his hand on the table and the china rattled. "How can you say that? I have lifted my daughter out of poverty and given her everything she wants!"

"You can give her everything she wants, but Frederica has given everything she had to that child. She almost gave her life."

"What do you mean?"

"She nearly died in childbirth. The baby had not turned, and I had no money for a doctor. Even after she was delivered safely, I thought she wouldn't survive, she lost so much blood. But do you know what kept her resolve?"

She paused, eyes narrowing as if reliving the moment. Hawthorne's throat turned dry, and his chest tightened at the thought of her dying in childbirth, lost and alone.

"A single name," the old woman continued. "That's what kept her alive. May God forgive me for betraying her confidence, but you deserve to know. During her confinement, she uttered that name over and over until the moment the child left her body. When she thought death awaited her, she prayed for forgiveness, pleading that the one person she loved more than her own life would find happiness."

She sat back, as if the effort of speaking had drained her. The room fell silent, save for the ticking of the clock over the fireplace.

He pushed his plate away, his appetite gone.

"What was the name?"

She gave him a look of contempt and shook her head.

"Mrs. Beecham, please."

Her anger seemed to dissipate at his quiet plea, and she spoke more softly. "Think what you want of her, but she's never said a word against you. She used to say that, save her father, you were the best man to walk upon the earth. If you knew her at all, you'd have no need to ask whose name she cried when she was near death, no need to ask who she longed to see again, who she has never stopped thinking of."

"Tell me," he whispered.

"Hawthorne," she said. "The name she kept crying was Hawthorne."

She struggled to her feet and shuffled out of the room, leaving him alone with his conscience.

CHAPTER THIRTY-FOUR

GEORGIA CLUTCHED FREDERICA'S hand as they descended the stairs. Her daughter might have blossomed in London, but she still lacked the confidence expected of a child of her rank. Miss Jones had spoken of the remarks some of the other children had thrown in her direction while out walking. Only yesterday, Georgia had returned from Hyde Park with her governess, quiet and subdued, and asked Frederica if she knew what a bastard was.

But Georgia had a good friend in Amelia Trelawney.

And Frederica had a friend in Amelia's father.

She pushed open the parlor door. Ross leapt to his feet, and Amelia ran toward Georgia, squealing with excitement.

"Can I play in the park with Georgia, Papa?"

Georgia's smile disappeared, and Frederica took Amelia's hand. "Why don't you explore the gardens here? You can pick some flowers for your papa."

"Oh, yes!" Amelia said. "May we be excused?"

"Of course," Frederica said. "Georgia, take Amelia to the kitchens. Mrs. Miller is making your favorite shortbread."

The two girls skipped out of the room.

"Shall I ring for tea, Mr. Trelawney?"

"Later, perhaps," Ross said.

"I can ask Hawthorne to join us. He's in his study, and I'm sure he'd wish to see you."

"No," he said. "It's you I came to see. I'm concerned for your welfare."

"I'm quite well."

"But are you happy? Let me be frank. We're friends, are we not? Since you returned to London with Georgia, Amelia has come out of her shell. And your company has helped me, also."

"I can't see how."

"You understand, as most women don't, that there's more to life than society. They see you as inferior, but they're wrong. You're so far above them, they are not even fit to tread the ground you walk on." He took her hand. "That's why I must speak the truth. My friend acts like a cad toward you."

She snatched her hand away. "Mr. Trelawney..."

"Can you not call me Ross?"

She shook her head. "I won't use such familiarity with you. Neither will I let you disrespect my husband. You know what I did to him. You were there when I left."

"So, you'd let him continue to punish you for it? How many years will you endure it? Ten? Twenty? The rest of your life?"

His words ripped her open and exposed her deepest need—the need to be loved. But she had long ago sealed her fate by destroying the man she loved.

"I'm sorry." She shook her head. "My priority is my daughter's happiness."

"What about yours?"

"Georgia makes me happy," she said. "I treasure each day with her, the day she learned to walk, her first word, her first tooth. If she's happy, then so am I."

Admiration shone in his eyes.

"Frederica, don't you know I long for your happiness?"

"No," she said. "Don't say something you'll regret later."

"I can't keep it to myself anymore."

"Please, no!"

"I love you, Frederica. Don't you know, I love you?"

⟫⟫⟩✕⟨⟨⟨

HAWTHORNE'S BLOOD FROZE at his friend's words, and his fingers curled around the door handle.

Giles gave a nervous cough. Curse that bloody butler! Always appearing where he wasn't wanted.

She let out a cry. "Why could you not have left it unsaid?"

"Because you deserve to be loved!"

Treacherous bastard! While Ross had comforted Hawthorne on the return of his wayward wife, he'd been seducing her behind his back.

Ross spoke again. "Why do you endure his treatment of you, Frederica?"

Frederica, indeed! How dare he!

"Please, Mr. Trelawney," she said, "you must go."

"Not until you answer me!" Ross cried. "I've seen it with my own eyes."

"Stop it!" she cried.

"Why?" he roared. "I saw de Blanchard with his hands all over you, and so did Hawthorne. But he accused you of seducing the man! Ye gods, he almost offered you to him! Do you value yourself so little?"

A sharp intake of breath made Hawthorne look round. Giles stood behind him, disgust lining his features.

"Why?" Ross's voice reverberated through the door. "Why subject yourself to such treatment?"

"Because I love him!" she screamed. "I know he'll never forgive me for leaving, but I did it for him. Everything I do is for him!"

She gave a cry, and Hawthorne heard a scuffle and splintering china. He pushed through the door to find his wife struggling in Ross's arms, a broken vase at their feet.

"Get your hands off her!" He leapt forward, curled his hand into a fist, and smashed it into his friend's face. Ross released his grip on Frederica and fell back.

"On your feet, and fight me like a man!" Hawthorne roared.

"No!" Frederica pushed him back. "Let him go."

"Get out of my way, woman," he snarled.

"Will you strike me as well?" she asked. "Go ahead. It's nothing compared to what you've already done." She opened her arms as if in offering. "In fact, I'd welcome it."

His anger left him. *Dear God*, did she think he'd hit her?

"Mr. Trelawney is misguided," she said. "Let him go, and I'll have nothing more to do with him."

Hawthorne nudged Ross with his foot.

"Get up," he said. "Be thankful my wife pleads your case."

Ross stood and wiped his nose. He held his hand out to Frederica, but she refused it with a shake of her head.

"Just go," she said. Her voice was cold, but Hawthorne knew her too well. Her body vibrated with distress.

"Giles," Ross said, "be so good as to find my daughter. I'll wait in the hall." The butler nodded, and the two men left.

Frederica remained, her body trembling, as if holding a storm at bay. Hawthorne moved toward her.

"Are you all right?"

She lifted her gaze to him, her eyes red-rimmed.

"Frederica, what can I do?"

"Nothing," she said coldly. "There's nothing you can do which will hurt me any more than you have already."

She picked up the pieces of the smashed vase. She gasped, and a droplet of blood appeared on her hand.

"Here." He held his hand out. "Let me take care of that."

"No!" She pushed him away. "You've done enough. You have

exposed me to the derision of the world. Good men like Mr. Trelawney see me as a creature to be pitied. Others, such as de Blanchard, think I'm easy prey. With none to protect me, I must fight for myself. Even if that means fighting you, Hawthorne."

Guilt burned his insides. He'd wanted her to suffer as he had suffered. To teach her a lesson. But that didn't make him a man in search of justice.

It made him a monster.

She was his wife to love, honor, and keep. Yet, he'd been neither loving nor honorable. He'd used their child as a weapon to cow her. She had every right to hate him, but she could never hate him as much as he hated himself. To hear Ross' words, his friend's declaration of all of Hawthorne's sins against her laid bare…

The look of disgust in the butler's face as he heard every word, paled into nothing compared to Hawthorne's own self-loathing.

He reached toward her, but she blocked him with her hand.

"Leave me alone."

Her footsteps disappeared up the stairs, but before Hawthorne could follow her, Giles placed himself in his path.

"Let her go, sir," he said. "I'll send Jenny up with a brandy later."

Giles was right. The least Hawthorne could do was give her some space.

CHAPTER THIRTY-FIVE

FREDERICA DIPPED HER brush in the water. The paint dissolved, turning the liquid a soft shade of peach to match the color of Georgia's skin.

"You can move now, angel."

Frederica had learned to capture her daughter with quick sketches, but there was nothing more fulfilling than the deep observation from painting a portrait.

The child stretched and reached for her doll. Hawthorne had bought her all manner of dolls, each one more elaborately attired than the last, and Frederica encouraged her to play with them in his presence. But when the two of them were alone, Georgia always reached for her old doll, which Frederica had bought with the proceeds from the sale of her first painting. The material was a base cotton compared to the fine silks of her other dolls, frayed around the edges and faded through years of washing. But Georgia loved it just the same.

Georgia chatted to her doll while Frederica cleaned her brushes and tidied up her sketches. She opened her paint box, and a piece of cloth fell out. She picked it up and brought it to her lips, inhaling to savor the faint scent. Hawthorne's discarded necktie. Her daughter would, one day, find a husband and home of her own, and would have no more need of her. But this small, inanimate piece of cloth would stay with her forever.

She folded the necktie, placed it in the box, and shut the lid.

"Papa!"

She jumped at Georgia's excited squeal, her heart racing with anticipation. Hawthorne liked to spend time with their daughter late in the day, before Miss Jones readied her for bed. He rarely ventured into the parlor this early, when he knew she'd be there.

"Mama has been painting me!"

Frederica stood and reached for her sketchbook.

"Don't leave on my account."

A hand rested on her shoulder. "May I see?"

"Of course."

He moved beside her and ran his finger along the edge of the painting. "You've captured her likeness well."

"Thank you."

She remained still, waiting for him to leave or to tell her to move. But he did neither. His shadow stretched across the table, silent and unmoving. At length, he traced the rest of the outline of the painting, then took her hand.

Her body jolted at his touch, her skin pricking with the sensation. She swallowed and remained still, tensing.

"Shh." His whisper touched her like a soft caress, and he turned her hand over and ran a fingertip across her palm, over the callouses she'd gained through years of hard work. He sighed, then traced a path across her palm and stopped at her wrist where the scars from her childhood had faded, but would never disappear.

"Papa, what are you doing?"

She snatched her hand away.

"Did you see the marks on Mama's wrists?" Georgia asked.

"Yes," he said quietly. "Do you know how she came by them?"

"She told me she played a silly game and cut herself."

His gaze focused on Frederica. "Is that so?"

"I thought it a good lesson for Georgia," Frederica said, "on the folly of childish games."

He reached for her sketchbook. "Is this the sketchbook you had as a child?"

"The very same."

"May I look inside?"

"Papa!" Georgia laughed. "You need no permission!"

"I rather think I do."

He flicked through the pages, leafing through sketch after sketch of studies of hands and poorly-executed likenesses. Further into the book, her accomplishment began to flourish. He paused at a drawing of Papa, then continued through the book until he reached another sketch. The edges of the paper were frayed, so often had she looked upon it. He ran a fingertip across his likeness before moving on. Sketches of a baby came next, each one depicting Georgia's development into the child she was now. He gave a gasp in acknowledgement of the memories he'd missed.

The next few sketches were of Mrs. Beecham, followed by blank pages, until he reached the final sketch on the last page of the book. He ran his thumb over the date.

November 1815.

She had drawn it from memory a year after she'd left London.

His features had matured from her earlier sketch, but the likeness was still there. The eyes looking out from the page were filled with warmth. The mouth, upturned in a smile, drew the observer in. It was the face of a man the world could trust. The face of a good man, a man in love.

"It's you, Papa!" Georgia cried.

"Aye," he said, "but it's been drawn with too sympathetic a hand."

He closed the sketchbook. "I always believed artwork said more about the artist than the subject."

"Perhaps Mama will give it to you."

"No, little one," he said, smiling. "I think your Mama should keep it." He lifted Georgia up and kissed her on the forehead.

"Be a good girl for your Papa and run along," he said. "Miss Jones awaits you in the schoolroom."

The child kissed him back and ran to embrace Frederica before leaving the room. Frederica rose from her seat.

"If you'll excuse me…"

"No."

She froze at his soft command.

"Will you stay and take tea with me?"

"Very well." She moved to ring the bell, but he caught her hand. "I took the liberty of asking Harry to bring us some."

As if he'd been eavesdropping, the footman appeared, brandishing a tray. As soon as he left, Hawthorne poured a cup and handed it to her.

"I can't make fine speeches, Frederica," he said. "I never could, not in relation to myself. But I find I miss your company."

A spark of hope flared within her.

"I don't see why we can't be civil to each other. For Georgia's sake."

"For Georgia?"

He sighed and sipped his tea. "No matter what I do, she'll always be seen as a bastard."

She flinched at the hateful word. "How can you say such a wicked thing?"

"It's true, nonetheless," he said. "Whoever her father may be, the law will never view her as legally mine, because she was born out of wedlock."

A flare of anger ignited in her at his veiled insult. "Whoever her father may be?" she cried. "Surely you don't think…"

"What was I supposed to think, Frederica? You abandoned me the night before our wedding, straight into the arms of Markham!"

"I did not!" she cried. "I hated him. I still do!"

"So, where did you go?"

She closed her eyes, reliving the memory, the hot, thick summer air, the blisters on her feet from running, the greed in the pawnbroker's eyes as his fingers curled around the sapphires. And the inn—the drunken laughter, the stench of horse manure, and the dingy little room where she'd hidden to wait for the coach.

"I took the first coach to Falkirk."

He leaned forward and his demeanor changed into that of the magistrate facilitating a cross-examination. As countless witnesses must have done before him when trying to prove their innocence, she straightened and met his gaze unflinchingly.

"I pawned the necklace, then waited at the Saracen's Head for the Falkirk coach."

"Which pawnbroker?"

She fisted her hands. "Am I on trial? Shall we continue our discussion in your courtroom?"

"Of course not," he said, "but you owe it to my mother's memory to tell me the truth about her necklace."

"What about my father's memory?" she challenged. "Did he deserve to be forever known as a murderer, vilified in death and buried in an obscure little graveyard in London, away from his true home, lest his reputation taint the Hampshire air?"

A flicker of guilt crossed his expression, then he looked away and sighed.

"It was a Mr. Wilson, on Drury Lane," she said.

"Thank you," he replied. "Why did you go to Falkirk?"

"Papa took that coach when he conducted business in Scotland. And it seemed like the best place to go, as far away as possible from…"

"From me?"

"From *him*," she said. "But I was never free, was I?"

"You were free, Frederica," he said, "free to marry me or leave me. You chose the latter. I would have protected you from him. I *wanted* to protect you."

"You wanted to own me," she said. "We live in a world where a woman is considered her husband's property. If she defends herself, he can correct her with a stick. If she seeks freedom, she's branded a harlot because a woman's reasons for flight must always be due to her desire to leap into the arms of the next man. Yet her husband is at liberty to offer her to others with no damage to his reputation. How do you rate *your* choices, Hawthorne? Will you take me on the morning room floor, or will you whore me out to your friends?"

He flinched and shook his head.

"I'm sorry for being so cruel," he said. "I wanted to hurt you, to make you feel some of the pain I endured. But it was wrong of me. In future, in public I shall treat you as befits my wife."

He took her hand, and a shock of recognition rippled through her at his touch, igniting hope and desire.

"We must bury the past," he said. "I wish to focus on the future—my work and my daughter. As her mother, I want you to be part of that. From now on, I promise to protect you as a husband ought. I feel nothing but shame for taking you the night we returned from the ball."

She curled her fingers round his. "Hawthorne, that night was…"

"It was a mistake," he interrupted. "I lost control, but I assure you, I'll not do so again. And from now on, I will protect you from the attentions of others."

His next words crushed her hope.

"I promise, that while I have breath in my body, Frederica, no man—I or any other—shall touch you again."

CHAPTER THIRTY-SIX

HAWTHORNE HELPED HIS wife out of the barouche and almost missed her quiet word of thanks.

Summer was coming to an end, and the trees in the park had entered into that brief phase of brilliant color before shedding their leaves. It had always been Frederica's favorite time of year, her artist eyes able to capture the reds and golds which dressed the landscape.

Georgia ran ahead with her governess. A bird flew out of a nearby bush, and Frederica shrank back. Hawthorne held out his arm, and she took it, giving him a lifeless smile.

"I wonder if you might indulge me with a painting, my dear," he said. "I recall your skill at capturing the colors at this time of year."

"Thank you." Though polite, her tone was flat.

But bland civility was all he'd offered her. How could he expect more from her? They continued along the path, their stiff, overly-polite bodies in sharp contrast to Georgia's excited movements and animated voice. The rays of the morning sun picked out the shades of red in her hair. It was as if he saw his little changeling darting through the woods once more.

More visitors appeared as the morning wore on, mostly couples taking an early stroll, but the occasional, solitary man, perhaps making his way home after a tryst with his mistress. The Serpentine ran parallel to the path, and a pair of swans glided along the water, seemingly effortless. Hawthorne knew beneath the water's edge they propelled themselves forward with a frenzy as if, like Hawthorne, they understood the need for a calm exterior to conceal the turmoil within.

As they rounded a corner, he spotted another couple walking toward them. Frederica tightened her grip on his arm.

"Georgia," she called. "Go and look at the swans."

"But Miss Jones wants to show me her favorite part of the park."

"Do as you're told!" Frederica snapped. "Miss Jones, take her to the water *now*."

A passing gentleman stopped and stared at her.

Hawthorne bent his head and hissed in her ear. "Hush! Do you want all of society to hear you speak so?"

She said nothing but stared straight ahead at the approaching couple.

"I say, it's Stiles! What an extraordinary pleasure to see you out and about, and with your wife, no less! At least I presume she's your wife? It's so difficult to tell when all manner of *females* can be seen on a gentleman's arm."

Roderick Markham still bore the countenance of an angel. In contrast, the woman on his arm bore a gray, lifeless complexion. Her dress seemed to hang on her body. She'd always been a thin, but today, she looked on the brink of disappearing altogether. Her gaze flicked between her surroundings and her husband, as if she needed to continually verify his approval.

Miss Jones looked up, and her gaze lingered on Markham, before she resumed her attention on her charge.

"What a delectable little child!" Markham said.

"Don't look at her," Frederica snarled.

Markham chuckled. "Your daughter, I presume. Of course, the question on everybody's lips is the identity of her father."

"How dare you…" Frederica said, but Hawthorne interrupted her.

"That's enough. Markham. Retract that slur, or I'll hold you to account for it."

Markham fisted his hands, and Alice winced.

"You have my apologies, Stiles," he said. "You're not to blame for your wife's indiscretions. She told me she wrote you such a pretty note to say goodbye before she jilted you. I suppose I should be affronted that she did not go to the trouble of doing the same for me when she sold herself to the next man, but whores are plentiful in London, are they not?"

Alice showed little reaction to her husband's words. Markham's infidelity was well known, but it was another thing entirely to boast of it in front of his wife.

"I didn't leave with you," Frederica said.

"A flat denial is what I expect from a doxy," Markham said. "What tales did she weave to entice you back, Stiles? Did she use the brat or merely her body?"

Hawthorne suppressed the urge to obliterate Markham's grin with his fist. "I have no intention of relating our history to you."

Markham let out a laugh. "Perhaps my little bird has picked up a few tricks in addition to the skills I taught her."

"Stop there, Markham," Hawthorne barked, "unless you wish me to call you out."

"I used every inch of her body," Markham said with relish. "And she let me do anything I wished to heighten my pleasure."

Hawthorne caught a blur of movement at his side, then, with a scream of rage, Frederica smashed her fist into Markham's jaw. Markham staggered back with a groan.

"Roderick!" Alice clung to his arm, and he shook her off with a violent gesture.

He wiped his mouth and advanced on Frederica. "I shouldn't expect anything else from a scrubber's brat, the daughter of a murderer!"

"That's enough!" Hawthorne roared. He pulled off his glove and slapped it across Markham's face. "I'm calling you out. It's about bloody time I taught you a lesson!"

"Nothing would give me greater pleasure," Markham said.

"No!" Frederica placed her body between the two men.

"Stand aside," Hawthorne said. "This is a matter between gentle-men. I must settle this once and for all. Markham's had this coming for a long time."

She placed her hand on his chest and looked up at him, her eyes shimmering with fear.

"Please…"

"Frederica, I must settle this," Hawthorne said. "Don't you under-stand? It's a matter of honor, your honor."

"I rather wonder at your notion of honor in relation to a soiled whore," Markham said. "But I take pride in finally understanding what she values above all." He gestured toward Hawthorne's coat. "I find myself admiring the buttons of your jacket, Stiles. Perhaps when we've settled the matter, you'd be generous enough to let me inspect them at close quarter."

"That's enough!" Frederica cried. "Markham, leave us alone. Take your wife home, she looks unwell."

"Who are you to judge my wife?" Markham asked. "And I shall go where I please. If your husband is a coward then, by all means, you may go."

"Coward, how dare…"

Frederica tugged at Hawthorne's sleeve. "Please, Hawthorne, come home with me."

Markham folded his arms and stared at Hawthorne, as if in chal-lenge. "Are you so much of a milksop that your wife orders you about?"

"Of course not," Hawthorne said. "I'll see you at dawn. Name your weapons."

"Hawthorne, no!" Frederica said. "If you do this, I will leave you and take Georgia with me. And this time, we'll disappear for good. As God is my witness, I swear, you'll never see your daughter again!"

The angry resolve in her voice told him she would carry out her threat. As he had used their daughter to cow her into submission, now she turned the same weapon on him. But who was she protecting? Him, or that bastard, Markham?

A small crowd had formed, mirroring the day he'd confronted Markham in the park, five years ago, shortly after Stanford died. Now, as then, they whispered to each other, relishing the second act of their entertainment.

"Well, really!" a woman exclaimed to her partner. "I must say, Countess Stiles is more entertaining now than she ever was. For amusement value, if nothing else, I daresay a little pollution is permissible among our ranks."

Hawthorne recognized Lady Wilcott. Doubtless, she was congratulating herself on marrying off her daughter to another. A ripple of amusement threaded through the crowd.

Anger boiled within him, and he fisted his hand, unable to fight the urge to destroy the smile on Markham's face. But before he could strike, cold, determined fingers curled round his wrist.

"Don't touch him."

The iron-like grip of her fingers was matched only by the steel in her voice.

"As my wife wishes," he said.

She loosened her grip, and he shook her hand off. Then he took her arm and led her toward the barouche.

"Our excursion is over," he said. "Miss Jones, bring Georgia to us immediately!"

Frederica remained silent for the journey home. Georgia was quiet at first, but at encouragement from Miss Jones, chatted about the swans in the park.

After Hawthorne escorted his family to the front door, he returned to the street.

"Hawthorne?" his wife called after him. "Where are you going?"

"To my club," he said. "I need a drink. In peace."

"Promise me you won't confront him."

"After you publicly ordered me not to?" he said. "Is your desire to protect him that strong?"

"I did it for you, Hawthorne."

"Just like you left me," he said, "and threatened to do so again. All for my benefit."

"You can think what you like," she said. "As long as you're safe."

Before he could respond, she disappeared inside the house.

IF HAWTHORNE THOUGHT brandy a great healer, it wasn't working. He was on his fourth, and despite a blurring around the edges of the images of his two companions, he felt no softening effects.

His friends provided no comfort. Ross sat opposite, flaunting the bruise on his face where Hawthorne had punched him, Westbury watched him with a cold expression in his clear blue eyes.

Westbury visited Whites so rarely, he should at least be enjoying his time here. Rumor had it, the scarcity of his visits was due to his wife's influence. Hawthorne had to admit the duchess was intriguing, but she was merely a woman. Did Westbury remove his balls as well as his greatcoat each time he entered the marital home? Perhaps he kept them in a dish by the front door.

Hawthorne waved the butler over for another brandy.

"Don't you think you've had enough, Stiles?"

Ignoring the accusatory tone in Ross's voice, Hawthorne barked his order at the butler. As soon as he shuffled out of earshot, Westbury leaned forward.

"Your friend is right, Stiles. Brandy won't solve your problems."

"It makes them feel a damn sight better."

"Only temporarily. You of all people must understand that."

"I fail to see what business it is of yours, Westbury."

"I was the one who fished you out of the Thames after you'd indulged in several bottles of the stuff." Westbury cast him a sharp glare, then turned his head away. "But my opinion doesn't count, I suppose."

Hawthorne snorted. "A man ruled by his wife? What value should I place on anything you say?"

"There was a time when you listened to my counsel," Westbury said. He nodded to Ross. "And his. Trelawney has always seen the good in a woman, even that vapid creature who rejected him for Markham."

Hawthorne jerked involuntarily at the mention of that hateful name.

"And there it is," Ross said. "Your jealousy of Markham."

"I'm not jealous!" Hawthorne snapped.

Westbury drained his glass and stood. "I see no reason why I should continue to waste my time here. I'd rather spend the evening with my wife."

"*Your* wife is a good woman," Hawthorne said.

"And so is yours!"

"That's not what you said at the Wilcotts' ball."

Westbury's eyes flashed with anger. "That was before I spoke to her. Shall I tell you what happened at the ball, Stiles? I told her how much she'd hurt you. I even insulted her, and do you know what she did?"

Hawthorne shook his head. The last thing he wanted to hear was the details of an argument between his wife and his friend.

"She told me I was a good man," Westbury said. "She said that no matter what I thought of her, she would always have admiration and respect for the man who was there when you needed him. Now, I love my wife to distraction, and I'm sure you ridicule me for it. You're too damned blind to realize you're in possession of just such a woman."

"She left me," Hawthorne growled, "much as your wife left you."

Westbury nodded.

"Frederica knew I loved her," Hawthorne said.

"Did she?" Ross leaned forward, brows furrowed. "Or did she think you just viewed her as a trophy which you fought over with Markham?"

Hawthorne sipped his brandy and leaned back in his chair, the leather creaking. He closed his eyes. "I told her I'd forgiven her."

"And have you?" Westbury asked. "Assuming, of course, there was anything to forgive in the first place."

Hawthorne drained his glass, the brandy giving him much-needed lucidity, as if his rational mind, which harbored the prejudices of the aristocracy, now cracked and crumbled to reveal his heart. Instead of trying to understand her, he'd let his pride eat away at the one pure thing in his life, the love he bore her. Ross had been right. He *was* jealous of Markham, a boyhood rival he'd thrashed at Eton, a man he loathed. That loathing had nourished the devil on his shoulder, giving it a voice to whisper in his ear.

Frederica was no society lady driven to further her position. She was his little changeling, her heart as pure as the snow which adorned the landscape in winter. That purity had been tainted over the years by the footprints of others. And none more than his, which had trampled her soul.

And yet, she still loved him, still defended him. Markham had shot and killed Frederica's father for trying to defend her honor. But Frederica didn't share society's obsession with honor. Instead, she valued life and love. Her outburst in the park that afternoon was not from a lack of understanding of society, but out of her need to protect someone she loved.

And that someone was him.

What if her flight from him five years ago had been driven by such a fear? Had Markham threatened to shoot him? Manipulate him into a duel?

What had she said about him to Ross?

I know he'll never forgive me for leaving, but I did it for him. Everything I do is for him.

The brandy turned to cold acid in Hawthorne's stomach, and he set his glass aside.

"I say, old chap," Westbury said. "Are you all right?"

Hawthorne leapt to his feet. "I'm going home."

The time for speaking was over. He had wronged the finest woman in England, and his place was by her side. He prayed he was not too late and that she would forgive him.

CHAPTER THIRTY-SEVEN

FREDERICA SET HER charcoal aside and inspected the sketch. The light had long since faded. Harry had lit the candles, but the flickering yellow flame gave her a headache compared to natural light.

"Begging your pardon, ma'am."

Jenny stood before her.

"You were so engrossed in your sketch, I didn't want to disturb you. If I may be so bold, I wonder at your ability to capture his likeness from memory."

"You're very kind, Jenny, but it's not really from memory. Whenever I close my eyes, I see him."

"Oh, my lady…" A thin hand covered hers as they shared a brief moment of female solidarity.

Jenny might be inferior in social position, but she was richer than Frederica in what mattered. Harry had recently offered for her hand, and Hawthorne had granted it, giving them his blessing and a guarantee of employment for life. They had reason to think him the kindest man in the world.

And he was, which made Frederica's pain all the more intense— that such a good man could not find it in his heart to love her as he once did.

"I came to tell you Mrs. Beecham is retiring."

"I'll be along directly. Could you bring Georgia? She'll want to say goodnight."

The old woman sat in her chamber propped up against her pillows. She reached out to Frederica, thin, bony hands clinging to her as if in a last desperate attempt to cling to life.

"My dear child."

The pain of future loss throbbed at Frederica's temples, and salty moisture stung her eyes. Mrs. Beecham had outlived expectations, so Doctor McIver kept saying, but that wouldn't lessen the pain of her passing.

The old woman smiled as if she read her thoughts.

"What have I told ye, lass, about grieving?" she said, her Scottish burr more prominent when she was tired. "I have no intention of leaving you yet, not until that young man comes to his senses."

"I've hurt him too deeply, Mrs. Beecham."

"As he's hurt you, my dear," the old woman replied. "As others have hurt you. But do you harbor hatred? No, you don't."

Frederica sighed. "It's different for him, he has a position to maintain."

"You think the Almighty judges us for our circumstances of birth? If that were so, I should be terrified of facing Him. Yet, I do not fear my passing. I've done my best to live a good life, to care for those I love, including you and your wee bairn. I may know little, but I understand much. That young man cares more for you than he wishes to admit. I see him struggle with it when he thinks no one watches."

She squeezed Frederica's hand. "I'm determined to live to see the day when he admits it. Then my work in watching over you will be done."

"I can take care of myself, Mrs. Beecham."

"That ye can," the old woman said softly, "but we all need love in our lives."

Her eyes glistened with moisture, and she wiped them away.

"Be off with ye, lass. I can't spend my time blathering when I'm in need of sleep."

"Goodnight, Mrs. Beecham." Frederica kissed the old woman's forehead.

She closed the door behind her and padded along the corridor toward her chamber.

Rapid footsteps approached, and she turned to see Jenny, her face creased in distress.

"Oh, ma'am, it's the little mistress!"

"Has she been taken ill?"

"I can't find her!"

"Have you asked Miss Jones?"

"Miss Jones is nowhere to be found. She must have taken Georgia out."

"Where would she go?"

A memory assaulted her mind, cold blue eyes following her daughter in the park, and the memory of his words…

Even a soiled whore always has something to lose… It's just a matter of discovering what that is.

"Markham…"

She ran toward the stairs, screaming for Giles. The butler appeared in the hall.

"My lady?"

"Fetch my cloak, immediately!"

"For what purpose?"

"Just do it!" she screamed.

He took a step back.

"It's the little mistress," Jenny said, panting.

"We must fetch the master," Giles said.

"What good will that do?" Frederica asked sharply. "You'll trawl the clubs and gaming hells, and for what? So he can admonish me on my failings? There's no time for recriminations. I must find her now!"

Harry appeared with her cloak and handed it to her. She could not miss the tender expression which passed between the footman and Jenny. Pulling her cloak around her, she pushed past Giles, and ran out the front door.

Where would she even begin to look?

The streets were empty. The windows of the townhouses she passed were ablaze with light. Silhouettes moved and laughter filtered through the doors—society families enjoying soirees to mark the end of the season—evenings of insipid, vacuous gossip and bland conversation.

"Well, how fortuitous!"

Her body froze at the familiar voice, and a man emerged from the shadows. This was no ordinary predator that would move on and seek better quarry.

Roderick Markham smiled. "Does the esteemed earl let you roam the streets unfettered? But I suppose you cannot help your nature. Once a street whore, always a street whore."

She bit her tongue, fighting the urge to defend herself. What good would it do? He would not listen to reason or give mercy. His face might be that of an angel, but his soul was as black as the night.

"I have to thank you, my dear."

"What for?"

"I wondered how I might entice you out. I'm grateful you spared me the bother, and came of your own free will."

"What would you know of free will?"

"Still stubborn, I see, but that will change."

"My husband..."

"Has, according to my source, been in Whites all day," he interrupted. "Anything to delay having to return to the slut he married."

She froze at his next words.

"I have the brat."

He drew near, and her skin crawled as soft fingertips caressed the back of her neck.

"That's it, little bird," he whispered. "You want her to live, don't you?"

Defeat rested on her shoulders, rooting her to the spot.

"What do you want?"

"Now, *there's* an interesting question."

Before she could respond, pain exploded in the back of her head, and she pitched forward into darkness.

⟫⟪

As HAWTHORNE APPROACHED the townhouse, the front door opened to reveal Giles, together with the young couple whose love Hawthorne had, until now, envied with a passion. But no more. He was in possession of such a love.

Frederica. His Frederica.

The butler's expression was grave, and the couple beside him exchanged fearful glances. A sense of foreboding slithered through Hawthorne's body.

Something was wrong.

"Giles, what's happened?"

"Her ladyship's gone."

Dear Lord, had she carried out her threat of that afternoon? Had she taken the child?

"And my daughter?"

The maid began to cry. "She's not here, sir. I'm so sorry!"

"Has my wife taken her?"

"Your daughter disappeared," Giles said. "Your wife left in search of her. Alone."

"Why did she not look for me?"

The butler shifted from one foot to another. "Perhaps you should ask yourself that."

"I don't like your tone, Giles."

"Forgive me, sir," the butler said. "She wanted to find the child as swiftly as possible, with as little recrimination from you."

The maid and the footman shared a glance, which sent a spike of guilt through him. Frederica couldn't trust him, and they knew.

"Do you know where she went?"

"No," Jenny said. "She left in such a hurry. But she mentioned a name."

"And what was the name?"

"Markham."

Hawthorne's stomach twisted sideways.

Markham...

Markham had been watching Georgia in the park. What had he said about Frederica?

I pride myself in finally understanding what she values above all.

Hawthorne hadn't understood it at the time, but what if it was a warning?

Or a threat?

A cry erupted in his mind. Markham had Frederica and Georgia. They might die. *She* might die, never knowing how much he loved her, the woman to whom his soul had been irrevocably bound since they were children.

"Sir, shall I summon the carriage?" Giles asked.

"No," Hawthorne said, his voice hoarse. "There's no time."

"Sir!" Harry said. "Take this, you might need it."

Hawthorne blinked at the object in the footman's hand.

A loaded pistol.

He grasped the handle and sprinted out the front door, following the path Frederick Stanford had taken nearly six years ago. And for the same reason, to save the person he loved most in the world. On that night, Frederica had lost her father.

Tonight, she might lose her life.

CHAPTER THIRTY-EIGHT

D ARK SHAPES SWIRLED around Frederica, black feathers beating to the pulse of pain in her head.

She opened her eyes, and an angel stood before her, a beautiful, smiling angel with eyes the color of ice. Behind him, exotic plants curled upward, tendrils weaving their way through the air. The last rays of the setting sun cast a red glow through the glass roof overhead, and feathered shapes flitted to and fro.

A wave of panic rippled through her. She was in an aviary.

She tried to move, but he caught her wrists and forced her back, slamming her against the wall.

"Still fighting, I see."

"And I'll continue to fight you with my dying breath."

His smile broadened, but his eyes remained cold and hard. "You'll soon learn the benefits of being more *open* to my affections."

Before she could respond, a cry rose overhead, and a mother's instinct made her look up. A thin iron ladder crawled up the wall to a high platform.

"Georgia…"

"Yes, little bird."

"What have you done with my child?"

"You mean the brat you've foisted onto Stiles?"

"She's his daughter."

He let out a laugh. "The odds are against you being able to identify her natural father."

"I've never been with anyone except him!"

"We can soon change that."

Her skin crawled, and she fought the urge to retch. Beyond Roderick Markham on the aviary floor, lay a body, limbs twisted as if it had been engaged in a macabre dance. Pale, sightless eyes looked upward. Blood coated her lips where she had bitten her tongue, purple to match the lesions on her throat.

It was Georgia's governess.

"Miss Jones!"

He tightened his grip on her wrists, running his fingernails across her scars.

"Foolish little slut," he said. "Willing to do anything for a few shillings. But aren't all women the same? They'd sell anything for the right price. If you don't want the brat to suffer the same fate, I suggest you give me what I want."

"What is that?"

"What's rightfully mine," he said. "Victory over Stiles." He traced the outline of her lips, then forced his thumb into her mouth.

"You want to bite me, don't you?" he said. "I see it in your eyes. Do it, and your little bastard will suffer."

Another flurry of wings beat at the air, and blurred shapes flew overhead. Roderick's smile broadened, his teeth glittering.

"I must remember to thank Lord Mulberry."

"Lord Mulberry?"

"Edward Langford, Lord Mulberry," he said. "Not especially bright, but very talkative about his childhood and the *little grub* he used to tease. He told me a very interesting story about a disused outbuilding, a flock of birds, and a common little slut who aspired to mingle with her betters."

He gestured around him. "Do you like my aviary? I invested in some more livestock especially for you."

Another cry rose up in the distance.

"What have you done to her!" Frederica cried.

"All in good time, little bird."

"She's my daughter, you've no right to torment her!"

"Your daughter's life is a privilege you must earn," he said smoothly. "I'm prepared to be generous if you're prepared to be *accommodating*."

"What must I do?"

"What a charming offer, my dear."

Choking down her hatred, she held her breath.

It was all a game to him. He was stronger than her in body, but if she could make him think she yielded, she might be able to seize an opportunity, however small, to defeat him. The prey might overcome the predator.

Thick, hard fingers circled her throat.

"Kiss me."

She shook her head, and his grip tightened. "If you continue to resist, let me provide a little incentive."

He circled his free hand around her arm and pulled her toward the iron ladder.

"Look up. Look up and see your reward."

Through the mesh of the platform, a shape moved.

"Georgia!"

"Mama!"

"Dear God!" she cried. "She could fall!"

Her captor laughed softly. "I've secured her well. You think I'd risk damaging the goods?"

"Why put her up there?" Frederica asked. "She's terrified!"

"Security, my dear," he said. "You cannot reach her without me." His eyes darkened. "Now, kiss me."

The air thickened with the sour male scent of him, the stench she had forced into the back of her mind.

"It's time to stop denying me, little bird," he said. "Not even that pathetic creature I married can give me the pleasures I intend to take from you."

Hatred fueled her strength, and she pushed him back but could not free herself from his grip. "Do you force yourself on Alice?" she spat.

"She knows where her duty lies and spreads her legs at a word from me. But she's a bland little creature who's failed to give me an heir. Child after child of mine she's killed before it's even born."

A rush of wings beat in the air behind him, and she shrank back. His fingers dug into her, claw-like in their sharpness, mirrored by the claws which flashed past her. A larger shadow shifted outside, but her vision, blurred by fear, couldn't discern anything other than a dark form.

"You'll be mine," Markham said. "You'll take pleasure from serving me and comfort from saving the life of your brat. I hear Stiles is rather fond of her, even if he loathes his wife."

He squeezed her throat. "They're better without you, little bird. You're nothing but a disgrace, the by-blow of a scrubbing maid, a madwoman…"

Another cry rose from above her, ripping through her heart.

"Mama!"

She lifted her leg and rammed her knee into his groin. He loosened his grip and staggered back, fury raging in his eyes.

"Bitch!" he roared. "You'll pay for that! You should have stayed with me when you left Stiles, not run off into the night like a thief. Admit you came back for me. Admit it, and I'll let you live."

"I didn't come back for you!" she cried. "I came back for him! Everything I did was for him!"

"But he doesn't love you."

"That's where you're wrong, Markham," a deep voice said.

Hawthorne appeared behind Roderick, the pink sunlight forming a halo around his hair. Beside him stood a woman, thin and gaunt, as if she would disintegrate at the lightest of breezes.

"I'll thank you to take your filthy hands off my wife."

HAWTHORNE APPROACHED MARKHAM, his body as tight as a bow, ready to let the arrow fly. The bastard had his filthy hands on Frederica, but what made Hawthorne any better?

Markham's wife trembled beside him. When Hawthorne had arrived at Hackton House, beating on the doors, roaring to be heard, Alice had initially resisted him. But her terror of her husband had won, and she'd led Hawthorne to the aviary.

"You don't want your wife, Stiles," Markham sneered. "Why not let me have her? I'll make use of her."

"Like you *make use* of your own wife?"

Alice flinched as Markham's gaze landed on her.

"What are you doing here, bitch?" he snarled.

Hawthorne touched Alice's shoulder in a gesture of reassurance. "You're not worthy to be called a man, Markham, if you cannot treat your wife properly."

"And how do you treat *your* wife?" Markham sneered.

Frederica remained in Markham's grip, eyes glistening with fear, a helpless little creature in the jaws of a predator, thinking she had none to champion her.

Hawthorne's conscience stabbed at his heart. He had led her to this. Her gaze darted about, lifting up to where Alice told him Markham had secured Georgia, before it settled on Hawthorne himself.

"I love her," Hawthorne said, keeping his focus on her. "I always have. She is everything to me. Everything."

Markham ran a fingertip along her chin. "But she abandoned you."

"And I understand why," Hawthorne said. "She sacrificed herself for me, because she believed I valued my career and social position more than I valued her. And because she feared for my life, feared what you would do. I had the best woman in all England, yet I was weak enough to let my doubts get the better of me. And you exploited that, didn't you, Markham? That, and the rivalry which has plagued us since our schooldays."

He held his hands out, palms up. "My wife is innocent," he said. "You and I are the guilty ones. She is far superior to either of us, and I have loved her since I was capable of understanding what true love means. A love that great, that deep, can never be destroyed, Markham. Not even by you."

Markham wrapped his fingers round Frederica's throat.

"Stay back, Stiles, unless you want her to die."

Hawthorne drew his pistol and aimed it at Markham's head.

Markham barked with laughter. "You don't have the mettle! If you shoot me, it would ruin your precious career."

Hawthorne cocked the weapon. "My career means nothing compared to the woman I love. What matters most is that I endeavor to deserve her. I would gladly face the gallows for her."

"Would you die for her, Stiles?"

Frederica's gaze met Hawthorne's, and she shook her head, a gesture he recognized for what it was. She was pleading with him not to risk his life for her.

"Always," he said.

She blinked, and a bead of moisture splashed onto her cheek. Her lips moved in a silent whisper.

Hawthorne...

"Then so be it." Markham sprang forward and rammed Hawthorne with his body.

He fell back and crashed to the ground, Markham on top of him. His hand tensed on impact, and he dropped the pistol. An explosion rang out, followed by splintering glass. Shards fell from the roof, and a flock of birds flew into the air, screeching.

Hawthorne lashed out, and his fist connected with Markham's jaw. With a roar, Markham rained blow upon blow on him. Hawthorne lifted an arm to defend himself and with a scream of fury, Markham dealt a kick to his stomach. Alice stood paralyzed by fear. In the background, another figure moved toward him, fighting off the birds which swirled around in the air. His little changeling, his avenging angel, advanced on Markham from behind, then launched herself at him.

"Roderick, behind you!" Alice screamed.

Markham turned just before Frederica reached him, and tossed her aside as if she were a child. Fury twisting his features, he advanced on Hawthorne once more. Hawthorne pushed himself up and tried to stand, but was too late. The last thing he saw was a polished boot, then his head shattered with pain and he fell back, his mind tortured with one final thought before oblivion claimed him.

He had failed to save her.

CHAPTER THIRTY-NINE

FREDERICA SAW HER husband drop to the ground. Alice stood beside him, whimpering. Markham nudged Hawthorne's body with his boot.

"Roderick..." Alice moved toward him, hands outstretched. "Roderick, are you hurt?"

"Get back into the house."

"But..."

"I said, get back into the house!" Markham roared. "Foolish bitch, why can't you do as you're told?"

"But I've just saved you from..."

"Who brought Stiles here?" he asked. "I told you not to admit anyone tonight. Go back to the house and I'll deal with you later. I've not finished here yet. I must deal with the brat."

"Georgia!" Frederica sprang into motion, but Markham was too quick for her. He sprinted toward the ladder and began to climb.

"Mama! Help me!"

"Don't worry, little brat," Markham called, mock concern in his voice. "Soon you'll join your Papa."

Alice let out a wail. "Roderick, be careful!"

By the time Frederica reached the ladder, he was almost beyond her reach. She grasped the rungs and pulled herself up in pursuit. He was bigger and stronger, but she had climbed trees most of her life, which gave her an advantage. As he neared the top, she had caught up with him. She reached up, and her fingertips brushed his boot.

He lifted his foot, then stamped on her fingers. Hot, sharp pain burst in her hand, and she lost her grip and swung out into the air while she clawed at the rung with her other hand. She kicked out with her legs until she found a purchase. Ignoring the flames of agony in her hand, she reached up again and grasped his ankle. He kicked out, but she tightened her grip and pulled. Cursing, he slipped and crashed onto her.

She held on to the rungs while he clawed at her, but he lost his grip and, with a scream of rage, he fell. His screams were cut short, and she looked down to see his crumpled form on the ground, a pool of dark liquid already forming under his head. Alice flung herself on top of his body.

Beyond Alice, blurred shapes moved, morphing into human form. With screeches and a flurry of wings, a flock of birds flew up in front of them, up toward where Frederica clung to the ladder. Her limbs went rigid with panic until a plaintive voice cut through the nightmare.

"Mama!"

She pulled herself onto the platform. At the far end, Georgia sat, her hands bound. Frederica crawled along the platform until she reached her daughter and wrapped her arms around her, breathing in the scent of her child.

"I'm here, angel," she whispered.

With trembling hands, she fumbled at the knots. Markham had tied them so tight, they chafed against Georgia's skin, leaving marks to mirror those on Frederica's own wrists. She tore at the bonds with her teeth. They worked loose, and she drew the trembling, crying child into her arms.

The platform shook, and she looked up to see a man crawling toward her.

"Stay back!" she cried.

"It's me," a familiar voice said. "Don't you know me?"

She blinked, and her eyes focused.

"Mr. Trelawney?"

He held his hand out. "Give me the child."

"No!" she cried. "I've lost my husband. I can't lose my child as well."

"Hawthorne's perfectly fine," Ross said. "See for yourself. Westbury's with him." He pointed to where Hawthorne sat far below, another man kneeling beside him.

"We must get you down," he said, his voice tight. He wiped his forehead. "It's bloody high up here, Countess. Do me a favor, and let me help you before I pass out."

Georgia shifted in Frederica's arms. "Uncle Ross?"

"Yes, I'm here," he said. "I need a brave little girl to help me climb down to your Papa. Can you do that?"

He held out his hand, and Georgia took it.

"Climb onto my back and hold tight."

She did as he asked.

"Good. Now, off we go." He swung his leg out while Georgia clung to him.

"Clever girl," he said before turning his gaze to Frederica.

"Countess, wait for me. As soon as Georgia's safe, I'll return for you."

"I can take care of myself," Frederica said.

His eyes lit up with a smile of warmth. "Yes, you always could, couldn't you? And those around you. I regret my outburst which cost me our friendship, and will always envy those fortunate enough to have you to take care of them."

"You've not lost my friendship," she said. "Nor will you ever."

He nodded, then climbed down the ladder. She followed.

As soon as her foot touched the ground, strong arms plucked her off the ladder.

"I don't need help."

"Bloody hell," Westbury's cursed. "You're as stubborn as my Jeanette."

He set her down before addressing Ross, who had turned pale.

"I told you I should have gone up instead."

"I didn't realize how high it was," Ross said. "It's worse when you're up there. Here you go, little angel." He set Georgia down.

"Papa!" The child ran toward Hawthorne and threw her arms round his neck.

"My angel." He embraced his daughter as if his life depended on it.

Markham's body lay beside him. Westbury stood over it, hands in his pockets, and poked it with the toe of his boot.

Frederica averted her eyes. "Where's Alice?"

"Gone," Westbury said and pointed outside. Two footmen were walking back to the house, carrying a limp form between them. "She appears to have had a mental breakdown. I've told them to send for a doctor."

"Poor, Alice," Frederica breathed, "he must have been unbelievably cruel to her."

"She made her choices," Ross said. "She deserves everything she gets."

Frederica recoiled at his bitterness. "How can you speak so?"

Westbury placed a hand on her arm. "If you side with the devil, you must pay the price."

"For pity's sake, Westbury, leave my wife alone!"

Hawthorne, Georgia clinging to him, was struggling to stand.

"Sit down, Stiles," Westbury said. "You're in no fit state to move."

"You've no right to tell me what to do."

"I've every right," Westbury said. "If we hadn't come looking for you out of concern over the amount of brandy you were drinking, you'd be dead. And so would your wife."

"That's enough!" Hawthorne growled. "Come here, Frederica."

She hesitated, and he let out a sigh.

"Then I'll come to you." He limped toward her.

His nose was swollen where Markham had struck it. She reached up, succumbing to the instinct to soothe his pain.

"You've always felt my pain, haven't you?" he asked quietly.

"Hawthorne..."

He caught her hand, brought it to his lips, and placed feather-light kisses on her knuckles.

"I cannot live without you, Frederica."

She closed her eyes, fighting against the call of her heart which willed her to believe him.

"Oh, little changeling!" he cried. "A part of me always knew deep down that you didn't leave me of your own free will," he said. "You cannot understand the depths of my shame when I think of the cruel things I said. They were born of anger and loss, my love, not of hatred. The mere thought you wanted another, it almost killed me. Your note when you left..."

His voice tightened, and his body shuddered. She tipped her head up and brushed her lips against his.

"Did you never understand the words I'd written?" she whispered. "I remember them as if I'd written them yesterday. "I have only ever wanted one man, and nothing you can say or do will change my mind. If I cannot be with him, I would rather be alone.'"

She caressed his cheek with her thumb. "You were meant to think it was another. I wanted you to let me go, for your own sake, for your career, your reputation, and your life. But I couldn't bring myself to write an untruth. Those words were about you, my love. I have never loved anyone but you."

"Oh, Frederica!"

He pulled her to him and fisted his hand in her hair. He took her mouth with his, the lips of a man starved. With a groan, he kissed her, sweeping his tongue across the roof of her mouth, as if devouring her.

"Ahem..."

He broke the kiss, and she shrank back, shame heating her face. Westbury watched them, arms folded, but eyes were full of mischief, not disapproval.

"Ross and I will deal with things here, Stiles," he said. "I suggest you take your wife home and made amends."

CHAPTER FORTY

Hawthorne kicked open the bedchamber door. Beads of perspiration adorned his forehead, but he held her firmly as he had during the journey home.

"Hawthorne, we can't!" she cried, "I must check on Georgia and Mrs. Beecham."

"The old woman's fine, my love, and our daughter's with Jenny."

He sat her on the bed and kissed her. "Would you deny me the chance to atone?"

"I'll deny you nothing," she said, "but you're hurt."

"There's no greater cure than the attention of a loving woman."

"At least let me fetch Doctor McIver."

"I have no intention of letting the good doctor join us," he said, a twinkle of mischief in his eyes before his tone sobered. "Besides, he's tending to the duchess. Markham has a lot to answer for."

Frederica shuddered at the memory. By her own hand, she had pulled Markham from the ladder where he'd plunged to his death.

Hawthorne kissed her knuckles. "It was an accident, my love."

"Are those the words of a husband or a magistrate?"

"Both. You've nothing to fear and nothing to reproach yourself over. You saved two lives, our daughter and the duchess. Had Markham lived, do you think Alice would have survived his fury?"

"Will she recover?"

"McIver's an excellent doctor, but her wits have been snapped.

Ross believes she deserves her fate, but I wouldn't wish residence at Bedlam on anyone."

"Bedlam. Dear lord…"

"Let us not speak of it."

He traced a line along her arm, his touch sending ripples across her skin. Strong, deft fingers peeled off her dress and tugged at the laces of her corset. His breath quickened as he removed her undergarments, and he reached for her breasts, cupping them in his hands, caressing her tender skin. Small whimpers resonated in her throat, and she let out a little mewl of pleasure as her nipples hardened to painful, needy little points. She leaned back, pushing her chest upward, offering them to him.

"I've missed you," he said hoarsely, "missed the taste of you."

With the slow, relaxed motion of a powerful animal, he peeled off his jacket before removing his cravat and unbuttoning his waistcoat, dropping the garments onto the floor, where they landed beside her own.

He sat back and held his hand out. "Come to me."

Her skin tightened at the command, and her body moved with the instinct to obey. She crawled toward him. Ugly marks covered his torso, bruises where Markham had kicked him, and she placed her hand on his chest. The soft, rhythmic beat of his heart pulsed against her, the lifeblood of the man who had been prepared to die for her. She ran her hand across his chest, and he drew in a sharp breath.

"Does it pain you?"

"No more than I deserve."

She leaned forward and pressed her lips against the bruise, inhaling the musky, male scent of him. How many years had she held his discarded necktie, the ragged cloth she had treasured, to her lips to recapture his familiar scent, even after it had long since faded?

Gently, she pushed him back on the bed.

"Let me ease your pain."

She climbed on top of him and peppered light kisses across his chest, flicking her tongue out to taste the salt of his skin. A small growl erupted from his throat. His muscles tensed as he fisted the sheets in his hands, body vibrating with unmet need.

"I've missed the taste of you, Hawthorne."

She ran her hands across his body, circling each bruise with her fingers before tracing the line with her tongue. She ran her fingertips over the soft, downy hair which grew thicker the further down she moved. His skin was on fire, a heat which grew hotter as she reached the nest of wiry curls where his manhood jutted out. She circled his girth with her hand, and he let out a groan.

"Frederica…"

"Hush," she whispered. "Let me tend to you."

His breath quickened as she ran her hand along his length and circled the tip with her thumb.

"Have I eased your pain?"

He groaned in response. She lowered her head and took him in her mouth, and he shuddered, his legs shifting with the tide of need as he moved to chase the pleasure he sought.

She swirled her tongue around the tip, and he cried out.

A hand fisted in her hair and pulled her back.

"I cannot last much longer," he said. "I need to be inside you. Now."

She straddled him until she felt his manhood against her center, where she was already slick with need. He lifted his hips to sheathe himself fully into her, but she resisted, rocking her body back and forth, chasing her own pleasure.

"Would you torment me?"

"Did you not always say the longer the denial, the greater the pleasure?"

"I have been denied you long enough."

"Then you shall be denied no more."

She drove her body down and impaled herself on him. He let out a cry as she withdrew. He held her firm while he thrust upward, slamming their bodies together. In a swift movement, he rolled over until he was on top of her, pinning her to the bed with his body.

He twisted his mouth into a devilish grin.

"And now, my love, it's time to make reparation for your earlier denial."

He withdrew slowly, then plunged into her again and again, increasing the pace with each thrust until his body burned inside her. Exquisite agony morphed into pure pleasure, and she cried out with the force of it. The wave crested, and her body disintegrated around him. With a roar of completion, he drove into her one final time, and she screamed his name as waves of pleasure ripped through her.

He clung to her, his body twitching with the aftershocks of his climax. At length, he lifted his head, and their eyes met. In the candlelight, his eyes looked pale, almost amber. Then he kissed her and sat up. He took her hand and traced the scars on her wrist with his fingers.

"I have a confession to make," he said. "Your scars, the birds..." He shook his head. "I can keep it from you no longer."

He blinked, and shame filled his expression. "When I see what Markham did to Alice, what it's done to her mind—I'm as much of a monster as he, for what happened to you when you were a child. Coward that I am, I concealed my part in it for so many years."

She placed a hand on his. "Say no more, my love," she whispered. "I know what happened. I have always known."

"Why did you say nothing?"

"It served no purpose," she said. "Why should you be held to account for a childhood prank devised by your friends?"

"But I abandoned you on your father's doorstep."

She lifted her hand to his face and caressed his cheek, brushing away a bead of moisture with her thumb.

"You took me home, Hawthorne," she said, "to Papa. You did the best thing you could have done for me, and I thank you for it."

Their fingers interlocked, and he smiled. "It is a fortunate man indeed who secures the heart of a good woman," he said. "And I consider myself the most fortunate man in all England. I pray that one day I can prove myself worthy of you."

He reached across to the table beside the bed and picked up a box.

"I have a gift for you." He handed it to her. "Open it."

She lifted the lid to reveal a familiar row of sapphires and diamonds.

"Is this…?"

"Yes," he said. "My mother's necklace. I found it."

"How?"

"I traced it from the pawnshop to a merchant in Hammersmith." He smiled. "I managed to persuade him to part with it when I explained it was a family heirloom meant for the neck of the most beautiful woman in England."

"I'm sorry I pawned it," she said.

"You must never be sorry, my love. You did what you had to out of love. I return it to you now, as a token of my love."

He lifted his hand and traced the outline of her face, then cupped her cheek, caressing her skin with his thumb.

"Forgive me, my love. Forgive the harsh things I said and did. Despite what I led you to believe, I have only ever loved one woman, and that is you. My own little changeling."

"I never stopped loving you, Hawthorne," she said. "My only consolation after I left was that you might find happiness with another. I could live in peace if I knew you were happy."

"Then you've just proved what I always believed," he said. "You will always be a better person than I." He blinked, and a tear fell onto his cheek.

She wiped away with her finger. "Shed no tears for me, my love."

"Selfish creature that I am, I shed tears for myself," he said. "I don't deserve you, for I had no wish for you to be happy with another. I only wanted you to be happy with *me*."

"And so I shall."

He pulled her to him, and she rested her head against his chest. Within moments, she drifted into a contented sleep, safe in the knowledge that nothing would ever part them again.

EPILOGUE

Hampshire, England, a few months later

THE MORNING MIST had yet to clear. Moisture penetrated Hawthorne's coat, bleeding through to his skin. The watery light from the sun created a backdrop of gray, picking out the blurred shapes of the trees. Gravel crunched underfoot as he continued along the path. Another, larger shape materialized through the mist. The Stiles family chapel.

Throaty caws echoed above, and dark shapes circled in the air. The woman beside him stiffened, and her gloved fingers curled around his arm. In her free hand, she held a posy of wild flowers. Shortly after their retirement to Radley Hall at the end of the Season, Hawthorne had made arrangements for Stanford's remains to be moved from the cemetery in London and interred within the family crypt. Since then, she had visited the building each week without fail.

"Frederica."

She relaxed her grip and looked up at him, her clear eyes giving a burst of color to the otherwise gray landscape.

"Are you well, my love?"

She lowered her gaze to her belly where her pregnancy was already beginning to show.

"Always, when I'm with you."

As they neared the building, the crows dispersed, and he led her inside, shutting out their caws of protest.

Their footsteps echoed as they descended the steps into the crypt.

At the bottom of the steps, she paused beside Adam's memorial, the brother who had died before he'd had a chance at life. She knelt beside the stone, uttered a quiet prayer, and placed a flower beside it. Then she crossed the floor to a stone memorial illuminated in the diffused sunlight from a single window. A cluster of flowers lay at the bottom, already withering. She replaced the blooms with the posy, then traced the inscription with her finger.

Here lies Frederick Stanford,
Beloved father of Frederica,
Born into eternal life to look upon the blessed.

"Hello, Papa."

Hawthorne stood back as she spoke to her father, telling him about his grandchildren—the exuberant little girl who currently slept at Radley Hall under the watchful eyes of Mrs. Beecham, and the grandchild to come. It was her moment, her time alone with her beloved Papa, and Hawthorne had no right to intrude.

When she finished, he helped her up.

"Come, my love. I've something to show you."

He led her further into the vault where another stone had been inserted into the wall. A delicate pink marble, the inscription had been freshly cut.

"Hawthorne, what's this?"

"I had it made," he said. "For you."

A small cry escaped her lips as she read the inscription, and she sank to her knees.

In memory of Mary White
Beloved mother of Frederica
Who, through suffering, delivered grace and salvation unto the world.

"My mother," she choked, "but she was nothing to you, she…"

"She was the woman who bore you, my love. She brought you into the world and thus delivered my salvation. You are a part of her and, as your mother, I would honor and love her memory, as I love you. There will always be a place in my heart for her."

Her body shook, and he pulled her into his arms.

"Hush, my love," he said. "Let me heal your pain. Let us heal each other."

He placed a kiss on the top of her head and breathed in the scent of her. "We must look to our future, Frederica. We have our beautiful child, and are soon to be blessed with another. But today, let us mourn the passing of our lost loved ones."

"Thank you."

He took her hand, and her fingers curled against his, drawing strength from him as he had always drawn strength from her. A ray of sunlight stretched across the room. The light diffracted to form a myriad of colors which illuminated the letters on her mother's stone.

A sign from heaven. Perhaps Frederick Stanford was declaring, from beyond the grave, that Hawthorne had finally proved himself worthy of her.

He drew her to him and brushed her lips in a soft kiss.

"Come, my love," he said. "Let's take you home."

Hand in hand, they ascended the steps and walked out into the light where the mist was already beginning to clear.

The End

About the Author

Emily Royal grew up in Sussex, England, and has devoured romantic novels for as long as she can remember. A mathematician at heart, Emily has worked in financial services for over twenty years. She indulged in her love of writing after she moved to Scotland, where she lives with her husband, teenage daughters and menagerie of rescue pets including Twinkle, an attention-seeking boa constrictor.

She has a passion for both reading and writing romance with a weakness for Regency rakes, Highland heroes, and Medieval knights. Persuasion is one of her all-time favorite novels which she reads several times each year and she is fortunate enough to live within sight of a Medieval palace.

When not writing, Emily enjoys playing the piano, hiking, and painting landscapes, particularly the Highlands. One of her ambitions is to paint, as well as climb, every mountain in Scotland.

Follow Emily Royal:
Website: www.emroyal.com
Facebook: facebook.com/eroyalauthor
Twitter: twitter.com/eroyalauthor
Newsletter signup: mailchi.mp/e5806720bfe0/emilyroyalauthor
Goodreads: goodreads.com/author/show/14834886.Emily_Royal

Made in the
USA
Middletown, DE